All th
You D

Preeti Shenoy has authored fifteen bestsellers and ranks amongst the highest-selling writers in India. She has been featured on the Forbes India longlist of the most influential celebrities in the country.

She has received numerous awards for her literary works, including the Popular Choice Fiction Award, 2021, by AutHer Awards, as well as the Most Popular Self-Help Book of 2021 by Amazon India. Additionally, she has been awarded the 'Indian of the Year' award for 2017, and the Business Excellence Award by the New Delhi Institute of Management.

Preeti is also an avid fitness enthusiast, as well as an artist specialising in portraiture and illustrated journals. She enjoys travel, blogging and yoga.

Connect with Preeti:
Website: www.preetishenoy.com
Email: ps@preetishenoy.com
Twitter: @preetishenoy
Blog: blog.preetishenoy.com
Instagram: @preeti.shenoy and @preetishenoyart
Facebook: http://preeti.io/fb
Snapchat: preeti.shenoy
LinkedIn: https://in.linkedin.com/in/preetishenoyauthor

By the same author

When Love Came Calling

Praise for the author and her works

One of India's most popular authors. – *Cosmopolitan*

India's top-selling female author. – *BBC World*

Feel-good air, crisp and easy-to-grasp writing. – *New Woman*

Quick-paced read. – *DNA*

Positive and full of life. – *Financial World*

Woven intelligently with simple language ... leaves a profound impact. – *Exotica*

Amazing how deftly she weaves her stories. – *Eve's Times*

Keeps the reader hooked from the first page to last. – *Afternoon Voice*

Magnetic, engrossing and unputdownable. – *One India One People*

Intense fiction that plays with your emotions. – *The New India Express*

Preeti Shenoy makes it work. – *The Hindu*

Has something for everyone. – *The Hindu*

Heart-warming love story. – *Bangalore Mirror*

Show-stealer. – *Deccan Chronicle*

Keenly observant mind. – *DNA*

Wonderful, passionate, common story. – *The Sentinel*

PREETI SHENOY

All the Love You Deserve

Never give up on
your dreams!
With love
Preeti Shenoy

First published by Westland Books, a division of Nasadiya Technologies Private Limited, in 2023

No. 269/2B, First Floor, 'Irai Arul', Vimalraj Street, Nethaji Nagar, Alapakkam Main Road, Maduravoyal, Chennai 600095

Westland and the Westland logo are the trademarks of Nasadiya Technologies Private Limited, or its affiliates.

ISBN: 9789357769020

10 9 8 7 6 5 4 3 2 1

Typeset by R. Ajith Kumar, Delhi

Printed at HT Media Ltd, Greater Noida

For Purvi and Atul,
who keep me young

Boarding

Every takeoff is optional.
Every landing is mandatory.

–Rules of the Air

1

Sujit

Some chapters in your life should stay closed. They are done. Over. There's nothing you can do about them because they have already been written. But Dr Harsh doesn't think so. His deep-set brown eyes are filled with compassion as he looks at me on Skype.

The only reason I'm taking these free therapy sessions, offered by the Samajam, is because Amma insisted. 'What do you lose by trying therapy? We don't even have to pay for it. Dr Harsh is one of the best in India,' she said.

It was only to placate her that I booked online slots with Dr Harsh. I thought he would be a boring middle-aged man who'd give me sermons on facing grief and becoming the 'man of the family', just like all my relatives did after Achcha passed away. But Dr Harsh turned out to be surprisingly young, sharp and astute. He never tells me what to do but asks questions that make me think. So, I continue with the free therapy, much to Amma's delight.

'Look, Sujit, whatever happened to you in the past, it happened only once. But each time you think about it, the pain comes only because of the "story" you make up about it. They are stories, not facts,' he says.

'I am not making up any story! All of it happened exactly like I told you.'

'I am not for a moment insinuating that you're being untruthful. Let me explain what I mean.'

Dr Harsh loves to use long words like 'insinuating'. I make a mental note to look up the meaning of the word later.

The sweltering summer in Kochi is getting to me. I feel sweat trickling down my armpits underneath the T-shirt I am wearing. I wish for the hundredth time we could afford air-conditioning. I wipe the sweat off my forehead with a hand towel.

'Are you with me?' he asks.

'Uh-huh.' I nod.

'If you pass a stranger on the street, would you remember them?'

'Unlikely, unless they were dressed in a Kathakali costume.'

'Exactly! When you pass strangers on a street, it is unmemorable, because there is no strong emotion attached. Consider a teacher humiliating a student in class. We know how traumatic that feels. But two students might deal with it in two completely different manners. One might feel bad but move on. To the other, it might be a disaster he will never recover from. The second student has made up a "story" about it, and because of this, he is trapped in a pain cycle, as he believes his story to be true. Do you get what I am saying?' Dr Harsh asks, his voice gentle, persuasive.

I nod though I do not fully agree with him. He notices immediately. The slightest change in my facial expression, and he knows.

'I can see you don't entirely agree with me. But it is imperative that you release the emotion. Unless you do, you won't be able to move on. You are permitted to feel negative emotions. But do not attach stories to them.'

I nod. A second word gets added to the mental notes I am making: 'Imperative'.

He is urging me to let go of the narratives I am holding on to. But it's not easy.

'No matter how you look at it, I was an asshole back then and that is a fact,' I say.

'Sujit, remember what we discussed about using unkind terms like "asshole"? Be kind to yourself. Would you use a term like that to describe your closest friend if they made a mistake?'

'I'd use a worse term.' I fidget in my plastic chair and stare at the fan.

Dr Harsh chuckles in response.

But I wasn't joking at all. Dr Harsh realises this and says, 'Look, Sujit, I recommend you write a letter to her. Tell her what you feel, but don't send it yet.'

A knock on the door interrupts us. 'A minute,' I tell Dr Harsh. 'You can't come in here, Ravi. I am busy,' I yell. I had specifically told my brother not to knock during my session.

'Sorry Chetta, I didn't know,' comes a small voice from the other side. Instantly I regret my angry tone. It's not Ravi. It is Sindu and she is the sweetest kid on this planet. Losing our father has hit her really hard. I can see how she has changed. She has become quieter, timid, and she hardly speaks these days. 'Molle, it's okay. I'll finish soon, okay?' I say, my voice a lot softer now.

'Okay,' she says, and I can hear her footsteps as she walks away.

'Sorry about that,' I tell Dr Harsh.

'Oh, that's okay,' he says. 'How is she doing? In the last session you mentioned you were concerned.'

'Achcha's death has hit her hard.'

Dr Harsh knows everything about my family, which comprises Sindu, my half-sister, Ravi, my younger brother, and Amma. Though she didn't give birth to me or Ravi, she has raised us as her own. My biological mother passed away when I was six and Ravi was two. My father remarried a year later, and in a few years Amma gave birth to Sindu, the baby of the family. With Achcha's death I've become even more protective of her.

'To deal with the death of a parent is arduous. That's why you should cut yourself some slack,' Dr Harsh says.

'I am trying. You were saying something about writing a letter when we were interrupted.'

'Yes, Sujit. To release the past you must first accept it. Write down everything you feel in an email. Don't add the "to" address, you may accidentally dash it off.' He smiles.

But I am too engrossed in what he is saying to smile back. He continues, 'You could ask for her forgiveness if you regret what you did. Till you face it and process it, it would be hard for you to eliminate the distress you feel. Keep this mail for ten days. After ten days, if you still feel bad and need closure, then I suggest you send it to her.'

'I don't think she will ever talk to me,' I blurt out.

'What do you lose by trying this?'

'Mmmm ... I don't know.' I look away. Even thinking about it is painful for me. We have spoken about it a few times in the previous sessions; Dr Harsh knows the extent of my trauma. This is even harder than talking about my father's death, the primary reason for enrolling in these sessions.

'She can't think any worse of you than she already does, right?'

'Look, doctor, it isn't about what she thinks of me. It is about what I did.'

'Sujit, you are not the same person you were then. Don't you agree?'

I look at him mutely, having no words to reply with. I wonder if it's a coping mechanism; I don't want to think about my father's death, and so I am focussing on this.

'That's why I suggest you get it out of your system by writing. Tell her your side of the story. And you don't have to send it out if you choose not to.'

'Let me see what I can do,' I reply on a long exhale.

'It's only when we let go of painful memories that we move into a painless present. And, Sujit, you're making a lot of progress. Is there anything else on your mind?'

I glance at the time. We've come to the end of the session.

'Is there's anything else you want to talk about? Don't worry about the time.'

'No, doctor, thank you. We'll speak again next week.'

I know how tightly packed Dr Harsh's schedule is and I do not want to eat into anyone else's time slot.

He gives me a quick look. 'Alright, take care, Sujit. Think about everything we discussed, okay?'

'I will.'

2
Puja

'Get up, Divya! You haven't moved from here since morning. And it's nearly 4 p.m. now.' I try to be gentle. As annoying as she can be, it is very hard for me to see my 'perfect' sister crumble like this. I *have* to intervene.

I walk to the floor-to-ceiling windows that open out to the sea-facing deck and part the curtains. Divya squints as the bright sunlight hits her eyes. 'Don't,' her voice is half whimper, half plea.

'You can't just lie like this! This really isn't the end of the world.' I sink into the sofa opposite Divya.

'Let me be, Puja. Please ...' Divya uses her palms to shield her eyes.

'Look, Divya, do you know how many people have died in this pandemic? We should feel blessed to have all this,' I say, but the moment the words are out of my mouth, I regret them. Quite the wrong thing to say. This is exactly what our parents have been saying to Divya ever since she was laid off from her job. I sound like their mouthpiece.

'Yeah, yeah, we are blessed to have our twenty-second floor, ten thousand square feet penthouse overlooking the ocean. It's even named "Life is Paradise". A paradise indeed,' Divya replies, oozing sarcasm.

I take it as a good sign. At least she is speaking. This is more like the old Divya I knew.

'Ummm, let's go to the deck. Shanti Chechi is getting the deep cleaning of the sofas done today. They will be here any minute.' I deftly change the topic.

I walk on to the deck and sink into a wicker chair. I hear Divya getting up from the sofa and am glad she is following me. The outdoor garden coolers are on their highest setting, yet I fan myself with my hand. The heat is killing me. Kerala summer has been unusually blazing this year. Divya sits down next to me, her expression sullen and sad.

I want to put my hands around her and hug her, and tell her to cheer up. But we don't do such things in our family unless it's an exceptional situation—like the time I ran away to the UK and gave my family a proper scare. Things have changed so much since then.

Shanti Chechi serves us pakoras, pazhamporis and tea, all of it arranged prettily on a portable trolley she wheels out, along with plates, ketchup and cups. The smell of deep-fried golden pazhamporis and crispy pakoras makes my mouth water. Divya's too.

'Oooh, thank you, Shanti Chechi,' I say as I bite into a pazhampori. Divya follows suit.

It is after Shanti Chechi goes back inside that Divya starts talking. 'Look, if I could just get back into an office, *any* office, I wouldn't be worrying about my daily existence. It's been two and a half months since I was laid off. I am not even able to get an interview. I reek of desperation!' She is gazing at the ships, unable to meet my eyes.

'You're not the only one who has lost a job. Look at it this way, at least you had a job through most of the pandemic. I agree it is ironic that you lost your job just when things started opening up. But it's only been two and a half months. I've graduated and done *nothing* for one whole year now. I am stuck too.'

Divya bites a pakora harder than necessary. 'But it's not like you wasted one whole year. You did all those courses on social media marketing, and one of them was from Wharton!'

'Only because I didn't know what to do,' I say earnestly. 'All those random short courses on everything. Secretly, I am so sick of it all.'

'Sucks, doesn't it?' Divya says, picking up her cup.

'It does, but we have to pull ourselves out of it. Even if you don't feel like it, I want you to dress up. Wear nice outfits like you used to when you were working.'

There I have said it. It's the first time in my life I am advising my older sister. And she is actually listening to me.

'Look who is talking! You are lounging around in this crop top and shorts, with uncombed hair, and you want *me* to dress up?' she retorts.

'This is how I usually dress! You can't compare yourself to me! Come on, Divya, even your wedding being called off didn't affect you this badly.'

She looks away into the distance. I have addressed the elephant in the room—the break-up. Her fiancé Karthik—who I'd nicknamed Kar-dick—turned out to be a two-timing bastard. Divya had found out through a common friend, and she'd broken off the engagement as soon as she knew. It was hard for my parents too, as he was the son of one of Achcha's good friends, which made things *very* awkward.

'It did affect me, you know. But I buried myself in work. That was how I could cope. Now you know why losing even this affects me so much.'

'I know.' I nod. 'Are your sessions with Dr Harsh helping?'

Divya takes another sip of tea and I do the same. Even though it is hot outside, the warm tea is comforting.

'I'd have been in a worse state if not for him. He is compassionate and isn't preachy. He is totally worth the crazy amount he charges,' Divya says. 'Enough about me now, what about you? What's the scene with Arush?'

I sigh.

'What? Don't tell me there's nothing between you two now? That would be such an anti-climax considering you ran away from home to visit him.'

'What can I say? We talk ... but it has been over two years since we saw each other.'

'Well, it's over two years since *anyone* saw each other in person. This pandemic has been the pits.' She rolls her eyes.

'We talk and email each other, but I feel there's something missing.'

'Don't tell me it's because of Jenna. If the guy is cheating on you, I swear I will travel to the UK this time and break his nose. I've had enough of cheating bastards.'

'No, no, there's nothing like that between them. They're just friends,' I reply quickly.

'Ha! That's what I believed about Kar-dick too. I was naive and trusting. You can never be too sure. Just be alert.' Divya's voice is bitter.

I am suddenly filled with doubts. What if Divya is right? What if there's something brewing between Arush and Jenna, and I am unaware. The very thought is unbearable but I can't do anything about it other than hope it isn't true.

The other thing that worries me is how Divya seems to be withering away right in front of my eyes. I decide to speak to my parents about it.

I get my chance the next day when Amma returns earlier than usual from the hospital, and Divya is in her room.

'Amma, you're back early!' I follow her into her bedroom.

I am genuinely pleased to see her. I am proud of the work she has done during the pandemic, the lives she has saved risking her own, not caring about the danger of being in the Covid-19 wards.

'Yes, I have taken four days off. Combine it with Sunday and we have five whole days,' she beams.

'That's nice! How come?'

'They hired two more doctors, and they will cover for her,' Achcha informs me as he enters the bedroom.

'Also, I have so much accumulated leave, I had to make use of it,' she says.

'I wanted to speak to you both about Divya,' I tell my parents as I sit down on the sofa in their bedroom. 'I'm worried about her.'

'She has been this way ever since she lost her job. I've noticed too,' Achcha says.

'She stays cooped up in the house. If she at least dressed smartly and got out a bit more, she might feel better,' Amma says.

'Exactly what I told her!'

'Now all of us have been vaccinated, maybe we can go somewhere. It will be a nice break for Divya too,' I suggest.

'Maybe we can go to some resort in Kerala itself since Amma has only a few days,' Achcha says.

'Let's go to Varkala. A new luxury resort belonging to one of my patients has opened there. He told me we are welcome anytime. I'll call him and make the booking,' Amma says.

'That's sorted then. Tell Divya and start packing!' my father tells me.

I haven't heard my parents sound this excited for a long time. We babble happily.

3

Arush

The lockdown has divided us into two kinds of people. The first kind copes by doing productive things like exercising, making art, reading and taking courses. The second kind copes by doing absolutely nothing. No prizes for guessing which category I fall into. My paints and my creativity have both frozen.

I've become an expert onion chopper, a waiter, dish-washer and general handyman though. The situation has forced me to.

'Arush, do you want me to chop that while you peel the ginger?' my aunt asks.

'No, Mami, it's fine. I can do it,' I reply. My eyes sting as I chop the onions at my uncle's restaurant.

'Such a blessing having you here. Really, I don't know what we'd do without you,' she says as she stirs the dal in the pan.

I detest being here. The very smell of spices hitting hot oil and lentils in a pressure cooker is nauseating. There's nothing more I want to do than get out of this place. But how can I *not* help out? After everything our families have been through, I have no option but to assist my aunt. Without this restaurant she will drown. Her son who is in the US has asked her multiple times to shut it down and move there, but she won't hear of it.

'What do you know of our early struggles setting this up? It's easy for you to tell me to close it. Do you know it's only because of this that we could afford to send you to the US?' she yelled at him on the phone. She resents the fact that he couldn't come for his father's funeral. Though I want to point out to her that it's not his fault that the pandemic took away my uncle, I don't. I pretend I haven't heard.

It's been almost a year since we lost my uncle, but I still have nightmares about it. I wake up sweating and it takes me a while to fall asleep again. The horror of that day, when the hospital called us, is etched in my brain.

The pain is raw. I don't know how my aunt copes. The worst part is that it's only after a person has gone that you realise how much they mattered to you. While my uncle was alive, it wasn't as if I chatted with him everyday. But he was always around. Now there's a kind of emptiness when I go to their place. My aunt's eyes have lost their sparkle. Everything is shrouded in a thin layer of grief.

At last, I am done chopping and my aunt thanks me. Both of us have cleaned up the kitchen, washed the vessels and made every surface shining and spotless. I tell her that I will be back the next day as I leave for my home, which is next door.

'Arush, there you are! Did you eat something at Mami's place?' my mother asks, as I let myself in with my key.

'Not hungry, Ma,' I say as I head for the shower. The smell of the spices gets into my clothes, my hair, my nails and I need to wash it all out.

'Arush, you've become so skinny. You need to eat properly at your age. I've made biryani ...'

I shut the door to the bathroom and her voice trails off. I don't want to be rude, but today I am in no mood to even listen to her. I am exhausted. Physically and emotionally. I want to crawl under my duvet and sleep. But I can't. As soon as I finish my shower, I have to head over to my parents' saree shop and help them out. The shop is one of the most popular shops in Derbyshire that sells Indian garments. They need me there.

Now that flights have resumed, the first shipment of sarees from India has arrived. Business has just begun to pick up after two years of very little sales. The existing stock had been depleted. I know Dad had to make many calls to make this shipment happen and how important the reopening is for my parents.

At their request, I designed little flyers announcing the reopening of the store, and Jenna helped me distribute it among people visiting the gurudwara. We stood outside in the cold for about four hours and every Indian who visited the gurudwara that day went back with a flyer.

My parents are excited about the grand reopening. Mami is supplying the snacks from her restaurant and she thinks it is good publicity as all the customers will get to sample the food, and will also know that the restaurant is opening after being shut for months. It feels nice to see my family bustling about and working hard. After months of depressing news all around, it is good to see a glimmer of hope on their faces.

The flyers are the only design work I've done ever since I graduated. Jenna, bless her, keeps trying to motivate me. She drops in every now and then, and shares the work she has been producing.

Puja, in her own way, tries her best too but over video calls and emails. It's just not the same as meeting her in person. I am tired of this long-distance thing we're doing. I want to see her. I want to hold her in my arms, kiss her and thank her for all her long emails.

But I have no idea how I can travel to India anytime soon. My life now seems to be tied to my aunt's restaurant and my parents' saree shop.

Puja also doesn't understand why I am unable to paint anymore. I've tried explaining but she insists that I try again. Painting is not about 'trying.' Painting isn't like cooking, where you chop up a few ingredients and follow a recipe. How can I make her understand that after seeing my family in so much pain, after taking on a lot of responsibility for my aunt's restaurant and my parents' shop, art has lost its power to soothe, to comfort. Art doesn't come to me anymore.

Puja has asked me to take grief counselling many times. She recommends Dr Harsh, who her sister Divya is speaking to. When I hear what he charges, I am shocked. I tell her that I can take free sessions here in the UK, but I don't want to.

It's not therapy I need. I just need my family's financial situation to improve. I wish I had not overheard Dad speaking to Ma about how the money situation is very tight, and how the savings we have will last only for two months if the business doesn't pick up. I am worried. I haven't shared this with Puja because she will offer to send me money and that's the last thing I want.

Also, I've read up all about the grieving process and it is going to take time to heal—whether I speak to a grief counsellor or not.

Jenna understands. She lost her grandmother and she is grieving too. But, at least, like she says, her granny lived a full life. Unlike my uncle, who was only fifty-one.

Jenna has inherited her grandmother's cottage, and she says every room contains her memories. I've been urging her to redecorate it and get rid of her granny's stuff. We must let go of the past at some point if we have to move on. But Jenna can't bring herself to do it.

So, we all go through grief in our own way, doing what we can to cope.

I am tired of it all.

But there's nothing I can do except go on.

4

Puja

'Hey.'

We have spoken so much on the phone over the last two years that by the very tone of Arush's greeting, I can say what kind of a mood he is in. Today he is definitely feeling sadder than usual. I know.

'How are you doing?' I ask.

'Same, nothing much. The saree shop is reopening soon.' He sounds unenthusiastic.

'That's really good!' I reply, trying to inject some cheer into him. But it doesn't seem to have the usual effect. On most days he cheers up quickly when we speak, but not today.

'Suppose so. Jenna and I stood outside the gurudwara and distributed flyers.'

The moment I hear that, my intention of cheering him up vanishes. Jealousy shoots through me. He and Jenna stood together for hours, distributing flyers? How come I was hearing of it only now? The sane, logical part of my brain tells me I ought to feel happy that he didn't have to do it alone, and had a friend with him. Given the dreary cold there, I'm sure it wasn't easy. But I am too jealous to be gracious. It takes a huge effort on my part to *not* make a fuss about it and to pretend all is okay. I want to tell him that he is spending a lot of time with Jenna. Too much for my liking.

'Alright,' I say, forcing myself to sound normal.

I don't think it occurs to him that I could be jealous. He doesn't make any attempt to hide anything they do together and is always telling me when they meet, what they do. And Jenna is such a sweet person. I remember how she'd helped me plan the surprise I had sprung on Arush, when I turned up in the UK out of the blue, and how sweet it was of her to drive me to his place.

But that was *before* the pandemic. Now everything has changed. Doing long-distance is hard without the added complication of a very pretty female friend who can see him whenever she wants to.

'Jenna is struggling you know, with her gran's death and all that,' he says.

'What are Jenna's plans?' I ask. I didn't mean to ask that but I just said the first thing that came to my mind, to suppress the green monster.

'Eh?' Arush is genuinely puzzled.

'I mean, for the future. Is she planning to work, study further, what?'

'Umm, I don't know. This pandemic has thrown everything off gear. She has to first clear out her gran's cottage. Her mother is exhausted from working overtime in the hospital in London, and so won't be able to help her. The amount of people lining up for psychiatric help is insane,' he says.

'I know. My mother says the same. Apparently cardiac problems have risen steeply after the pandemic. She has got back to her normal duties now, which she says is a relief from being posted on the covid ward.'

'Yes, it's tough. The medical profession itself is so demanding. Jenna hasn't seen her mom for over eight weeks now.'

'I didn't see my mother for over three months at the peak of the pandemic. Even before the pandemic she was always busy. But that's a doctor's life for you,' I say, trying to subtly make the point that Jenna's mother is only a psychiatric nurse in the UK, while my mother is one of the leading cardiac surgeons in India, and therefore my mother is more stressed than hers. I don't even know why I am saying all this! So silly and immature of me.

But Arush doesn't notice at all.

'I have no such problems. I am around my parents all the time, and now my aunt too.' He gives a forced laugh.

'I've been meaning to ask, how is that going? You mentioned she might get a helper. It will be better for you then, right?'

'It's not so easy, Puja. Business has to pick up. Even the minimum wages for a helper here are pretty high. Not all of us are rolling in money, you know,' he says.

I detect the brusqueness in his tone. But what irks me is the reference to my money. This is not the first time this has happened. He has brought it up in the past too.

I take a deep breath and decide to raise it with him. 'Listen, Arush, you've mentioned my money earlier too. Is it bothering you?'

He is silent for a few seconds. Then he says, 'I am sorry, I didn't mean it as a jibe like that. Maybe it is because everything comes easy to you. You don't have to struggle like the rest of us. You decided to fly to the UK on a whim, spending how much, three thousand pounds? Do you know what a lot of money that is? I mean, it's enough for a family to start a business.'

'Arush, this is so unfair. You are talking about a time *before* the pandemic, when I flew to see *you*. And don't you remember, you acted like a jackass?'

'Look, Puja, I apologised too. Why are we discussing this now?'

'Because you brought it up.'

'Come on! I did not. You are the one who is saying stuff about money.'

'Because you always make a reference to the money I have. I didn't ask to be born rich, okay? And just because there's money in my bank account, it doesn't mean I don't have any problems at all,' I reply.

'Puja, let's have this conversation another time. I do not have the energy for this right now. I have to help my parents for the grand opening.'

Something inside me explodes. How can he brush me off like this? Like I am a spoilt rich brat who doesn't know what he is talking about. He doesn't have the 'energy'? What does he even mean?

And the thought that he will be spending more time with Jenna—I am sure she will be helping him at the opening —makes me even more angry.

'Great. Have a good opening,' I say and hang up abruptly.

I take a few deep breaths. I don't know what just happened and how things escalated the way they did. After a few minutes of fuming, I check my phone to see if there are any messages for him. But there's nothing. I decide that I am not going to be the first one to text him.

Later, after dinner, our parents ask us if we're done packing, as we're leaving the next day for Varkala. Divya already has.

'I'll pack now,' I tell them.

Long after my parents have gone to bed, Divya asks me what happened.

'What do you mean?' I feign innocence.

'Come on, Puja the Hooja, you can't fool me. I can see it written all over your face. The moment you walked out of your room, I knew something was wrong.' Divya's scrutiny is hard to escape.

'Is it that obvious?'

'Of course not, silly! Amma and Achcha won't be able to tell. But I knew immediately,' she declares in a way only siblings can.

'It was such a silly thing. I had a fight with Arush,' I sigh.

'I don't know how it escalated. I think I was jealous of Jenna. and I let that kind of dictate how I behaved. But he wasn't being too nice either. I am not going to text him first.'

'Yes, make him sweat a little,' Divya agrees. She is quiet for a few seconds. Then she says softly, 'I gave Karthik too much. I was dancing to his tune all the time. And see what happened.'

'Leave it, Divya. No need to give any mental space to that idiot,' I say, properly enraged on my sister's behalf. Also, she has just started coming out of her down-in-the-dumps state and I don't want her to slip back.

'Not going to think about him.' She shakes her head.

I kind of like this version of my sister. The pandemic has made us closer, and I like how we're there for each other now, unlike before.

The last thing I do before falling asleep is checking my phone for any messages from Arush.

There aren't any.

5

Sujit

Dear Puja,

I am not even sure I will send this to you. I am writing as a part of 'therapy'. Now that I have written the word 'therapy', I feel it sounds dumb. Therapy is for people who can't cope, and I don't think I am one of those.

Yet I must say Dr Harsh (my therapist) makes a lot of sense. He suggested that I write whatever is on my mind, keep it with me for a week or ten days, and send it to you if I still feel the need to send it. So here goes:

I am sorry, Puja. I unconditionally apologise. Please treat this as the equivalent of falling at your feet and begging for forgiveness. If I met you in person, I think that's what I'd still want to do but I don't think I will have the guts to do it in public.

I've been wanting to tell you how sorry I am for a long time. But I never got the chance to. I even thought of making a fake account and contacting you. (I know you've blocked me on Snap and Insta.) Even if I did reach out to you with a fake account, I doubt you'd believe me or forgive me, the asshole because of whom you went to jail. I never in a million years thought that was how it would turn out.

Believe me, Puja, I never ever intended for it to happen. I panicked. And I did something ridiculously dumb. It has haunted me ever since. Also, I feel like I was a silly teenager then, and even though we are both of the same age, I feel this pandemic has forced me to grow up.

I lost my father just before the final exams. It came as a total shock. He had recovered from Covid-19, and he seemed to be doing fine. He was having a bath when he slumped over and died in the bathroom. When he hadn't emerged even after an hour, Amma found it strange and told me to check, I had to break open the door. It was one of the worst days of my life.

It's a miracle I managed to clear the final year exams. My marks aren't great—but the fact that I even passed comes as a relief to me. Turns out my father had been laid off five months back, and he was under huge stress. He hadn't told any of us, and we discovered all of this only after he passed away.

Dr Harsh says that bottling up things is one of the worst things you can do to yourself. That's what my father had been doing.

Anyway, coming back to that fateful day when you were arrested because of me, all I can say is I was involved with the wrong kind of people back then. I feel very ashamed to admit it to you that I was a lowlife back then. I feel I must tell you the whole story in order for you to even try to understand why I did what I did.

Damn, this is hard. Now I know why Dr Harsh wanted me to write. I am not great at writing. So, forgive me if this email is disjointed.

Deep breath.

I first tried weed in Class 9. One of the older boys (you may not remember him—he was in 12th when we were in 9th; his name was Karan) gave it to me and I joined them at the lake behind our school. My mind exploded as I never knew this kind of a thing existed. It was such a fabulous feeling—it was like I was watching someone else, but I was also in control, and I was that person! Everything was moving in slow motion. I remember giggling at everything, and afterwards eating like I was starving for years. Somehow it made my shitty life more bearable.

The next day, I read up all about it. Everything I read said that weed is not physically addictive. In fact, it had medicinal value and could be helpful to treat a lot of conditions. I also read about how in India, ancient rishis used it and all of that. I was convinced it was harmless. Except, I was making a monumental mistake.

I went back to Karan for more. Pretty soon, I became psychologically dependent on it. I thought I had it all under control and I fooled myself into believing that I could quit whenever I wanted to. But that was not true at all. I was smoking up more and more. Gradually, I became a daily smoker. My life revolved around getting high. If I didn't smoke, I got very strong cravings, became irritated easily and couldn't sleep. I stole small amounts of money from my father—a hundred here, a fifty there, amounts that he wouldn't miss. I was clever enough to not take too much.

It was my addiction that made me start selling it. They were small sales. I would buy a bag of weed, break it up into smaller amounts and I'd sell it to friends. I'd make small amounts of money, enough to keep my own supply coming in.

In the first week at college, I met a big-time supplier. He fronted me the same amount of what I bought. If I bought half kg, he would give me another half kg on consignment. I would sell that and I'd pay him back.

I began selling more and more: to office goers, students and even bored housewives. You'll be surprised at the number of people who smoke this. Stoners have a way of finding other stoners.

In Wayanad that day, while we were at the trek, I was carrying a very little amount that I thought would suffice for me for the rest of the camp. I also had a small amount I thought I could sell. I did manage to sell it to Leah and Oshan, and they thought it was pretty cool. They'd both said it was the best weed they smoked ever.

Then my supplier called me, asking if I would carry back a couple of kgs of really top-class stuff grown in the mountains. My supplier's contact gave it to me that night, just outside Ashwathy Bhawan, when you were at dinner with Arush. I took your backpack when I went to meet him, which is what I regret the most. I don't know why I did that, I think it is because I didn't have a bag, and yours was the only one I had. I carried it back to my room in your backpack and thought I'd break it up into bits the next day, and hide it in my suitcase. I thought I'd make a weekend trip to Kochi and hand it over to my supplier, or I'd ask him if I could sell half of it. But before that I wanted to see for myself what this thing was. I did smoke up that night, and, my god, it was gold.

The next thing I heard were the police sirens. I panicked as I knew they were probably on to me. I didn't feel safe at all. I threw the bag out of the window and rushed out.

I was horrified when I read about your arrest in the newspaper. I owed a shit ton of money to my supplier. His contact who gave it to me thought I was playing him. My supplier didn't believe that the police had actually seized it till he read the newspaper. Anyway, these people are ruthless. All they wanted was the money or the stuff. I had neither.

When Leah, Oshan and Arush set the trap for me, and lured me to that empty plot of land in Jew Town, I was so desperate for a sale. A sale meant I could clear the debt I owed these guys. They didn't trust me enough and so they sent those two guys to follow me. Even I wasn't aware they were following me. Then Arush screamed all sorts of things, like he had called the police, and that set them off.

Puja, I yelled at a shopkeeper to call the ambulance because I knew Arush was hurt. I watched you giving statements on television and I felt like I didn't deserve to live. It was the worst feeling in the world. You were getting entangled in this for no fault of yours. Arush could've been killed—all because of me. That really shook me up badly.

I'd had enough of this life. I felt horribly guilty. This violence, gang fights, owing people money, I was sick of it. But I didn't have the guts to tell my father. So, I told my mother.

Without my father's knowledge she sold off her two gold bangles, the only ones she had, and gave me the money. That broke me, Puja. You see, she is not even my birth-mother. She is my stepmother, whom my dad married a year after my mother died.

I quit cold turkey that day. It's the hardest thing I have done. The withdrawal symptoms were terrible. My mother saw how much I was suffering; she said I absolutely needed a change of environment where I knew nobody. She sent me to her sister's place in Pune. Her sister's husband runs a yoga school, and she thought it would be good for me. I went for her sake. Even in the train, when I was looking at passengers, my mind was quickly analysing potential customers. I had to force myself to stop thinking that way. I had to remind myself why I was leaving that life behind.

My aunt and her husband were very sweet to me. The facilities at the yogashala were minimal. They gave me wholesome vegetarian food.

The rules were strict: I had to be up at 5.30 a.m. We had an hour to assemble at the shala. Then the whole day had set routines.

That month there cleansed my whole system. I decided I would never touch that shit again. I changed my phone number.

I can tell you it is the hardest and yet the best thing I have done in my life. For the first time in many years, I was drug-free and I could think of a life that did not revolve around getting high. I read some good books.

Then the pandemic hit, and my father died.

So now you know my whole story.

I feel terrible for what happened to you and Arush. There are simply no excuses for who I was back then.

I have changed now. I am no longer that person.

I am truly sorry, Puja. From the bottom of my heart.

Please forgive me if you can.

Sujit.

7
Arush

Why is Puja annoyed? I don't get it. I've already apologised for bringing up her money. That wasn't cool at all. In fact, it was downright rude. I have made a mental note to never bring it up again. I replay the whole conversation we had in my head. I still don't get why she hung up so abruptly.

Mami calls me to help in setting up the food tables and chairs. One of my father's friends from the Sikh community, who has a furniture rental agency, has offered the chairs and tables. He even sent his two sons to help us. My parents, my aunt, my father's friend's sons—everyone pitches in. In no time the tables and chairs are set up.

Mami has gone all out for this event. In addition to the scrumptious feast she has been making—rotis, naan, shahi paneer and butter chicken—she also wants to give a little takeaway packet to every guest who attends the event. 'The packet will contain two samosas and chutney,' she says.

'Isn't it a bit too much, Pammi?' my mother asks my aunt.

'Param always said that we have to spend money to make money,' my aunt says recalling my uncle's words. 'All this stuff we are giving away for free costs only a little more than what it does to put an ad in the local paper. This is targeted marketing, as every person who comes here would be interested in Indian food. An ad in the paper—who knows who would even see it. Besides, think of the word-of-mouth benefits we will be getting once they taste all this.'

'Alright, let's do it then. We will all help. Once they taste what you make, the orders will come pouring in,' my father says.

Jenna says she will come over to help. She has become such a good friend over the past two years that it's hard to think of a time when she wasn't around. Rhea, my little sister—who at eight is growing up fast—practically worships her and follows her around like a little puppy whenever she visits. She even asked Ma about getting her hair dyed blonde. 'I want blonde hair and blue eyes like Jenna' she had declared one day.

I had sat her down and explained what genetics is, and why British people look a certain way.

'But we are British too, aren't we?' Rhea had asked.

'Yes, but we are of Indian origin. Dad and Ma came to Britain in a ship when they were very young. All our relatives are in India,' I explain to her. Then I'd proceeded to give her a little history and biology lesson, till she yawned and asked me not to be 'such a professor'.

On the day of the grand opening, all of us wake up early. Jenna arrives on the dot at 6.30 a.m., like she said she would. She takes me by utter surprise, as she is dressed in a light purple salwar kameez. She is even wearing a bindi. And, good heavens, what's with the Indian jewellery? I've never seen Jenna like this. I gaze at her in surprise.

My aunt and my mother chuckle in delight. My mother says she looks stunning.

'Your aunt lent me this. I think it belongs to her daughter,' Jenna says as she grins from ear to ear at the look on my face.

'Mona didn't take any of her Indian clothes when she left for Australia,' my aunt says. It occurs to me that Jenna has become so comfortable around my family, that she was able to plan all this behind my back.

We sit in a large circle, my parents, my aunt, Rhea, Jenna and me. My aunt hands out food-handling gloves and kitchen caps that we put on. Jenna is chattering away nineteen to the dozen with my folks. 'You must make a trip to India when we go. You can come with us,' I hear my mother saying and my jaw drops.

'Really? I'd love that. But I don't know, let's see,' Jenna says.

Once we are done with the food packets, we help my aunt arrange the packets in wicker baskets and line them up on tables at the entrance so that we can hand them out to the guests as they leave.

We gobble the breakfast which my mother has prepared. It is scrambled eggs with an Indian touch; she calls it egg bhurji. My mother adds garam masala and coriander leaves to everything she makes, and Jenna loves it.

'I think secretly I am an Indian trapped in a white person's body,' she says.

'And I think I am a British person trapped in an Indian body,' Rhea says and we all laugh.

Soon a lot of people from the neighbourhood and from the community start arriving. My father plays Punjabi songs on the speaker which I have set up. It isn't very loud because we don't want out neighbours to complain, even though we have taken permission from the city council for holding the event. A large, broad white ribbon is tied across the entrance of the store.

When most of the guests have arrived and have been seated, my father makes a little speech. He thanks the community for the support they extended during these extremely hard times and he talks about how happy he is to be reopening the store.

Then he says, 'I would like my good friend, Nik Mehta, to cut the ribbon. All of you know, Nikhilesh owns one of the biggest travel agencies in the UK. Apart from that he owns multiple businesses. His success is an inspiration to all of us. We all came here, leaving our motherlands, to fulfil a certain dream. Nik is a living, shining example of that dream. But before he cuts the ribbon, I request Nik to address this gathering.'

All the guests burst into applause and I join in, thoroughly surprised to see this side of my father.

Nik stands up and the first thing I notice about him is his height. He is towering over the others and is a good three inches taller than my father who is almost 6 feet tall himself. He walks briskly to the front of the shop. The streaks of silver in his hair glisten in the sunlight. He has tiny laughing eyes, as though he just heard a joke. In a well-fitted suit, every inch of him exudes success. He is one of those people who automatically commands respect when they walk into a room.

'A very warm good morning to everyone present here, even though the sun in Britain is never warm,' he says and that instantly elicits chuckles from the audience.

'Satyam, Shivam, Sundaram!' he continues. 'This is a Sanskrit mantra, which means Truth, Godliness, Beauty. It is something that has stood by me in my darkest times. If you carry these words in your heart and infuse them in your work, no matter what adversities you face, you will get through them and shine. Be truthful to who you are. We need our authenticity. That is what people will gravitate towards. Be honest and fair in your dealings with others, and you will find beauty in your work, in life, and in everything you do.'

Nik Mehta goes on to tell us how his parents arrived in Britain in a ship, with many other Indians, with just three pounds in his pockets to work in Britain's foundries at a time when the country desperately needed people from its former colonies to regenerate the post-war economy. He talks about how Indians did the work that the native British people did not want to do. His father lived in a four-room house with twenty-eight other people. They took turns sleeping on the beds available as they did day and night shifts. He talks about how determined he was to give his parents a good life. Then he goes on to elaborate how his business grew. 'The Indian community can achieve great things because we have a secret weapon that no one has,' he pauses, 'it is called hard work.'

By the time he finishes, every single person is visibly moved and inspired at the same time.

When Nik Mehta cuts the ribbon, Jenna clicks photos and records videos with her DSLR camera. At college, photography was one of her electives, and she is excellent at this.

When we are inside, my father introduces me to Nik.

'Remember Arush, my son?' he asks.

Nik stares at me and breaks into a wide smile. 'Oh my god, Arush? The last time I saw you, you were about this high,' he says and makes a gesture towards the floor. 'You were furiously pedalling your tricycle.'

I smile because I don't know what to say.

My father then introduces Rhea to him who smartly shakes his hand. My sister is not shy at all.

After Nik goes around the shop, my father asks him to join everyone for lunch. My aunt, my mother and Jenna are standing behind the table, serving everyone who has helped themselves to plates. Almost every single person makes a remark about how wonderful the food is. After the meal is done, Rhea and I stand behind the table with the wicker baskets and hand out the samosa packets as the guests leave.

As Nik leaves, he asks me, 'So your father tells me that you designed the invitation for this opening?'

I nod.

'It was a unique and eye-catching design, I must say. I loved it.'

'Thank you so much, Mr Mehta,' I say.

'Nik, just call me Nik,' he says. 'What are your plans for the future, young man?'

'To be honest, I have no concrete plans. Before the pandemic I intended doing my master's, but now I am not so sure. I've been so busy helping my aunt and my parents,' I tell Nik.

'Well, things are opening up now, and if you are in the market for a job and are willing to move to Birmingham, this is a good time. We're, in fact, looking for someone in design for my company,' he says.

A job offer? So casually and quickly? Based on just one design of mine? I thank him. I can't believe my luck! I tell him that I will get back to him, and I ask for his email. I note it down in my phone.

I want to look up the company, the pay, and what they do. I need to speak to my aunt. To my parents. Only then can I decide. The prospect of a job buzzes like a bee inside my bones.

Once the guests leave, we get busy. We wash the plates, the large vessels my aunt cooked in, clear the tables and fold the chairs. It takes us a few hours and we work like robots. Jenna stays back and helps with all of it. Before she leaves my parents thank her; she says she is happy to help.

'You know we have no leftovers? Everyone took a second helping,' my aunt says. She is bursting with pride and happiness.

'I saw some taking a third helping as well,' my mother says.

'Pammi, get busy. You're going to have a big crowd at your restaurant,' my father says.

'Ah, may it be so. I will look forward to that,' she says.

I am exhausted with the day's events. In bed that night, the phone vibrates when I am almost asleep. At last, Puja has reached out, I think, and reach out for the phone. Not Puja. The text is from Jenna.

'Today was such a different experience. I loved it.'

I want to reply, but I am too tired. I place the phone back on my bedside table and go to sleep.

6
Puja

We are on our way to Varkala when Sujit's mail arrives.

Achcha, who has given our driver Antony a few days off, says he is immensely enjoying driving this car. He is humming Bob Marley's *Buffalo Soldier*, nodding and shaking his head. Amma grins watching him. Divya stares out of the window as we speed towards Varkala. Even though I have lived all my life in Kerala, watching the beautiful bright green fields lined with coconut trees whiz by is exhilarating.

That's when it pops up. A notification saying I have a new email. For a few seconds I just stare at the sender's name. I can't believe what I am looking at. Sujit? Why is he sending me a mail? After so long? I have blocked him everywhere—Snapchat, Instagram, WhatsApp. But it hadn't occurred to me to block him on email as well. Curiosity compels me to read his mail.

When I finish reading, I wish I'd never opened it. The raw honesty in his mail has hit me hard. I feel terrible for him. I feel his pain, his helplessness, his anguish. All of it. I can imagine what a humongous effort it must have been for him to write this.

I had no idea about his family background, how he lost his mother at a young age or about his father remarrying. At school, he'd always been 'the trouble-maker Sujit' and none of us thought anything beyond that. We had just accepted that it was the way he was. But now I am seeing another side to him. I can't even imagine what he must have gone through to find his father dead in the bathroom. I involuntarily shudder. Losing a parent is one of my biggest fears.

I thought I had closed the chapter on Sujit and moved on. But the way he has explained all that he has been through, and his genuine apologies throw me off track. His therapist is the same as Divya's. I sit in silence not knowing what to do, my head spinning with whatever Sujit has written. I stare out of the window, trying to process it all.

It is only when Divya nudges me that I see that my mother has opened a packet of murukkus and is offering me some.

'Dreaming of Arush?' she teases me. I am yet to get used to this—the fun playful person that she can be. She has changed so much ever since I ran away to meet Arush in the UK. Gone is the strict, pushy parent who wanted me to get into IIM. She says that it doesn't matter what we do, the important thing is to be happy with the choices we make. The pandemic has altered all our perspectives, hers more than anyone else's. She said that in her entire medical career, she had never witnessed so many deaths at the hospital. This experience has made her think about what really matters in our lives.

Looking at her happy face, I force myself to smile and I help myself to a murukku. I'm quiet the rest of the way.

Divya types a message on her phone and shows it to me. She has typed, 'What is wrong? What happened?'

I take her phone and type, 'Will tell you later.'

Divya and I communicate this way when we don't want to share something with our parents. It started when we were all locked in during the pandemic, and we've continued it.

The boutique resort we check into is beautiful, done up entirely in the traditional Kerala style, with sloping roofs and red tiles. Divya and I are in a luxury double room, and Amma and Achcha are in the suite next to it. Our doors open to an unhindered ocean view; I think about how much Arush would enjoy this. Then I am annoyed with myself for even thinking about him. It's been more than thirty-six hours and Arush hasn't texted. It makes me even more determined to dig in my heels.

I. Am. Not. Going. To. Message. Him. First.

Divya reclines on the bed, which has intricate wooden carvings. I open Sujit's mail and push my phone into her hand.

'You want me to read this?' she asks as she takes my phone.

'Yes. It's a mail from Sujit who has suddenly reappeared.'

'That jerk because of whom you were arrested? *That* Sujit?'

'He isn't a jerk. Read the mail.'

I notice her facial expression change with each line she reads.

'Oh, my!' She shakes her head. 'I had no idea ...'

'Yeah, exactly what I felt too.'

'And Dr Harsh, he is quite something if he got him to write that mail. You know he told me the same too. To write to Karthik if it would give me closure.'

'Did you?'

'No, too painful. I am still furious and yet to process the whole thing. Your boy here, Sujit, it would have taken him a lot to write this.'

'I know. I feel so bad. I feel we judged him harshly.'

'Don't forget you went to jail because of him.'

'Yeah, Divya, but he suffered more than me. I mean, yes, it was scary. But Achcha came immediately and bailed me out in a few hours. And Arush getting beaten up ... a little bit was his own making too. What was the need to trap him like that? In a way, don't you think Arush was asking for it?'

'Hmm ... I guess that's one way to look at it. And it's clear from Sujit's mail that he feels horrid about that too and regrets it big time.'

I bit my lip. 'Yes, he does.'

Divya hesitates. 'Do you think he is lying? A small chance? I'm just playing the devil's advocate here.'

'I don't think so. Why will he write to me after nearly two years? Also, if he is lying then he should become a film script writer. It doesn't seem like a story someone can make up just like that.'

'You're right. It sounds sincere. He is pleading with you, actually.'

'Yes, he is'

'Are you going to write back and tell him you forgive him?'

'I forgave him long time back, Divya. I put it behind me at that time itself. Still, I am not sure whether I should write back.'

'I think you should,' Divya says.

'Really? Why?'

'It will give him closure. He seems to be struggling with the guilt.'

But before I can say anything, our parents enter our room through the connecting door.

Both Divya and I gape at Amma. She is wearing jeans and a T-shirt! We've only seen photos of her in jeans from her college days. Her usual outfit to the hospital is salwar kameez, which Shanti Chechi lays out for her. Divya lets out an appreciative whistle and Amma grins.

'Wow, Amma! You look smart,' I say.

'What did you girls think? Only you can be fashionable?' she asks, smiling. Her patient who owns this resort, Mr Nandagopal, has arranged for a kayaking afternoon in the mangroves for all of us. He has spoken to Mr Nambiar, the owner of the kayaking company, and blocked it exclusively for our family.

'What VIP treatment we're getting because of Amma,' Achcha says.

'Nandagopal feels I saved his life. But, honestly, it's not in our hands. We doctors are just the instruments. Any other surgeon would've performed exactly what I did.' Amma shrugs.

A hotel car takes us to the kayaking place down a narrow road snaking through verdant green fields lined with coconut trees. Juxtaposed against the bright blue sky, it is almost like a postcard. As we pull in, the person in charge is already waiting to greet us. Both Divya and I look at each other. It's the same thought that's running in both our heads: this guy is hot! He is in a sleeveless T-shirt, and his muscular biceps glisten in the sunlight. His vest is low-cut and I am sure Divya hasn't missed his taut chest muscles. His hair and shoulders are wet.

'Hello, welcome, I am Benny Kuruvilla, the manager, instructor and guide, all in one,' he says, pushing back his damp hair from his forehead. He has a charming smile too.

'Hello, Benny. I'm Chaitra, this is my husband Krishnan and my daughters, Puja and Divya,' Amma introduces all of us.

'Nambiar already told me,' Benny says. He walks with us towards a cabin, in front of which is a shallow pond. Multi-coloured kayaks, bright red, lemon yellow and light green, are scattered across the edge of the pond. He asks Achcha to fill a form, which is a disclaimer that he understands the risks associated with the sport. He has to write his name and phone number and names of the people who will be kayaking.

'Er, I have a request,' Benny says. 'I had already booked a client for kayaking today. He is leaving back for Mumbai early tomorrow, and this is his last chance to kayak. He wanted me to ask you all whether he could join in with your family.'

Achcha looks at Amma who looks at us. I shrug. I don't mind at all if a person joins us. Neither does Divya.

'No problem, he can join us,' Achcha tells Benny.

'Okay, great, thank you!' Benny says. Then his voice drops a bit and he says, 'Could you please not mention this to Mr Nambiar? He was insistent this should be an exclusive tour.'

'Of course, it is exclusive. It is only our family. There's no one else here, no?' My father laughs and looks at us. He pats Benny on the back.

'Thank you, Sir. Give me two minutes.' Benny looks relieved and walks towards the cabin.

The guy who would be joining us emerges from the cabin with Benny. His medium-length dark hair is slicked back casually and he has a stubble-covered jaw. He is slightly shorter than Benny and it is obvious that this guy hits the gym regularly. While Benny has a rugged look about him, like he has spent a lot of time outdoors, this guy seems like he is the kind who'd go to a salon for a men's facial. He is well-groomed and casually stylish.

Divya and I look at each other again, and we both suppress a chuckle. Why are we behaving like this, like we've never seen guys, I don't know.

I drag her aside. 'Don't make me laugh,' I whisper.

'You are the one drooling with your eyes,' she says.

'I am not,' I hiss.

Benny says, 'This is Vihan Dixit from Mumbai.'

'Hi and thank you for letting me join in today,' Vihan says, flicking his hair back with his hand.

Divya looks at me again and this time I am unable to suppress a giggle, which I quickly turn into a cough. Being cooped up inside the house for so long is making us behave like idiots.

Benny guides us towards the shallow pool in front of the cabin for the training. He hands us all life jackets, which we wear. He gives us each a kayak paddle and makes us stand in a semi-circle with more than three feet distance between us. He shows us how to use the paddle.

'Left-right, left-right, you have to keep up the rhythm. Remember if you row on the left, the kayak will turn to the right, and if you row on the right, the kayak will turn to the left.' He asks us to mimic him as he swings the paddle gracefully on both sides like a dancer. When we copy him, our movements are awkward.

'Will we be alone in a kayak?' Amma looks nervous.

'Yes, Ma'am. You will be alone as we're not doing tandem. You have to steer the boat by yourself. How many of you know to row a boat?' he asks.

Only Achcha raises his hand. He grew up in a fishing village where children learnt to swim before they learnt to walk. Every house had a boat.

'Aah, don't worry, by the end of the day everyone here will be an expert in kayaking. Please tell others that you learnt to row in Benny Kuruvilla's class,' he says and all of us chuckle nervously.

'I don't even know how to swim. I don't think I want to do this,' Amma says.

'Don't worry, 99 per cent chances are that the kayak won't topple over,' Benny tells us.

'And what about that one per cent?' Vihan asks. 'I can't swim either.'

'That's what I am here for. I will be with you throughout. Trust me, it will be worth the effort once you see the mangroves,' he tells us.

Then he takes us all into the shallow pool and demonstrates how we are to get into the kayak and out of it and how to balance our body weight. He gently lowers himself and takes both his feet inside at the same time.

'Don't do this, else it will tilt and you will fall into the water,' he says and he steps into the kayak to demonstrate what we shouldn't be doing. The kayak topples and he splashes into the water. All of us gasp.

He emerges, laughing. 'Seeeeee? If you just step in like that, this is what will happen. I wanted you to see it so you don't do it.' He sounds gleeful.

'Is this Benny Kuruvilla high on something?' Divya whispers to me.

'Maybe he is. His eyes are a bit bloodshot,' I tell her.

Benny asks each of us to step into the shallow pond and makes us all get into the kayak. All of us are nervous, especially Vihan. Only Achcha is chuckling at our discomfort.

I try rowing just like Benny demonstrated. It is hard! I see others struggling too. But Benny is encouraging and patient. He rows to each of us, gives our kayaks a little push into the water to help us.

In about fifteen minutes we've all got the hang of it. This is incredible! I am actually on a kayak, rowing all over. Benny shouts, 'Woo hoo! Well done my friends. Now follow me.'

My arms hurt as I row. After five minutes we are in the middle of the backwaters and Benny stops and asks us to enjoy the surroundings and the greenery.

It is so silent. Green. Serene. A kind of peace that I've never felt before envelopes me. I feel fortunate to be experiencing this. No one speaks and I can see that they're all feeling the same. I reach out for my camera from the pocket of my shorts and shoot a few videos. After a few minutes, we continue rowing to the mangroves. I take a sharp breath when we reach and I stare in awe. It's nothing like I've ever seen before. I am looking at a forest in the middle of the water! A dense tangle of roots makes it appear as though the trees are on stilts. Narrow waterways form canals around these and we weave our kayaks into these tunnels of greenery. There are so many species of fishes and birds that I can spot. I can't name any of them but I'm filled with wonder as I watch. We maintain a silence, recognising how special this is.

At one point the water path is so narrow that my kayak gets stuck in the roots. I see that my mother and Vihan are also facing the same problem.

'Don't worry! I'll help,' Benny says as he rows towards each of us and expertly nudges our kayak with his paddle, and in no time we're on the right waterway again. He also asks for our phones and shoots a few videos of us. I click a selfie with Benny. Once we reach the shore, everyone is in a great mood and we pose for more pictures. I decide that I will post these as soon as we get back to the hotel. I want Arush to burn with jealousy.

Divya has hit it off really well with Vihan. They're both laughing so much and chattering away nonstop, standing under a tree next to the kayaks, under the moonlight and a million glittering stars. The scene looks like the cover of an album of love songs. The whole place around them is dark, and light from a lamppost illuminates both their faces. It looks so pretty that I take out my phone and shoot a small video clip. Amma looks at me and raises her eyebrows. I shrug and smile. It's been so long since we heard Divya laughing like this, and it feels nice. Achcha is walking just in front of us, with Benny. I can tell that he likes Benny.

'How did you get into this kayaking? What's your background?' I hear my father asking Benny.

'Sir, after my MBA, I was working in an Italian company and got a chance to travel. In Reno river in Bologna, I had my first kayaking experience. It totally blew my mind that something this magnificent exists in the world. I thought there are such beautiful rivers in Kerala, why don't we have kayaking here too?'

Benny speaks well and his voice is unhurried and deep. His accent is neutral, and I think that he would do well if he chose to be a radio jockey—he has a good 'radio voice'.

'With the savings from my job, I started my own company here in Varkala. We were doing really well too. In another six months, we would have broken even. Then the pandemic struck. I had to sell my company, and Mr Nambiar bought it. But I am too much in love with kayaking, and I continue to do this daily. It was one of the conditions when we made the sale, that I'd handle the day-to-day things.' Benny smiles.

I know he has won my father over. He loves entrepreneurs. And he loves people who are driven, and who speak well. Benny is all of it.

By now Amma and I are walking beside them. 'We both enjoyed it very much,' Amma says.

'Thank you,' Benny beams. 'The main thing is that a good instructor should have love for the sport. Then he or she should have a solid personal technique in both still and choppy waters. Here, because the water is very still, it's not so hard to row. Also, it's not just about kayaking. We need to have a great sense of empathy for people, and we have to understand each student, and work according to their potential. Sometimes we all need a little nudge. But for some people, the nudge might be too much force and they might see it as a shove. It's just like when your kayaks got stuck. We need to know where and how much to push. It's a lot like life.' Benny looks wistful.

How much this guy talks!

'Well said, well said,' my father agrees. I can see that he is enjoying this conversation with Benny a lot. By now we have all walked to the car that is waiting for us. We turn to look for Divya. She and Vihan are still near the kayaks.

'Divya, we're leaving,' I call out.

'Coming.' She waves as she and Vihan walk towards us.

'Guess what? Vihan is staying in the same resort,' she says.

'How did you come? Do you want to ride back in the car with us?' Amma asks.

'I hired a scooter and rode here.' He grins. 'Alright, I'll see you all around later,' Vihan says, but he looks at Divya as he says it. And I can't believe I am seeing Divya blush. My parents don't miss it either.

In the cart, my parents ask Divya what Vihan does. She says he was born and raised in Singapore, works for a foreign bank and is currently in Mumbai on an international posting. She tells us that he said there might be an opening in his bank for a job that fits her profile.

I decide to tease her a little bit.

'Love is in the air ....' I sing the classic song by John Paul Young. It's a song from the seventies and I know it because my father has played it a million times at home. Amma likes it too. They immediately join me. We all sing it badly, out of tune, looking at Divya as we do so.

'Enough! Stop it, you all,' Divya says but she is smiling.

When we reach the resort, our parents say they are exhausted and go to their room. Divya is excited as Vihan has asked her if she wants to go for a walk. She tells me not to wait up, and that she will let herself in with her key card.

I check my messages. There still isn't any from Arush. I lie in bed wondering if a long-distance relationship can fade away if both involved don't talk to each other or communicate for a while. I idly scroll through my phone, pleased with the videos I've shot. During the pandemic, one of the courses I did was a mobile videography course and I've made use of everything I've learnt. I open Instagram, find a trending song, and about thirty-five minutes later, I've made a smart, well-edited fifteen-second reel that captures today perfectly.

Then I use the hashtags, post it and go to bed thinking that Divya must be having a really good time with Vihan.

8 Sujit

Now that I have sent the mail, I feel like an idiot. It has been two days and there's no reply from Puja. I check my Instagram fifty times a day to see if she has unblocked me. She hasn't.

I tell this to Dr Harsh at our next session. 'I shouldn't have sent that mail.'

'Why? What is it that you feel?'

'Every single thing I say cannot be analysed precisely, Doc. I just feel like an idiot,' I reply, annoyed at his question.

'Hmmm. Was it because you expected her to reply?'

'It might sound stupid, but yes, I guess that's what I was hoping for.'

'No, it's not stupid at all. We all need acceptance from our peers. That's how our brains have evolved over millions of years. We are herd animals and when we are rejected from the herd, it can impede our survival. That's why we so desperately want to "belong" to a group.'

But his telling me a scientific fact based on Charles Darwin's theory of evolution doesn't help me at all. 'I don't think it's about belonging. I never was a part of her circle. It's not that I am seeking acceptance into some cool kids' gang like in college,' I say.

'I find it interesting that you mention this now and you phrase it that way. Did your college have these cool kids' gangs? Were you ever a part of them?' Dr Harsh looks curious.

'Hell, no. I was never a part of that inner circle, but they would all come to me, for getting you-know-what whenever they had a party. I was never invited to any of those parties though. They only needed me to get them their shit,' I reply, my voice lowering instantly, remembering all the times in college that I'd sold stuff to the rich kids. They were such fools and I could easily make money off them by selling it to them at four times the price I got it for.

'Did it kind of make you feel powerful? And now that you don't deal or do the substance anymore, do you feel that some of the power has been taken away?'

I sit still for a few seconds thinking about what he just said. Then it hits me that he is absolutely right. Damn! This Dr Harsh is good. That's exactly what it is all about, but even I hadn't realised it, till he phrased it this way.

'I suppose yes. Though it didn't occur to me till you said it,' I admit.

'No one likes to *not* be invited to things, Sujit. It's natural. But now that you know it, you can be more aware of every action of yours. You've given up the substance, you want to move on with your life, you have made major changes. You might *want* acceptance from Puja, but ask yourself whether you *need* it? Can you function without it? Does it consume you to the point where you can't think of anything else?'

I think about that for a moment. 'I'm able to function,' I tell him.

'So, you do have it under control then?'

I nod.

He then asks me that else is troubling me. I tell him it's the whole job search issue. I've been looking for jobs. I only have a graduate degree and that simply isn't adequate to get management-level entry jobs. Most of them ask for an MBA. Now that Achcha is no more, I don't have the luxury of going in for an MBA degree. I need to take care of Sindu, Ravi and Amma who has been a housewife all her life.

'Ever thought of starting something of your own? That way you don't have to depend on someone else for a job,' Dr Harsh says.

'You mean like a business?'

'Yes. Some kind of a business.'

'No. No one in my family has done that,' I say and my mind immediately starts assessing as to how in the world would I ever raise funding, what business could I start even if I wanted to. The idea itself seems very alien.

'Then maybe you can be the first, Sujit,' he says. 'You set your own working hours, you are your own boss. Do start thinking about it.'

I tell him I will.

Long after the session is over, his words keep playing in my head. Talking to him is helping me a lot more than I was initially willing to admit. It has given me a new way of looking at things. I am starting to feel better about myself, after every session with him. I am surprised to find that the grief that I am carrying within me is losing its sharp sting. It's suddenly becoming more bearable. That night I sleep much better than I ever have.

The next morning, at breakfast, I tell Amma that I am glad she forced me to take those sessions.

'I also want to talk to Dr Harsh,' Sindu announces through a mouthful of idiyappam.

'You want to talk to him? Why?' I ask, surprised.

'Because I want to ask him what to tell Urmila when she wants to copy my homework. I work hard and do it. Every day when I go to school she asks if she can copy it. Just because she is my best friend, I don't think she can do that, no?' Sindu says, her eyes blazing with indignation.

I nod gravely. I can see Amma and Ravi suppressing their amused smiles.

'Best friends can't take advantage of each other. Maybe you can tell her that if she keeps copying, she will never learn to do the homework herself, and by allowing her to copy, you are actually kind of making her "dumb". Doing homework makes us smarter,' I say.

Sindu is satisfied with that. 'Yes, Chetta, that's what I will tell her.'

How I wish my problems in life were as simple as hers. She leaves for school and Ravi leaves for college. Amma then asks me if I will get some kudampuli from my dad's sister's house, which is about two kilometres away. 'Jayashri Chechi told me she will give me some, as her mother-in-law sent some to her from the village. And it is of excellent quality.'

I groan. 'Amma, couldn't you have told me this yesterday evening? It's going to be too hot to cycle now. I will get roasted in this heat.'

'She called me only this morning. I was planning to make your favourite fish curry for lunch. But if you can't—'

'No, no. I will get it.'

Amma's fish curry is legendary. It's worth cycling five times in the heat just for a spoonful of that stuff.

I pack water in my backpack—I am going to need it if I am cycling in this scorching heat—and set out towards Jayashri Chechi's house. By the time I return back from her home with the kudampuli, I am drenched in sweat.

As I enter the home, I am shocked to hear Amma crying in the kitchen. Long, racking sobs. My heart begins pounding loudly. What has happened now?

'Amma, what happened?' I ask as I rush towards her, dropping my backpack on the floor.

But she is crying so hard that she is finding it hard to speak.

'Amma, please tell me what happened. Is Sindu okay? Is Ravi okay?' My mind jumps to the worst possible things I can imagine. After Achcha's sudden death, I am aware that anything can happen at any time to anybody. Life comes with no guarantees.

Amma nods. Her face is pale and she looks shaken.

I heave a sigh of relief and fetch her a glass of jeerakavellam, which Amma always has on the stove.

'Here, Amma, have this,' I say as I hand it to her.

She takes it from my hand, trying to control her sniffles and then she drinks it all in two gulps. She inhales deeply. 'A man came here after you left. Looked like a proper goon. Said Achcha had taken a loan from his company and he was here to collect. He said the bank had sent several reminders, and tried the phone number as well, but the phone is switched off and there's no reply.'

'Didn't you tell him he passed away?'

'I did, Mone, but he didn't believe me. He asked me not to lie. He … he used very coarse language. His tone, it was not okay. He said we had to repay it immediately,' Amma's voice quivers as she speaks.

My blood boils when I hear that. How dare anyone come *here*, to *my* home and threaten *my* mother? 'How can he just turn up here like that and how dare he refuse to believe you, Amma?'

'I don't know. I never expected anything like this, and I don't even know if what he is saying is true.'

'Did you ask him to show any ID?'

'I did but he said he doesn't have to show me any ID proof and if I had any doubts, I can check with the bank that we borrowed from.'

'What did you tell him?'

'The truth. That I wasn't aware of any loan ... and that's when he said he knows ways to get the money from me. He said he will reach out to all our relatives and tell them we are defaulters.'

I want to find this guy and knock out all the teeth in his mouth. I want to bash his head in.

'I wish I was here, Amma. I wish you hadn't sent me to—'

But she doesn't let me finish. 'See, Sujit, there's no point blaming him. Maybe he is a recovery agent hired by the bank. I've heard horror stories of how they deal with defaulters. Let's go through Achcha's files and check if what he is saying is true.'

She has calmed down considerably now. And she is right.

'Let me get all his files,' I say as I walk to their bedroom where Achcha stored all the files.

An hour later, Amma and I are surrounded by financial records. We've spread it all out on the dining table. We have meticulously gone through all the old files Achcha has fortunately maintained, even though it's not in perfect order. We unravel a paper trail. We discover that he owes the bank Rs. 62,843. The letter also states that if we don't repay it within a certain date there's a penal amount in addition to the interest rate they are charging. I look at the figures. Why in the world did Achcha even borrow this amount? Was he that desperate for money?

'Amma, leave this to me, I'll handle it,' I say, standing up.

'What are you going to do, Mone?' Amma looks worried.

'Don't be worried, Amma. I'm going to their office, and I am going to talk to the manager. I'll take a copy of the death certificate with me and I'll see what can be done,' I say with a confidence I am not feeling.

The bank is about ten minutes away if I cycle. It's past midday. The harsh blazing sun beats down on me as I pedal furiously, taking out all my anger and frustration on the pedals. I feel the burn in my thighs. By the time I arrive at the bank I am drenched in sweat and look a mess. I don't have a tissue with me, and I wipe my face on my shirtsleeve.

I park the cycle and after chaining it to an iron railing, I enter the bank. There is hardly anyone there. An old man stands at the cash counter holding an umbrella which doubles up as his walking stick. He waits patiently as the teller counts the currency notes.

'Sir, you can also withdraw from the ATM machine outside,' she tells him when she finishes counting.

'Do you have any problem giving me my cash, young lady?' the old man asks her.

'No, sir, of course not,' she says as she hands him the money. He counts it carefully, keeps it in his wallet and turns around.

There's no one else at the other counters in the bank as I approach the teller. 'I'd like to speak with the manager, please,' I tell her.

'What is this regarding?' she asks

'I want to speak to him directly,' I say. I don't want to tell her about a goon threatening my mother.

'Young man, that's the manager's cabin,' the old man tells me, pointing to a cabin with his umbrella. When he sees me hesitate, he says, 'You don't have to ask her permission. It is their duty to serve you. Do you know these banks use our deposits to lend our money at high interest rates? That's how they make their money. But for us, these people here wouldn't even have jobs, Bah!'

'Go on, right there,' the old man urges me again.

And I walk towards the cabin, not sure whether to knock or not as the door is wide open. A lady in a maroon saree sits at the table and is writing. The nameplate reads Vijaya Kumari, Branch Manager.

'Excuse me, Ma'am,' I say as I gently knock.

'Yes, come in,' she says as she looks up at me. Her black-framed glasses remind me of my old school principal. But her eyes are inquisitive, not accusatory or judgemental. I walk in and she indicates the chair opposite her.

'I am Sujit ... Sujit Nair,' I say as I sit down. 'My father is Damodaran Nair.' My hands are icy cold and I clutch them tightly, thankful that they are hidden from her view because of the desk.

'Damodaran Nair ....' She frowns. 'I'm sorry I don't recall that name. Does he have an account with us? I've personally met all our customers,' she says, tilting her head, her eyebrows going up a little.

'He passed away some time back,' I say as I take out the death certificate. But I don't give it to her yet. I don't even know why I have taken it out without her asking for it.

'Oh, I am sorry,' she says. She seems to be genuinely sorry. She has eyes that reflect what's going on inside her head, even though the rest of her demeanour is professional.

'So, what is this about?' she asks.

'Ma'am, he had taken a loan from this bank. According to the records, he owes the bank some money. But this is no way to send reminders. A goon came to our house today and threatened my mother. That's simply not done, Ma'am. The fact is neither my mother nor I were even aware of the loan. When my mother asked to see his ID papers, he said there was no need for him to show her any of that. I've come to formally register a complaint and I want to sort out this issue,' I tell her. My anger is coming back at the unfairness of it all.

'This must be the third-party collection agents. He is not our employee. I apologise for the trouble he caused. This is not at all how it should be done. Give me a few minutes. Let me check the details.' Then she presses a few buttons on her computer as I wait. 'Ah, yes, I've got the details here. He had taken a personal loan just before the pandemic.'

'Yes, Ma'am, he had,' I say.

'May I know the cause of death? Did he pass away because of Covid?' She adjusts her glasses.

'He died of a heart attack within a week after he was discharged from the hospital because of covid-related complications.'

'I am sorry, that must have been really hard for you,' she says. Usually when people say it, they sound insincere. Not her though.

'Yes, it's hard, especially for my mother. I don't want her to undergo any more trauma than she already has. That collection agent or whoever he was—'

'That will not happen again. I will ensure that. And I think there's been some misunderstanding here about the total amount owed,' she says as she studies the figures on the computer.

'Oh, is it more?' I ask, bracing for the worst.

'No, in fact, it might be a fraction of what is mentioned here. The Kerala government has come out with a 5,600-crore rupee relief package for helping out the state economy impacted by covid. They have launched an interest subsidy scheme for all district cooperative banks. All the interest on defaulted loans as well as penal interest can be waived off 100 per cent.'

'Oh!' I am so surprised by this I don't know what else to say.

A security guard knocks on her door, interrupting us.

'Madam, your lunch is here,' he says, holding up a package.

'Leave it here, thank you,' she says, pointing to the cabinet on the side of the room.

The guard does as she asks and leaves the room. The aroma from the packet wafts across the whole room, and it makes my mouth water. My stomach rumbles, reminding me that it is time for lunch. I think it is fish I smell.

'I took over as branch manager only last month. The loan officer must have issued the standard directives for loan recovery from all debtors. But I can see this is a genuine case. Is there any other earning member in the family?' she asks.

Though the question is asked in purely an official capacity, it hits me hard. I feel ashamed to tell her that I have no job.

'Ma'am, I've just started my own business.' The lie slips out before I can stop it.

'What is the business?' she asks, instantly interested.

'It's very tiny, as we have just started. But we make the best fish fry in whole of Kochi. You taste it once and you will never eat fish anywhere else again,' I say. I don't know where any of this is coming from. But I know I sound very convincing. Years of dealing in weed has made me an efficient liar. I've lied numerous times to my school teachers and principal when they suspected I was dealing.

'Is that so? What is your restaurant called?'

'It's called A Fishy Business,' I tell her the first thing that comes to my mind.

'Aha! That's such a clever and creative name. You know, I love fish. In fact, the lunch I've ordered today is fish curry and rice,' she says.

I could tell by the smell. 'We also have good fish curries. Our speciality dish is thirutha curry. For fried fish, you must taste kalanji roast. The other thing we do best is kanava with kanthari chillies. Sorry, I am giving all the Malayalam names,' I say. I am totally getting carried away by my own lies. I'm naming all my favourite fish dishes that Amma prepares.

'That's okay. I am a Malayalee. Thirutha is grey mullet fish. Kalanji is Asian bass. Kanava is squid. Am I right?' Her eyes light up as she mentions the names of all the fishes.

'Wow, you are a fish connoisseur!' I exclaim. My brain is screaming at me to stop. But my motor-mouth doesn't listen. It's having too much of a good time.

'So where can I order from?' she asks.

'Eh?'

'Your restaurant, where is it located? Do you deliver here?' she asks.

That brings me crashing back to earth. I have to think quickly. 'Ma'am, as I mentioned, we've just started. So as of now, we only cook from home. It is a cloud kitchen set-up. But anytime you want, please let me know a day in advance, and I am happy to deliver it for you,' I tell her.

Phew, I think. That was close.

'Oh, sure, give me your number,' she says and she dutifully gives me a call and cuts it after it rings, when I tell her my number.

'Now you can save my number too,' she says.

'Ma'am, I also want to tell you, I will repay the loan my father took. Please give me a while.'

'About that, I think I might be able to waive it off. We will have some paperwork to do. Please give me a letter or send me an email explaining the whole situation, along with all the medical documents. And I'll see what I can do.'

'Really, Ma'am? That would be really good. I … I don't know how to thank you.' I am speechless. I blink back tears that unexpectedly rise. The relief is immense.

'No need to thank me at all. I am just executing what the government has put in place. This should have been done by the previous branch manager. Special loan melas are being held in all panchayats. You might even be eligible for a loan.'

I can't believe what I am hearing. Not only has she promised that my father's loan would be waived, I might even get money to start a business?

'Ma'am, thank you so much. I will come back to you in the future about that,' I say as I stand up.

'Yes, of course, and please convey my apologies to your mother,' she says.

As I cycle back home, my heart is singing with joy. All my lies have got me a waiver and an offer of a loan! But I am also scared. What have I got myself into?

My brain tells me, 'Don't worry. All you have to do is convince Amma to start A Fishy Business.' And this time my motor-mouth is absolutely silent. The sun is even more fierce as it blazes in the midday heat, but now I don't mind it at all.

9

Arush

When I wake up the next morning, the first thing I remember is I have a job offer. With so much happening last evening till I hit the bed, I never got around to researching Nik's businesses. I recall my father mentioning proudly that Nik has multiple businesses. Even before I brush my teeth, I reach out for my laptop from the drawer. That's when I realise that my art portfolio, which is usually kept in the top drawer of my desk, is missing.

Strange. I always keep it in the top drawer. Then I open my second drawer to look for it, and it's right there, on top of my art materials—my brushes and paints. I am always meticulous about how I store things and I frown as I replace my portfolio back in its right place in the top drawer. I hate it when things are not in their proper place.

I open my laptop and type in the search: 'Nik Mehta businessman Travel UK'. A long list of articles about Nik pop up. One catches my eye: 'Indian-origin businessman saves 640 jobs after buying company'.

The article goes on to say that Satyam House, owned by Nik Mehta, has been on a buying spree in England's steel sector. Satyam House bought the trade and assets of two companies to be merged and renamed SAT (Satyam Aluminium Technologies). They will use environmentally sustainable production technologies, and won't lay off any existing employees.

I read a few more articles about Nik's other businesses. He also owns a real estate business called Shivam Homes Limited. Their Instagram page has reels that are indoor tours of beautiful homes, along with their prices. The page is very nicely done and has over 370 k followers. Their homes range from ground floor one-bed maisonettes to five-bed homes with private saunas and fabulous gardens. His travel firm, Sundaram Travels, has been operating for over thirty years with around 280 branches in the UK. They organise tours to all parts of the world: India, Egypt and Spain feature prominently on their website.

The prices are also advertised and there's a little button that says, 'What is Sundaram? Click here'. When I click on the button, it takes me to a page where Nik is speaking. He looks directly into the camera and talks about how it is so important for him that anyone who books with Sundaram Travels has a 'sundar' experience; 'sundar' means beautiful in Hindi. He says it is easy to splash beautiful pictures of exotic locales but the real test is how 'sundar' is it to get there. How seamless is your travel? Do you have to wait at airports? Are there hidden charges at the attractions? Are there experienced tour guides who will accompany you throughout and make sure that you're looked after? He passion and sincerity shine through as he speaks.

No wonder Nik is this successful, the man simply exudes charisma. I had no idea he was such a big tycoon! I make a mental note to ask my father as to why he agreed to come for the reopening of a measly shop in Derbyshire. Now that I have seen what a huge success he is, my respect for him has gone up tenfold. Nik Mehta has a freshly minted fan.

I try to remember what he said yesterday at our shop reopening, and then it strikes me: 'Satyam, Shivam, Sundaram'. That was what he had begun his speech with. They were also the names of the three businesses he owns!

As I brush my teeth, I wonder what it would be like to work in one of his companies. What did he have in mind when he made me the job offer?

I join my family for breakfast. Mami has made aloo parathas and brought them over. As I help myself to the parathas, I tell my family that Nik Mehta made me a job offer.

'Ah, so he liked your portfolio then,' Ma says.

'What? He saw my portfolio?' I ask.

Then the penny drops. The portfolio that was missing from my top drawer and turned up in the second one. My parents must have shown it to him without my knowledge. The whole thing was a set-up?

'Yes.' Ma smiles. 'I asked Jenna to help me scan the best pieces of your work. We mailed it to him six weeks back.'

'Ma, what the hell! That's simply going too far. I know you are all tight with Jenna, but really she had no right to go through my stuff like that.'

'Why are you getting so angry? Jenna didn't go through your stuff. I took it from your room and gave it to her. I told her not to tell you.'

'But why? Why didn't you ask me directly?'

'We did. Don't you remember? We had this conversation three months back. I wanted you to take up a job and you said you'd rather help us and help your Mami in the kitchen.'

That's when I remember it. When Dad and Ma kept nagging me about work, I had said Mami needed me, and that I wasn't ready yet.

'That was a while back. This is simply not done. I don't like these kinds of surprises.'

'We did it for your benefit. And it's not like we read your private correspondence with Puja or Jenna or anything. It's just that we took your portfolio and sent it off. And, see, now you have a job offer.' Ma is unfazed with my annoyance.

'Arush, they are your parents who want the best for you. Don't be so mad,' Mami interjects.

'Thank you, I suppose,' I say finally.

'You're welcome, now are you going to take up that job or not?' Ma asks.

'But how will Mami manage the restaurant? And how will you manage the shop without me?'

'Last evening's reopening and catering was such a success, I've got three big orders already—an engagement party, a prayer gathering and a birthday party. All are orders for twenty to thirty people. They are paying me in advance too, and with the amount I have received I can easily hire a helper,' Mami says.

Then my father says, 'Also, now that the shop is reopening, Datta is ready to join back. He's been with us ever since we started the shop, and he is grateful that we paid him full wages during the pandemic and he wants to come back.'

It seems like they had already planned all of this. I feel a bit cheated that I was not included or consulted in any of these plans.

'It's high time you made your own life. If you want to work and explore things on your own, this is the time. You are young and have no responsibilities. I'd say you take up this job Mr Mehta is offering,' Mami says.

While I know they are right, one part of me still resists. I'd just gotten used to pandemic life, helping Mami, my parents, and not mingling or talking with anyone apart from my family members except Jenna and Puja.

The thought of joining a new job, moving to Birmingham, setting up my own home there, working under Nik, meeting so many new people, all of it seems daunting.

'Hmmm, I can't think right now,' I say.

When I go to Mami's place to help her in the restaurant, I discover that the new helper is doing the dishes. He looks quite at home too, in his apron and youthful cheer. As much as I hated helping out Mami, now that I have been replaced, I feel a slight sting of rejection.

'That was fast,' I tell Mami.

'The Indian network here is strong. I'd only mentioned in passing and this is Mr Daljit's nephew's friend who was looking for a job.'

She tells me that I can head over to help my parents, and there I run into Datta. I help unpack the large shipment of clothes that arrived that morning. Once I am by myself, I think about the job. Extra income would always help, and at some point, I'd have to start working. Now that things are returning back to normal, I can't stay at home forever. My family seems to be moving on, and I must too.

I compose an email to Nik, thanking him for his offer of a job and telling him I am happy to move to Birmingham. I ask him to let me know the next steps. Once I dash off the mail, I'm excited. I must tell Puja about this latest development.

When I open my phone, I see that Puja has posted some stories. When I look at what she has posted I can't believe my eyes. She and her sister are with two extremely fit, well-built guys, having a whale of a time. I did not even know that Puja knew how to kayak. She has never once mentioned it in all these years I've known her. In one of the pics, it is just Puja and this guy, and he has his hands around her shoulders and she is looking at him and laughing while he looks straight into the camera.

I have no idea who these guys are. I feel a buzzing in the back of my head. A red-hot haze wraps my brain; All thoughts stop. I collapse on the bed because my legs suddenly disappear from under me. I lie down and grit my teeth. Who the hell are these guys? Why hasn't Puja mentioned them at all? Why am I feeling this way? Like I want to kill them? This is insane.

Bloody hell. I can't allow this to happen. I must not let *anyone* have this kind of power over me. I have to deal with this, but I have no idea how.

I pick up the phone and call Jenna.

Jenna thinks that I should call Puja.

'Look, this is Puja we're talking about. Puja who flew over five thousand miles to see you,' she says.

'Two years back, Jenna. *Before* the pandemic.'

'How does it matter?'

'It does because the pandemic changed us all. We're not the same people we were. We're different now.'

'Of course, Arush. All of us have gone through unimaginable losses, unanticipated pain. That's all the more reason you should talk to her.'

'What do I even say? That I am burning with jealousy?'

'No! Tell her you wanted to hear her voice.'

'Oh, please, Jenna, that's corny! I never say such things.'

'Then make up an excuse! Think of something to ask her. It's not rocket science!'

I can almost see Jenna shake her head.

'Maybe I should tell her I'm moving to Birmingham.'

'You are? You decided to take up the job offer?'

'Sort of. Though I am yet to forgive you for collaborating with my parents.'

'Come on, Arush. Your parents called me to help in selecting your portfolio pieces. I could hardly refuse.'

'You could have discussed it with me!'

'And you'd have agreed?'

'Ha, no way. You know me a bit too well, Jenna.'

'That I do. That's why I am asking you to call Puja. Long distance *is* hard Arush. You *need* to speak every single day. How long has it been since you both spoke?'

'I feel horrid to admit it, but I haven't called her since the day she abruptly hung up'

'What?! How could you *not*? Such a lousy, typical *guy* move.'

'Ouch.' I hate it when girls gang up.

'Just call her, Arush. I've got to run. I had applied for a job some time back and I am to meet them in person today.'

'Oh really? What job?'

'It's an illustrator's position in a small publishing house that publishes children's books. Based out of London, but I can work from anywhere. Wish me luck!'

'You don't need it, Jenna. The job would be lucky to get you.'

Once I get off the phone with Jenna, I can't help thinking how lucky she is to be getting a job in the field we both specialised in at art school: illustration. A children's book publisher would probably mean creating quirky drawings for storybooks. How wonderful it would be to create those.

And here I would probably be stuck at a desk in one of Nik Mehta's companies. He has written back saying I'd be operating out of his travel branch office in Birmingham but would have to do some design work related to his other companies too. The design team is common for all his businesses and he says the sooner I join, the better.

I write back to him saying I am happy to. He connects me to the design head, Olivia Stevens, who welcomes me to the team, and 'looks forward to meeting me'. She connects me to HR who will take care of all the paperwork, compensation and benefits. Olivia also tells me I can take a company-owned accommodation if I wish to, as part of the package. I am stunned at how quickly all of this has happened.

While the thought of moving to Birmingham is still sinking in, I wish I'd thought of applying to publishing houses. How easily dissatisfied our minds are! Till such time Jenna mentioned her job, I was excited about Nik's offer. But now that I know Jenna is going to be illustrating, which is my passion—and hers—I want to do the same. Jenna's job sounds much better than mine.

When my parents come back home from the shop for the afternoon break, I bring up my moving to Birmingham. 'It's only forty-eight minutes by train from here. Do you think I should really move there? I mean, I could go from here to work and come back here every day.'

'If you stay here and commute, you'd be wasting at least two hours every day in travel. You're considering only the commute time, but there's also the time it will take for you to get to the station from home and then from the station in Birmingham to your office,' my father says.

Ma breaks it down further, 'If you have to get to work at 9 a.m., you have to be up at 6.00 a.m. You won't have time for breakfast. Doing that every day will be really tiring. If you finish by 6.30 p.m., then you're likely to get home only after 8. Not worth it.'

'Yes, you're both right,' I tell them. 'I am not sure what I'm going to be earning. I haven't spoken about any of that.'

'Don't worry, son. Nik pays his employees really well. He was telling me about how employee satisfaction is at the core of every business he sets up. The starting salaries are from 36,000 pounds per annum. Which is 12,000 pounds more than the average starting salary for freshers elsewhere. So, I'd say it's really good.'

'That's terrific, Dad! But is he giving me this job only because I'm your son?'

'No. He is a shrewd businessman. If he didn't think that you would add value to his business he wouldn't have hired you.'

'How do you know him, Dad? And why did he agree to come to our shop inauguration. I mean, he is super successful, owns so many companies.'

'Ah, son, that's a long story. We have a strong bond though we didn't keep in touch for over a decade. Some connections are like that.'

'You've made me really curious now.'

My father looks at Ma.

'I think we should tell him. Our children should know our struggles. We never talk about it because it's painful. But it is important,' she says.

My father squares his shoulders. 'I was seventeen when I left India. You know that my father died when I was born, and it was my uncle who raised me and my brothers. Then I lost two of my brothers. One died of typhoid and another of fever. I was all my mother had left. That year my uncle's crops failed and he threw me out of the house. There was nothing to eat, and too many hungry mouths. The dire poverty got to him, and he said I had to leave home and start earning. My mother tried to stop him by holding his feet, begging him to not send me away but he was helpless.

'I remember crying as the ship pulled away from India. India was getting smaller and smaller, as we sailed farther. I felt sad, broken. There were many of us who left India together. Your mother's brother, your mother, Balwinder uncle, all of us were on that ship. A person from our village who was in Birmingham had arranged our passage. It was a grey, drizzly day when we docked in London. The first thing I had to do was get a coat. I was shivering with cold. Almost all my savings went into buying a coat and shoes. For the rest of that month, I worked in an Indian restaurant in Piccadilly. After the customers left, we slept on the tables.' My father's voice cracks as he says this.

He takes a sip of the tea and continues, 'I'd made a promise to my mother that I would never cut my hair. And I kept that promise. I faced a lot of discrimination because of this. They wouldn't let me serve. The customers stared at me. I was allowed only to wash the dishes or peel the potatoes. One day we were short of staff and I was asked to serve. As luck would have it, the gentleman I was serving happened to be the owner of a flourishing Indian grocery shop on Grafton Street. We got talking, and I joined his store, initially as a clerk. I worked very hard. There was nothing I wouldn't do.

My mother died and I couldn't even travel to India as I had not saved enough money. She was my last tie to India, and when she died, something inside me died too. I never wanted to go back. But things were not so easy here either. The discrimination continued. Mind you, there was not much awareness back then like there is now. I was treated sub-par anywhere I went. Like I was something dirty. I could feel the stares, the open disapproval, the distrust. They couldn't see beyond my turban and beard. They never saw a human being, just a wild tribal from some foreign land.'

I feel horrified as I hear this. My parents have never told me this before—I had only known they had difficult times. But I never knew it had been this hard.

I look at Ma and she is blinking back her tears. My father is very emotional and I can see the pain in his eyes. 'But that gentleman was my anchor. He treated me so well. He had a son who was many years younger than me, and I would go to his house on weekends to tutor his son, teaching him Maths and Hindi. Can you guess who his son is?'

'Who?' I ask, although I suspect I already know the answer.

'Nik. I've known him since he was a child.'

'Wow. So that means he is younger than you?'

'Much younger than me.'

'But he looks older, Dad.'

'Must be the stress of running all his businesses. Even as a child he was always restless, his mind used to jump to the next thing. He is one of the smartest people I know.'

'Yes, he is impressive indeed. How did you to move to Derby?'

'A few years after working for Nik's father, I had enough savings. By then more people were arriving from India. Nik's father wanted to help them. He encouraged me to go into business myself. A friend mentioned how Derby has a lot of scope for business. That's how we moved here. We started the store with my savings.'

'Dad, Ma, what you both did is admirable. I can't even imagine enduring such hardships,'

'We did what we had to. We never thought of it much,' my mother shrugs.

After listening to my parents' story, moving to Birmingham no longer seems daunting. Compared to what they endured, I have it easy.

Now I feel more than ready to begin my new job.

10

Puja

Early next morning, I'm woken up by Divya.

'Puja the Hooja, open your eyes,' she whispers into my ear.

I open a single eye, pull down my quilt to see her bright smiling face.

'Please, Divya, let me sleep some more.'

'No! You've got to see this. Wake up, please.'

The excitement in her voice makes me open both my eyes.

'Here, I've made coffee for you,' she says as she hands me a steaming cup.

I lean against the headboard and gratefully take the coffee from her. If she has made coffee for me, it has to be important.

'What is it? Did Vihan declare his love for you and give you a diamond ring?' I ask as I take a sip. The coffee is a bit too strong and sweet, but it gives me the necessary caffeine kick.

'No, you idiot. Your reel has gone viral. You're famous! And look at your followers. They are increasing by the minute,' she says as she hands me her phone, which is open to my profile on Instagram.

I take it from her and gasp when my eyes land on the views that reel has gathered. '1.4 million views? I can't believe it,' I say, staring into my phone. Overnight, my followers have gone from 1,134 to 21,386.

'And look at the comments!'

'This is crazy!' I say as I scroll. The comments are increasing by the minute. I've never experienced anything like this before. The maximum views I've got on a reel are about 3.4 k, like for an aesthetic time-lapse of a sunset I'd shot from our balcony at home. Most people who have left a comment on my reel want to know the location, the cost of the activity and the place. That's when I realise I haven't shared that. I'd merely written a caption: 'Would you like to do this?'

I read some more comments. Most are about Benny being hot. I smile when I read that. Of course, he is. Many compliment me on the shot of Divya and Vihan in the moonlight. I am delighted when I read those. I loved that shot too.

There's also a shot of Benny kayaking. I'd zoomed out and captured the beauty of the lake. I'd then turned the camera around in selfie mode to include me as well. It ends with a cute frame of the four of us posing with our arms around each other. Amma had thought she is clicking a photo, and had recorded a video instead.

I play the reel again, trying to analyse why it went viral. I've captured the shimmering golden rays of the sun, the greenery of the mangroves, the moonlight shot of Divya and Vihan, and all of us posing and laughing. It's a perfect recipe—travel, love, laughter and friendship. The edits are on beat too, and the reel, apart from being slickly made, definitely tells a story. But I never expected this kind of reaction.

I scroll through some more comments and I am horrified to see comments saying Benny and I make a great couple, and that we're meant for each other.

'Oh no. Look at these comments. They think Benny and I are a couple,' I wail, handing Divya her phone back.

'I noticed those too, but that's social media for you. They think Vihan and I are a couple too.' Divya is nonchalant but it makes me uncomfortable.

'I had only wanted to make Arush jealous, but I think this has gone too far,' I worry. 'Do you think I should delete this reel? Do you think he has seen it?'

'No way, Puja! Why would you want to delete your first viral reel? Because you are afraid that Arush will misunderstand?'

'Yes.'

'If he has already seen this reel, it would have made him crazily jealous.'

'We haven't been communicating for a while. I haven't told him about Sujit's email. I haven't replied to Sujit either. We've been having so much fun here that I kind of mentally parked everything else.'

'Yes, it is nice, isn't it? This vacation really did us good. By the way, Vihan thinks I will get a job at his bank as they have an opening that matches my profile to a T and they give a preference for employee referrals. He's recommending my name.'

'That's really good news, Divya! I am certain you'll get it. You should have told me this as soon as you woke me up!'

'I was waiting to tell you this, but then I chanced upon your viral reel, and forgot about it.' She smiles.

'It'll come through, Divya, I have a good feeling,' I assure her.

On the way back to Kochi, Divya tells Amma and Achcha about the possibility of a job in the bank where Vihan works.

'Where's the position based out of?' Amma asks

'Mumbai. If I get it, I may have to shift there,' Divya says.

'Are you excited about the job or are you excited about moving to the same city as Vihan?' Achcha asks.

And before she can answer, as if on cue, the three of us, Amma, Achcha and I, start humming the same song we were singing last evening and Divya says, 'Please, you guys, stop it! I haven't even got the job yet.'

When we get home, Shanti Chechi welcomes us with tea. Once I'm in my room, I lie in bed, checking for messages from Arush. There aren't any. I check his art account on Instagram and there are no stories, no posts. Since he hasn't posted anything, I check Jenna's stories and there he is. Looking cute in his kurta pyjama as he stands sweetly with Rhea, handing out packets to the guests who are leaving. Looking at him makes me feel all warm and fuzzy inside. Rhea looks very pretty in her purple and golden silk blouse and ghagra. She has grown so much!

The next story on Jenna's feed takes me by surprise and my smile vanishes. It's Jenna in Indian clothes. I didn't even know she had Indian clothes. And she looks stunning. She has captioned the story 'Indian inside'. I replay the story a few times. And the same familiar ugly jealousy grips me tightly, rising inside me, surrounding me. I burn.

I now wish I hadn't checked her stories. It's unfair that she gets to spend time with Arush, while I am so far away. Is she only a friend as

Arush claims? Or is there something he isn't telling me? The thoughts spiral out of control.

Thinking about it is driving me crazy. I need to stop torturing myself like this. I remind myself that all I have to do is message him or pick up the phone and call him. But now there seems to be a kind of icy silence between us and I don't want to be the one chasing after him.

Then I think of Sujit. The poor guy deserves a response from me. He must be waiting too, and it's not right to make him wait. He needs his closure, like Divya pointed out. I open my Instagram and all other social media and I unblock him. Then I type a reply to his mail.

Dear Sujit,

Firstly, apologies for the delay in replying. I was out of town. I know how hard it is to wait for a reply, and your mail deserved a proper response. Also, it came as a shocker, and hence I took some time to think about it.

Dr Harsh is really a godsend and I'm glad you decided to do what he suggested. Therapy is neither dumb nor is it for 'people who can't cope'. It's for everyone really. A good therapist helps make our lives even better, and it's not only 'if you have a problem' that you need to go to a therapist.

Your mail—it blew me away. I'd no idea what you've been through. I'm sorry you had to go through it. I am so sorry about your father too. One of my biggest fears is losing either of my parents. I must say you're incredibly brave and resilient, and the fact that you cleared the final exams when so much was going on in your personal life is commendable indeed.

We all make mistakes, Sujit. Your mistakes took you down a dark path. But the important thing is you've given up that life now and got out of it.

Also, I am thankful you told the shopkeeper to call the ambulance, and Arush received help on time. I shudder to think what would have happened if—but hey, there's no need to think about it. It's all in the past.

I think the good thing the pandemic has taught us is that life is so fragile. It is meaningless to hold on to grudges. While I haven't undergone any of the things that you have, I've changed too. I think we all have.

I am touched that you shared so much with me. I can imagine how hard that must have been. You are lucky to have such a supportive mother. (Birth mother or not, it doesn't matter.)

Your mail makes it so easy for me to say, 'I forgive you, Sujit, let's move on.'

Take care,

Puja

I send it and I am surprised to see a reply from him, about ten minutes later.

Dear Puja.

Oh, what a sweet relief to get your email. Thank you, my friend, thank you. (If I may still call you my friend). I had been desperately checking for replies ever since I sent it. And I felt like an idiot for doing so.

Sujit.

I smile when I read it. And I reply instantly. 'Checking for replies is human! Just because you wait for someone to reply, it doesn't mean you are an idiot.'

His reply too arrives immediately. 'Just noticed that you unblocked me on Insta. Yay!'

I open my Instagram and message him: 'Stalker! How many times did you keep checking?'

He replies, 'Only 1,54,378 times.'

I smile when I read that. Sujit is fun to talk to. He'd always been a practical joker at school, making everyone laugh with his weirdest antics. But now that he has shared his story, I am beginning to see why he was probably acting up. Another message arrives from him. He asks me if my phone number is the same. I tell him that it is, and I quickly unblock him from my contacts.

There's a knock on my door.

'Come in,' I call out.

My father opens the door and comes into my room

'Molle, Benny is on the line, he wants to speak to you,' he says.

I make a face and frantic hand gestures to my dad to indicate that I don't want to speak to him. But my father hands me the phone.

'Hello?' I say cautiously. Like Benny will jump out of the phone and bite me.

'Hey, Puja!' He sounds cheerful. 'I am sorry to call like this.'

'It's okay. What is this regarding?'

'Your reel. It's absolutely fantastic! I've been seeing all the comments. I wanted to check if you could please tag us in your reel? That will really help us get more business.'

'Ah, okay. Yes, of course. I'll do that,'

'Thank you so much. Also, would you mind if I reply to the comments that ask where the location is? I'll reply from our kayaking centre's official handle.'

'I don't mind at all. Please go ahead.'

'Thanks so much, Puja. Alright then, bye,' he says and hangs up.

It's after he hangs up that it occurs to me that he would have also seen all the comments where people have said we make a good couple. I'm so mortified I want to disappear.

I have to speak to Arush and clarify that there's nothing going on between Benny and me. But it's the middle of the night in the UK, and I decide to wait till he wakes up to make that call to him. This silence between us has gone on for too long now. It's time to break it.

Cruising

Flying isn't dangerous.
Crashing is what's dangerous.

—*Rules of the Air*

11

Sujit

'Amma, trust me, many people will place orders. You have no idea how tasty your curries are,' I tell her.

Amma just shakes her head.

We've been arguing about this for the last forty-five minutes. I am glad I raised this topic with her only after I had lunch, a snooze and my evening tea. Her mood was upbeat when I told her about the possibility of the loan being waived off. But after she heard about how I lied to the bank manager about A Fishy Business, her good mood evaporated.

'I am not willing to commit any fraud. That's essentially what you are doing,' she says.

'Amma, you've been watching too many Malayalam soap operas. This is not fraud. No one is going to arrest me for this.'

'How do you know? You have lied to a bank manager.'

'Does the bank manager have a spy camera to see what's going on inside our house? Come on, Amma. You can't be this negative. For once, for once in my life, I have a great idea. And I am sure it will succeed,' I say as I bite into an achappam she has made. I can be as dramatic as her. The achappam goes crunch-crunch in my mouth, so perfectly crispy. 'Maybe we can offer free achappams with orders above five hundred rupees,' I tell her.

'*Onnupoda*! Free achappam it seems.' She shakes her head.

'Okay, okay, no need for free achappams. Just make two or three varieties of the fish curry tomorrow. I'll go to the market early morning and get fresh fish. Please do this much for me. Rest I will take care of,' I plead.

Sindu returns from school just then. She says she worked out a solution with her best friend about the copying.

'How did you manage that?' Amma asks her as Sindu takes her bag off her back, puts away her shoes and joins us at the table.

'She was copying only because she was not understanding anything. She said her father will drop her here and we will do the homework together. I will teach her and then she will learn it. There won't be a need to copy anymore,' she announces proudly.

'That's a wonderful solution indeed!' Amma says as she hands Sindu her glass of Bournvita.

Ravi comes back from college then and Amma goes into the kitchen to make tea for him. As he helps himself to the achappams, I narrate to him my plan to start a home food business. He is enthusiastic and thinks it is a splendid idea. Seeing both Ravi's and my excitement Sindu joins in too.

'Amma, please listen to chettan. Your fish curry is *adipoli*,' Sindu says and makes a circle with her thumb and forefinger and smacks her lips. Amma laughs.

'I'll help you tomorrow. I can grind all the masalas for you. I know people in my college hostel itself who crave for home food. They will definitely order Amma's fish curry,' Ravi says.

In the end, Amma cannot refuse the collective persuasion skills of the three of us. She reluctantly agrees to make three types of fish curry as an experiment. 'If it doesn't sell, you will be eating fish for the next two weeks. I am not going to make anything else,' she warns us.

Later that night, after Amma and Sindu have gone to sleep, Ravi and I talk sitting on our respective beds. Since the room is too small to accommodate two beds side by side, they are along the wall, perpendicular to each other.

'Chetta, we need a tagline for our business,' Ravi says.

'Yes, let's write down whatever we can think of.' I grab a paper and pen from the desk we share.

Both of us brainstorm. We come up with many taglines—some are outrageously boastful, some don't have a nice ring, and some are downright cheesy.

Ravi says, 'How about this as a tagline, "Nothing fishy about it"?'

'That's confusing as we aren't telling them what the product is about. Our tagline has to capture what is unique about the product,' I tell him.

'You paid more attention in Shankaran sir's class than I did.' Ravi smiles.

'Is he still around?'

'Of course. He remembers you and asked if I was your brother.'

'Marketing management was the only paper I paid attention to in college. It was my favourite subject.'

In the end we settle on a simple tag line.

A Fishy Business: *Lip-smacking fresh fish, hot from Amma's kitchen.*

Ravi loves it, so do I.

'Mission 1 complete, on to mission 2. Attack social media,' Ravi says.

We both go through our phones and find some old pictures of fish curries Amma has made in the past.

'These are not even shot with good lighting, yet see how nice they look. My mouth is watering just looking at the pictures', Ravi says. I agree wholeheartedly.

We open both an Instagram and a Facebook account, and we set it up so that they cross-post to each other.

'Should we start a twitter too? Only oldies are on twitter,' Ravi says.

'Why not? The more the exposure the better, and oldies are the one with cash,' I tell him.

'But isn't our target audience students?'

'Our target group is anyone who is willing to buy from us,' I tell him.

We upload the pictures with descriptions.

'How do we price it?' Ravi asks.

I have no idea either, so I look up some restaurants in the same area that are selling similar fish curries, and read out the prices to Ravi.

'They have small and large portions—how do we decide our portions?' Ravi asks.

'Let's just wing it,' I tell him. 'Once we get a few orders, we will get the hang of it.'

'Alright, we can adjust pricing according to demand,' Ravi says.

'So, you also have been paying attention in Shankaran sir's class!' I say and he smiles at me.

We price our fish curry a good thirty rupees less than what the hotels around us charge. We add pictures of rice too.

'Will we make a profit, Chetta? I mean, we haven't calculated the cost of anything. We're randomly pricing it.'

'I know the price of raw fish as I am the one who buys it from the market every week. Even if we take the cost of the masalas, oil and gas, I am certain that we will make a good profit,' I tell Ravi.

'Alright, we'll go by what you say. Now that the pricing is done, let's shoot a reel. That's the only way we're going to multiply our reach,' Ravi says.

'Reel? No way. I don't want to be in any video,' I tell him. I am too terrified of appearing on camera, I don't want my old customers to recognise me. I have deleted my old account, which had all kinds of hashtags relating to cannabis. In the new account I have only posted some colourful city shots of Kochi. There are no pictures of me.

'Okay, don't worry. I will be the face of this business. People are more confident to place an order when they can see a person behind the brand,' he says.

'You? You look too young. Why will they want to order from a kid?' I ask him.

'Chetta, you are very out of touch with social media marketing. Wait, let me shoot. Then you tell me,' he says.

I am surprised to see that Ravi has a tripod in his cupboard that he whips out and unfolds. He sets it up and attaches his phone to it.

'Where did you get that fancy thing from?' I ask, bemused.

'My friend Sinu is a content creator, and I help him with videography. He pays me a commission when he gets paid for making content. He does product photography. Working with him, I've learnt quite a lot. He gave me his old tripod some months back. I never used it till now. The only thing missing here is a ring light. Maybe we can invest in one, but for now this will have to do.' He switches on our study lamp and positions it expertly behind the camera after placing the tripod near the desk. Clearly, he knows what he is doing. He isn't camera-shy either, speaking confidently without even a script.

'In hostel and craving for some good homemade good? Working late and tired of ordering out? Want to eat the best fish in whole of Kochi, hot off Amma's kitchen? Check out the link in the bio and see the caption below,' he says as he points downwards.

I stare at him in surprise. I never knew he was so good at any of this. In no time, he has edited it and we upload our first reel, along with pictures of the food that Amma made earlier.

He also copies the profile link to A Fishy Business and sends it to me. 'Send it to all your friends, and ask them to follow the page, I am sending it to all my friends too,' he says as he gets busy with his phone.

'My god, Ravi, you're a pro!' I say, stunned by how efficient and methodical he is.

He bows. 'Thank you, but lots more to be done.'

He sends me the reel he just shot. 'Send this also to your friends, and tell them they have to pre-book the meal for tomorrow,' he commands. He has fully taken charge of it now.

I scroll through my phone, and I feel a little sad as I look at my contacts. Most of my contacts were my earlier customers for weed or my suppliers. I've deleted all of them. I spent almost all of my college life completely wasted and dealing in substance. While I feel relieved that I am out of that life, I don't have any friends as such. The only friend I can think of is Puja. I hesitate for a few seconds. Should I send this to her?

'Have you sent it? I have sent it to at least thirty people now,' Ravi says as he looks up from his phone.

I am too ashamed to tell him I have no friends. 'Yes, I'm sending too,' I say and then I hit 'Send'. As soon as I do it, I regret it, I want to delete it. I don't know why, but it seems too 'salesman-like', and I don't want Puja to think of me that way.

But I notice the two blue ticks; she has seen it even before I had a chance to delete it. Oh, hell. And she is typing a reply now. I stare in horror at the three dots and the word 'typing ...'

What in the world is she typing for so long? Then there is a silence. Has she deleted it? Oh no, here she is typing again.

The message from her arrives. She has typed a long one.

Hey Sujit, how wonderful to know about this! I just checked the Instagram page and I figured it must be your new venture. Of course, I recognised Ravi too, but he has grown up so much in the last 4-5 years. I haven't seen him since I left school. Hearty congrats and I would very much like to place an order from your restaurant. Every single thing looks tempting. I'd like two rice and two fish curries, please. By when will the delivery happen? By around 12? Let me know and I will text you the address. I've already made the payment using the UPI you've mentioned in your Insta. Congrats once again – this will be a roaring success!

I read it twice. She is being so sweet! 'Ravi, we've just got our first order and we've got the payment too!' I tell him. 'Two fish curries, two rice.'

'I've also got an order. This is from the hostel guys. Four fish curries, four rice. And they have made the payment too.' He grins.

'So, we won't have to eat fish curry for the whole week.'

'No, we won't. Amma isn't going to believe this.'

'Let's set the alarm for 5 a.m. tomorrow.'

The next morning, both of us wake up before Amma. I head out early so that I am at the market when the fresh catch comes in. Back home I see that Amma and Ravi have got out the banana leaves from the backyard. Amma prepares the leaves by heating them on the gas for packing the rice orders.

'Got good fish?' she asks and when I show her, she is happy with what I have chosen.

'How will we pack the curry?' I ask.

'For today we will have to pack it in our containers. You all will have to get the containers back. If we get repeat business, we will think about how we can pack it cost-effectively,' she says.

I marvel at Amma's expertise as she gets busy cooking. By 10 a.m., we have packed the orders. The ones for hostel students are in identical plastic containers, the rice packed in banana leaves. I tell Ravi that I will be at the college by 11 a.m. and hand it over to him at the gate, so he can give it to the students who have ordered. After that I will head over to Puja's place to make the delivery.

I check the address that Puja has sent me. I am shocked when I see it. I had no idea she was living in one of the poshest, wealthiest buildings in Kochi. Her building is a well-known landmark as it has homes owned by billionaires. I had no idea she was this wealthy. It is too far for me to cycle, and I will have to take the bus to reach her place.

I cycle to Ravi's college, hand him the packets and cycle back home. Amma hands me a massive steel tiffin carrier for the order for Puja. 'I have kept three types of fish curry and rice too. Tell them it is a complimentary sample. If they like it, they will order more,' Amma says.

'Okay, I will,' I say. I've taken care to dress smartly. Yet I feel like a poor relative, holding the large tiffin carrier with rice and fish curry, waiting at the dusty bus-stop to take the bus to go to Puja's home.

12

Arush

Birmingham, the UK's second largest city, has a very young and distinct vibe to it. The energy in the air is peppy, very different from Derby. At Derby our home is in a quiet residential area, and we hardly see anyone outside. Here, since I am living very close to my office and the city centre, it is busy, vibrant and there's always something happening.

As I walk towards my apartment I look around this new city, which is now my home. Every day there's something new to discover: a quaint alley with shops that sell quirky home décor, a restaurant I hadn't spotted earlier, a pub I'd missed. I love my flat, the office and my co-workers, the street food scene, the small independent restaurants and the bars, the canals with boats chugging up and down, and the pubs on the side of the canal.

The only downside about all of this is the work that I am doing. While I love the airy, sunshiny, spacious office, as well as my very comfortable desk and chair, and the very cool monitor, the actual work I've been assigned is dull. So far, I am only designing PowerPoint presentations and internal company communications.

I report to Kathy Hart who reports to Olivia. There's another fresh recruit who works alongside me. Daljit Hayre. Daljit joined two days after I did. When Kathy told me that someone called Daljit would be joining, I'd expected to see a girl. But Daljit turned out to be a guy and a pretty friendly one at that. He has never been to India, and when he got to know that I'd been there before the pandemic, he was so excited that he bought me lunch and quizzed me all about my visit.

Daljit doesn't mind doing the grunt work that we're both assigned. Mostly we get the jobs that other designers are too busy to do. Five different colour options for the same design that the senior designer made? Really? There's absolutely no challenge in that and it's boring. But Daljit doesn't care.

'Look, man, we're getting paid good money. If that's what they want, then that's what we do,' he said. I wish I could be like him.

The design department shares office space with Shivam Homes Limited, the real estate arm of Nik's business. On the floor below us is Sundaram Travels. Customers drop in, all day long for enquiries, and the prices of various packages are advertised with large posters. Kathy tells me that from next month onwards, when the package tours start, Daljit and I will have to design a lot of stuff for the travel business.

'Right now, we're just easing you in and ensuring that you're comfortable. We don't want to load you with work,' she says. Daljit looks at me, raises his eyebrows and smiles.

Once I get home, I make a video call to my parents. My mother promptly asks if I am eating well. They want to hear all about my work, but I don't have the heart to tell them that it is dull, and I hate it. I tell them it is good and I'll soon be designing travel posters, and also that I am enjoying it.

Jenna too is excited and happy for me. I'd called her shortly after moving here.

'How does it feel to be living on your own?' she'd asked.

'I can't believe it. I feel like a proper adult now.'

'I know, right? I've been feeling that way too ever since gran passed. It's like we're in charge, and every decision we make now is our own. You know what I mean?'

'Yes, I know. It's a different feeling altogether.'

'Did you call Puja?'

'No. I was just getting used to Birmingham and the job and living by myself. All of it is a lot, actually.'

'Come on, Arush. You're making excuses and you know it. If you do care about this relationship then call her. Don't put off these things. You never know what tomorrow will bring. I don't mean to be morbid but—'

'I know, I know. I'll call.'

As I shower and heat up the ready-to-eat rotis and leftover dal I'd got from an Indian takeaway, I decide that Jenna is right. This silence between Puja and me has gone on long enough. It's absurd that we're so close to each other, and yet playing these childish games of cold silence. I check the time in India. It's around 11 p.m., which isn't too late. Puja is a night owl and stays awake till two or three.

I don't know why my heart beats so fast as the call rings. This is hard. I wait with bated breath for her to pick up.

And then she does.

'Hey,' she says.

The minute I hear her voice, I know she is hurting.

'Hey, I am so, so sorry,' I tell her even though I have no idea for what I am apologising.

'It's okay,' she says. 'If you had not called, I would have. I am sorry too.'

'What are you sorry about?'

'About this radio silence. About not telling you stuff and waiting for you to reach out.'

We both want things between us to be okay. That much I can tell. We're both eager for things to go back to what it was before. I sigh in relief.

Then what she has just said strikes me. She has just apologised for 'not telling me stuff'. What does she mean? The image of her smiling with two guys comes to my mind. Is there something going on? I badly want to know.

Instead of asking her about it, I say 'Whoa, slow down. Apologising for so many things? I can't keep up.'

She laughs in response.

I am not able to join in the laughter. All I can think about is that photo. I take a deep breath. Then I say, 'Listen, I need to ask you something.'

'Oh, yes, I've been meaning to tell you,' she says. 'I am glad you brought it up. Just don't pay any attention to the comments.'

'What comments?' I ask.

'On the reel. Isn't that what you were talking about?'

'Reel? What reel?'

'Oh, so you haven't seen it then? You haven't seen my reel?' she asks. Why does she sound sheepish?

'Hold on, I am checking right away.'

'No, no, no! Please don't see it! Please, Arush.'

'Come on, Puja! You've made me really curious now. You can't do this. You can't bring it up and then ask me not to see it, okay?'

'Aaaaaah …' she mock-screams. 'I know you're on it right now.'

Of course, I am. She knows me well. I open her Instagram and I cannot believe what I am seeing. The reel is so beautiful, and it's gone viral too. It has both the guys from the stories she posted.

'Puja, this is insane! Your reel has 4.3 million views!'

'Yes, isn't it crazy?'

'And your followers have gone through the roof.'

'Can you believe a couple of travel companies already got in touch with me? They want to do a barter where they will send me stuff and in return I make a reel where I use the product.'

'Wow! So you are an influencer now? And I didn't even know. I've been so busy with my new job and moving to Birmingham that I only saw your stories. Somehow, I missed seeing this,' I tell her.

I don't tell her how jealous I got and that I am dying to know who the guys in the reel are. I want her to tell me on her own.

'New job? You moved to Birmingham? Arush, tell me all the details,' she demands.

I tell her everything—about how my parents secretly sent my portfolio with Jenna's help, about how impressed I am with Nik, and about how I am not really liking my job but I'm liking living on my own and how pretty and vibrant Birmingham is.

Puja listens intently. 'You know what, Arush, it doesn't matter if the job isn't exactly what you had in mind. It's nice that you have something. Look at me! I am still sitting at home with nothing figured out yet.'

'That's okay, Puja. Most of us are in the same boat. To be honest, if my parents hadn't set this up, I'd still be in Derby helping out at the shop and the restaurant. I had become a bit too comfortable. Initially I was annoyed with my parents as well as with Jenna. But now I can see that I needed that little push. Maybe you need one too?'

'I don't know, Arush. There's a lot happening at my end that I have been meaning to tell you too,' she says.

She tells me about their family holiday, and how she met Benny, and how Divya has hit it off with Vihan.

'I am a little ashamed to admit, I posted those stories just to make you jealous. I so badly wanted you to message me,' she says.

'And I was waiting for you to tell me about these new entrants in your life.' I smile.

'Just ignore all those comments on the reel, okay? About Benny and me making a good couple.'

'Oh! So that's why you didn't want me to see the reel?'

'Yes, I'm embarrassed. I don't want you to think there's something going on there. There isn't anything.'

'Of course! I trust you, Puja.'

Secretly, I am relieved that Benny is just a guy she met on a holiday, and she will not see him again. But I'm not going to tell her that. But what she says next makes me clench my fists.

'I've been meaning to tell you, Arush, but never got the chance till now. Sujit got in touch with me.'

'What? That ... that worm. How dare he!'

'Arush, he has changed. He wrote me a mail explaining—'

'Explaining what?'

'Shall I read it out to you?'

'Yes, please. I want to hear what he has to say.'

When she finishes, I'm lost for words. He does sound genuine and sincere. I feel bad for him.

'What do you feel about it?' she asks, her voice tinged with anxiety.

'I feel terrible to hear what he has been through but I also think it's good that he regrets it. It gives all of us some closure.'

'He's started a restaurant now.'

'A restaurant? Really?'

'Yes, home-cooked fish curry and rice. I've placed an order for some food. I'll let you know how it is,' she says.

After we hang up, I think about how hard it must have been for Sujit. If he hadn't yelled to the shopkeeper that day, and if the ambulance hadn't arrived in time, I don't know what would have happened. Also, I'd been so mad at him that I had lied to him, which is something I am not proud of.

But all of that was before the pandemic. We've all grown up so much since then. Sujit, like all of us, is struggling to stay afloat, and I hope his restaurant succeeds.

13

Puja

'I can't believe that something good is actually happening in my life. I mean the final confirmation interviews are still left but Vihan says it's just a formality,' Divya says as she neatly arranges her clothes in the suitcase. I am sprawled on her bed, watching her.

Unlike me, Divya is a very meticulous packer. She made a list of things to take to Mumbai the moment she knew that she had cleared the preliminary interviews at the bank.

'Excited?' I ask.

'I hate to admit it, but I am more excited about seeing Vihan than about the job. I can't even believe I am saying this. I was so career-oriented and focused before the pandemic. And look what happened after I lost the job. I sank faster than the Titanic,' she says.

'Hey, it's okay to feel excited about meeting someone you like. Don't be so hard on yourself,' I tell her.

'Now you're sounding like Dr Harsh.' She smiles.

Divya's flight is in the evening today. Amma bade her goodbye and wished her luck before leaving for the hospital. Achcha called from Thrissur, where he has a meeting regarding a potential business opportunity in Abu Dhabi. Vihan plans to meet her at Mumbai airport when she lands. She has booked a hotel near Vihan's place in Andheri. I've got so used to having Divya around that I can't believe I'll be without her in a few hours from now.

'I'm really going to miss you, Divya,' I wail.

'I'm going to miss you too,' she says.

'But you have a new job, new apartment, new guy. You will be busy. Whereas I am stuck in the same old rut. I feel a bit useless right now,' I confess my innermost thoughts to Divya. The fact that she is leaving is making me emotional.

She slants her head and looks me in the eye. 'It doesn't matter what you do. Just say yes to every opportunity that comes your way. If you don't like something, you can quit. You would have, at the very least, learnt what you *don't* like. And that's one step closer to what you may eventually want to do. Twenties are the time for making mistakes.'

When Divya puts it that way, it makes me feel slightly better. But a nagging feeling remains. 'By the way, Sujit got in touch yesterday. He has started his own restaurant.'

'What? Sujit has a restaurant now? That's impressive!'

'Yes, it is. He messaged me yesterday. His restaurant specialises in fish. The stuff he posted looked delicious. And I felt like I should support him, especially now that I know what he has been through. I ordered some for today's lunch. You can taste it before you leave.'

My phone buzzes. A notification from the building security staff pops up on the app. One of us has to approve the entry for a visitor. I look at the notification, and it says 'food delivery', so I approve it. The name of the delivery person says Sujit. I am confused whether the security guards have made a mistake. Perhaps the delivery person said that Sujit sent him, and they entered that name. Sujit couldn't possibly be bringing the food himself, I think as I hear the doorbell ring. I head out of Divya's room to see Shanti Chechi taking the nylon bag, saying 'Okay, give me a minute to return it. Please wait.'

She takes a large tiffin carrier out of the bag and says, 'The delivery guy wants this container back.'

'They gave it in a steel container?' I ask, surprised.

'Yes, he said they don't use any plastic,' Shanti Chechi says as she begins transferring the contents into our Corelle bowls.

The door is left slightly ajar, and through the gap I spot the person who has brought the food. Could that be Sujit? I am not sure.

I walk to the door and open it. I was right. It is indeed Sujit! Gone is the curly overgrown mop of hair he had earlier. His hair is cut short neatly, almost like a soldier's haircut. He is wearing a fitted plain navy blue shirt and faded jeans. I've never seen Sujit in anything other than oversized shabby T-shirts and shorts. I am surprised to see this version of him.

He is in front of the elevator, looking around nervously. He looks startled as he hears the door open and sees me. He is sweating and he wipes away the sweat with a tissue.

'Oh my god, Sujit! How nice to see you!' I am genuinely happy to see him.

He says nothing for a few seconds. Then he smiles at me and looks at the floor. There's so much sadness in his eyes, it makes my heart melt.

'How could you just stand there and not even ask for me or say hi?' I scream as I go up to him and give him a quick hug.

Sujit doesn't hug me back.

'Er ... Hi, Puja ... I ... I just didn't have the courage to face ... you. I ... I ....'

'Don't be silly! I am not a dragon that you need courage to face me.' I smile at him.

But he doesn't smile back. He looks away and stares at the floor. It makes me want to assure him that things are truly okay and I have forgiven him. I want to tell him to let it go. I want to tell him that we were all foolish when we were teenagers and we've all grown since then. But it is not a conversation we can have standing.

'Come on inside. I can't just let you stand there,' I tell him.

Sujit sits on the bench we've placed just outside our flat and removes his shoes. They are frayed at the edges, slightly torn at the toe and the rubber sole is worn out. He places them neatly beneath the bench as I lead him inside.

Shanti Chechi is rinsing the tiffin container that Sujit brought the fish curry in. 'It smells delicious. My mouth is watering,' I tell Sujit as I lead him to the living room. But Sujit doesn't even hear me. He stands rooted to the spot, gazing around.

'Puja, your home! It's straight out of a magazine,' he says as his eyes take in the floor to ceiling windows that give us an expansive sea-view. 'This is simply stunning,' he says, as he walks towards the window. The white and blue ocean glistens in the midday sun. Today the sky is bright blue and cloudless. Sujit stands there staring at the ships, saying nothing.

'Want to go out to the garden?' I ask him.

'Whatever you want,' he says, his voice almost a whisper.

I have never seen this side of Sujit. The Sujit I am used to is boisterous, loud with a devil-may-care attitude. But now he seems like an entirely different person.

Shanti Chechi appears with the steel container.

'Shanti Chechi, this is Sujit, my friend and classmate,' I tell her.

'Oh! I am sorry. I thought he was the delivery person,' she says.

'I am the delivery person, manager, owner, all of it,' Sujit replies with a small smile.

'What shall I make to drink?' Shanti Chechi asks.

'Iced tea, please, Shanti Chechi. Sujit, you're okay with iced tea?' I ask him as I lead him to the terrace garden.

'Anything is fine,' he says.

The garden coolers are on full blast, and I indicate the wicker chair that faces the coolers and ask Sujit to sit opposite me. I sit down, facing the second cooler.

'Puja, this home, this garden, it's like a luxury hotel,' Sujit says, sitting on the edge of the chair.

'My father got all this designed by some French designer. It's nice, I guess,' I say.

'Nice? That's an understatement!'

'I haven't done a thing to earn it. It's all my parents' efforts But you, on the other hand, you started your own restaurant? How cool is that! Tell me about it.' I'm trying to change the topic.

I can see that he feels a little out of place and is clearly bowled over by the opulence. Arush too had said that when he had first seen my home over a video call. I guess it takes people some time to get used to it.

Shanti Chechi arrives with the iced tea and Sujit immediately stands up to take it from her.

'No, no, please sit,' she says.

'Thank you, Shanti Chechi,' he says as she places the glasses on the table. She has also brought some banana chips and unniyappams. She places them on the table.

'If I eat all this, I won't be hungry for lunch, and my mother will be annoyed,' Sujit says.

'Please take some. I made these. At your age you should be able to digest even an elephant.' Shanti Chechi smiles and then excuses herself.

'These are delicious,' Sujit says as he helps himself to the banana chips.

'Yes, Shanti Chechi is a really good cook,' I tell him.

'My mother too,' Sujit says.

'So how did you start this restaurant?'

'Do you want the long version or the short version?' Sujit asks.

I can see that he is slowly getting used to my place now and he is relaxing a bit more by the way he is no longer on the edge of the seat and is instead leaning back a bit.

'Long version, please.' I take a sip of the iced tea.

'Alright, you asked for it.'

14
Arush

Even though Kathy has told us that there'll be more work for us, Daljit and I discover she is wrong. There's hardly any work at all. Daljit doesn't care. He plays games on his laptop, scrolls through social media and chats with friends. I am very uncomfortable about it. I decide that I'll raise it with Kathy soon. I don't feel good at being employed here and not having work to do, and yet collecting a pay cheque. I begin to wonder if Nik hired me as a favour to my father and I hate even the thought of it.

On Friday evening, we're told that the entire office—both, the design team and the travel team—has been invited to a team dinner at Bacchus Bar in Burlington arcade. When I get there, I find Daljit standing around and looking lost.

'Google Maps led me here but I can't seem to find where the place is,' he says

'Ha, I'm in the same boat,' I say as we look around. Then I spot a narrow entryway that leads underground. 'Here it is. So easy to miss this one,' I say as we walk down. Walking down feels like we're entering a cellar albeit a plush one. Adorned with old-fashioned artwork and relics, vaulted ceilings and dark wood tables, it exudes an ambience of luxury. When we mention the name of our company, the hostess leads us to our table, which is tucked away in a far corner.

I spot some of my colleagues. They're all dressed smartly, and I'm glad I chose to wear a formal shirt. Olivia spots us. 'Welcome, the babies of the team!' She introduces us to everyone from the travel team. There's Ruby Allen, Ella Scott, Alfie Jenkins, Naomi Jones and Joshua Bell. From the design team there is Sophie Baker, Pavi Allen and Jessica Lawson, apart from Kathy Hart, all of whom Daljit and I already know.

Most people in the company are young. The few older ones in the group have worked in the same organisation for many years. They've been here right from the time it was set up. They're a friendly lot, and it is easy to hold conversations with them. We discover that some of us live in adjacent buildings since we are using company accommodation. Naomi lives in the same building as me, on the floor below mine.

'How is it that we've never run into each other?' I ask her.

'Different times, I suppose? My job is to do walking tours, and my timings are not the regular office timings,' she says.

'Walking tours? That sounds like fun! How did you get into it?'

'I've always been interested in history. I'd come to Birmingham for a travel and tourism course, and was fascinated when I took a walking tour,' she says.

'With this company itself?'

'No, that was with a rival company,' she whispers conspiratorially. 'We weren't offering any walking tours then. That happened only when I suggested it, after I joined here. I'd applied for an internship as a part of my course. I discovered I really enjoying telling people about the history of Birmingham.'

'I love history too. Huge buff,' I tell her.

'Then you should definitely come on one of my tours,' she tells me. 'You'll enjoy it. I have one tomorrow morning at eleven. Join me if you don't have plans for the weekend.'

'I'd love to join. Thank you.'

'Alright then. I'll knock on your door at 10.30 sharp. Don't be late—or hung over.' She wags a finger at me.

'No, Ma'am. I will be on time,' I say and she laughs.

We place our food and drink orders, and we all move around, talking to each other. Then Olivia taps a glass and calls for our attention. We're all asked to introduce ourselves and tell everyone two fun facts about ourselves. The things people come up with are very creative. They range from 'I like sad music' to 'I've run the Edinburgh marathon' to 'I have eight sisters and three brothers.'

This is such an icebreaker and we're all learning about each other.

'I can touch my nose with my tongue,' says Naomi.

'No way!' We all scream. By now most of us are buzzed.

'Yes, I can' she says and proceeds to touch her nose and we all scream, 'Wooooo'.

When it is my turn, I say 'I used to have a pet iguana, I also got beaten up in India and landed up in a hospital.'

'Badass! The quiet shy ones are the most dangerous!' Naomi screams. Everyone agrees.

By the end of the evening, I am drunk, and it is with great difficulty that Naomi and I walk back home. The others are following us too, raucously singing songs, having a whale of a time.

When we reach our buildings, we all say goodbye to each other. Naomi and I step into the lift and when she steps out, she reminds me to be on time.

The next morning when my alarm rings at 8.00 a.m. I have to hit snooze thrice before I can even get out of bed. To ease a headache and the worst hangover ever, I gulp down a pint of water and make myself some dry toast. While at university, Jenna swore by this cure, and I am happy it still works.

By the time Naomi knocks on my door, I have showered and put on clean clothes. I still look like I've had a rough night while Naomi looks fresh and chirpy. She is wearing a mustard dress that complements her golden-brown skin, which glistens in the sunlight. Her crimped hair is neatly pulled back in a professional way, and her maroon jacket matches her boots.

'I feel underdressed now,' I confess, confronted by her dazzling smile and dancing eyes. I've worn a plain grey T-shirt, baggy pants and sneakers.

She chuckles. 'Wait till you see the tourists. You won't feel out of place then.'

We grab a coffee at a shop which, Naomi tells me, serves the best coffee in the city. The coffee makes me feel less groggy. We reach the Centenary Square, from where the tour originates, earlier than all the tourists who've booked it. Naomi reaches into her bag and opens a yellow umbrella with the name of our company on it. 'This way tour group can easily find us,' she says.

She has a list of people joining in with a few details about them. 'The people who book this tour have to fill out an online form first,' she informs me. 'Today, most are from the United States, two from Canada and three from France and two Indians.' Naomi tells me.

She puts on her bright yellow company lanyard tag and hands me one as well.

'But . . . but I'm not even a part of this. What if they ask me something?'

'Oh, don't worry. I'll answer them. You can just say you're assisting me.'

People start trickling in shortly, and once all the participants are there, Naomi introduces herself.

'Hello, all. I am Naomi—like the model Naomi Campbell. I don't have her looks but I promise you I am a lot friendlier than her,' she says and everyone laughs.

She asks everyone to tell us which country they are from and she makes a few pleasing remarks about their home country. Naomi makes everyone feel relaxed within a few minutes. She says if anyone has any questions, they are free to stop her at any point and ask.

Then she introduces me. 'This is Arush. He will be assisting me today,' she says. I look round the group and give a small wave, hoping my nervousness doesn't show.

But everyone is smiling, excited to start the tour. The two Canadians in the group are senior citizens in their late seventies. The lady carries a large bag, which looks heavy, and the gentleman accompanying her has a walking stick and a backpack.

When Naomi starts talking about the Centenary Square, there's a hushed silence. She is really good at this! I notice that the two senior citizens are finding their bags heavy. The lady has set hers down. I walk up to them, and offer to carry it for them, as we would be walking a fair amount for the rest of the tour.

'That's kind of you, young man,' the lady says as she hands over her bag. When she asks the old man to give me his backpack, he looks at me suspiciously.

'It's okay, John. He is from the same company, see?' She says as she points to my lanyard card. The old man studies it and only when he is satisfied does he hand me his backpack. I put it on my back, and carry the lady's bag on my shoulder.

Naomi talks about how the very spot we stand on was an area of high-density housing in the eighteenth century. She says, 'This might seem like an unrelated question, but you will see why I am asking this in just a minute. How many people use MS Word?'

Almost everyone raises their hand.

'Oh, good, we have quite a few tech-savvy people here,' she says and all laugh. She asks if we know of the font Baskerville and most do. She says it is thanks to John Baskerville, an English printer and businessman who first introduced this font, and she speaks about how his works are still the finest works in printing.

Then she points dramatically at a building to the left of us, and says, 'This, ladies and gentlemen, is the Baskerville House where John Baskerville lived and was buried.'

The whole group turns to look at the building. With this story that she narrated, a building which we would have otherwise just passed by has suddenly become meaningful to each of us.

She talks about the Baskerville wharf, and how an iron merchant bought it and cut a canal arm through it and constructed the wharf to increase his business. She points out the Hall of Memory, a monument that cuts into the Baskerville wharf and was built to honour those who died in World War I.

Every single person, including me, is captivated at how beautifully Naomi has brought the history alive, and also connected it to something we're all familiar with, the Baskerville font. I am full of admiration for her. She asks everyone to follow the yellow umbrella she carries.

I walk with the old couple at the end of the group so the gentleman can keep an eye on his backpack. I don't want him to think that I am running away with his bag.

We make stops at Jewellery Quarter and she guides us through a secret canal route that even the locals don't use. We pass by St. Paul's

Church and she points out the lovely Georgian architecture dating back to 1779.

Naomi leads us to a row of restaurants by the canal. She says we have a twenty-minute break, and we're free to go to any of these restaurants, after which the tour will resume. She emphasises that whatever is bought will have to be paid directly to the restaurant.

'Enjoying it?' she asks me as we both sit on a bench while the group scatters across.

'You are an excellent guide. I'm loving this,' I tell her as I notice the old lady trying to walk to the counter. But it is crowded with people from the group.

'Excuse me,' I tell Naomi as I walk up to the old lady and offer to get them what they want. They both want a cup of tea, and she hands me the money.

When I get it, the lady says, 'Bless you,' and the old gentleman reluctantly grunts a 'Thank you.'

When I come back to the bench Naomi says, 'You're really kind, Arush.'

I just shrug.

When we resume the tour, we make a stop at the Birmingham Cathedral, St. Chad's Cathedral and Victoria Square.

At each stopping point, Naomi narrates the history of the place, replete with interesting anecdotes, and points out many things about the buildings. She makes references to the popular TV series *Peaky Blinders,* which is set in Birmingham and many marvel at her references.

The tour ends at Chamberlain Square. She thanks each one for booking this tour. Then she says, 'While this is a free tour, we'd very much appreciate any gratuity you wish to pay. Birmingham is an expensive city, and if you have enjoyed this, please feel free to pay what you think it is worth.'

Almost everyone is the group tips Naomi. The tips range from 5 pounds to 20 pounds. She thanks each one. I notice some people in the group exchanging email addresses and phone numbers. In these two hours we've spent together, we've formed a little bond. It's funny how I feel a little sad as I watch the group dispersing.

The old lady takes out a fifty-pound note and hands it to me. I am shocked to see such a large amount. 'Ma'am, this is a fifty pound note,' I tell her.

'Yes, you're a good lad. Split it with your friend there. You both make a fine couple.' She smiles.

'But we're only colleagues,' I clarify.

'That's what John and I initially were, isn't it, John?' she nudges him and his face breaks into a smile. He looks like a different person when he smiles.

'Thank you, Ma'am,' I say as I watch them go on their way.

By now the whole group has left.

Naomi walks up to me and I give her the fifty pounds.

'Oh, my! That's generous. You keep it, Arush. You were so nice to them,' she says.

'She wants us to split it.'

'No, you've earned it. What did she say? I noticed them smiling.'

'She thought we were a couple,' I tell her, awkwardly.

But Naomi just meets my eyes and smiles. She is speaking to me with her eyes, telling me that she can feel a connection too. I look away in confusion, not sure of what to say or do.

'I think you'd be a natural at these tours. You should move to the travel division,' Naomi says.

'I'm not sure I'd be as good as you,' I tell her.

'If you're passionate about history and love the city, you'll be good. I was very nervous initially too. But you learn to pretend that it is the first time you are hearing a question which you've only answered a five hundred and thirty-six times before,' she laughs. 'You know, we're short-staffed in the travel department. Think about it. Once you decide, tell Olivia you want to move here.'

I tell her that I will carefully consider it.

'You'll be good at it, Arush. I've never seen anyone so compassionate, and you speak really well too,' Naomi piles on the compliments, her eyes shining with sincerity.

As we walk back together, I think about how enjoyable this has been. Perhaps I'll speak to Olivia and give this a try.

15

Sujit

I think Puja is my lucky charm. Ever since I visited her home that day business has exploded. I cannot believe how it has taken off like a rocket. I am so busy these days, I don't have time for anything other than looking after A Fishy Business.

Puja had been impressed—though I don't know why—when I told her how I was running the restaurant, and that she was one of my first customers. She called me that very evening, on the day that I had visited her. She said everyone in her family, especially her mother, loved the fish curry and rice.

'Listen, my mom wanted to check if you will deliver to her hospital. Her colleagues want to try it as well.'

'It's just me here for delivery. We're getting other orders from Ravi's college as well. So, it will be hard,' I'd said. She had been shocked when she knew that I was doing all the delivery myself.

'Look, Sujit, never pass up a business opportunity. If the customers love what you sell, you don't have to go anywhere. They will come to you. By that, I mean, they will get the food picked up or will pick it up themselves. Give them that option,' she'd advised, which was a great idea.

We did just that. Ravi made a reel saying since we're a small business we were unable to deliver. However, if anyone wanted Amma's legendary—yes, he used the word 'legendary'!—fish curry they have the option of getting it picked up by GoGet, a popular delivery service.

The bank manager too has ordered from us four times in a span of mere ten days! Within a week of setting it up, we are doing almost thirty orders a day. Word of mouth spread at lightning speed among the kids from Ravi's college hostel. Some of them asked if they could come home for dinner. They didn't care that our dining room was cramped, they just craved home food. When Amma okayed it, they came over in groups, though we were forced to restrict it to just six people at a time, because we can't seat more than that. Six itself is a tight squeeze. Our home is now a busy place with students dropping in for dinner, in batches. They have to pre-book. If we're unable to accommodate, they are disappointed but go only after booking for the next day. News of our business is spreading like wildfire.

Ravi and I help Amma serve, cook and clean. Sindu too wants to help, but we tell her to focus on studying. Besides, her friend's father is dropping off her friend daily. When he sees the bustling activity in our house, smells the fish curry, he wants to order too. He tells his neighbours, and they have begun ordering as well.

I think the reels that Ravi has posted are adding to the multiplier effect we're currently facing. He has created many reels that show Amma cooking and me getting the fish from the market, shots of me on the cycle going to deliver the food. Since I told him I didn't want to show my face, he shot it cleverly from the back, zooming in on my hands handing over the cash, choosing the fish, pedalling away, etc.

By Day 12 of starting the venture, we are up to sixty orders a day and are now struggling to keep up. There is a line of GoGet delivery boys outside our home, waiting to pick up Amma's fish curry and rice. Our days begin at 5.30 a.m. so that we can finish cooking in time. Ravi helps till he has to leave for college. After that it is just Amma and me. It is exhausting to cook in the heat, but there is a glow on Amma's face that was absent before. Every night we count the orders we have received for the next day, so we can plan the quantity to cook and the amount of fish to buy.

One morning when I go to the fish market, Thresiamma Chechi from whom I usually buy the fish gives me a wide grin. She and two other ladies are looking at a mobile phone that Thresiamma Chechi is holding.

'Isn't this your mother?' she asks as she turns the phone towards me. She is watching a reel Ravi has posted.

'Yes, Chechi, it is,' I reply.

'See, I told you it is his mother! I never forget a customer's face,' she tells the other two ladies. 'You started a business?' she asks me.

'Yes, and it's doing very well.'

'Ah! No wonder you are buying so much. I was thinking that maybe there's some wedding in your house and you have extra guests. I never thought about this,' she said.

'No, no wedding. We sell fish curry and rice.'

'How much did you pay?' she asks flipping her forefinger with her thumb.

'Eh? Do you mean how much it costs to order?' I ask her.

'No, chekka, I am asking how much you had to bribe to get the food licence,' she says.

It strikes me only then. Oh, hell. *We don't even have a licence.*

'These days it is very easy to get a licence. Everything can be done online,' I lie easily. I am not going to admit to her that we have been running a business without a food licence. I don't know how this very basic thing hadn't occurred to me. What an idiot I am.

It's the first thing I tell Amma when I get home.

'I don't think we need a licence, we are not running a hotel,' she says.

I look it up online, and I tell Amma that we do need a licence. The Food Safety and Standards Authority of India (FSSAI) lays out the entire procedure to obtain one. They even talk about 'food safety mitras' that the government introduced in 2021 to facilitate small businesses. But when I explain it to Amma, she brushes it aside casually.

'Amma, it says that we can be fined up to five lakh and six months in jail if we run a business without a licence.'

'Okay, we will see about that later. It's not as urgent as these orders. It is not as though someone will come today to check our licence.'

That afternoon, after all our orders are done, and before the evening rush starts, I think about the licence again. Amma isn't much affected by it, but I am terrified. Things have just started looking up, and it is best to operate with a licence. I am not so sure if obtaining a licence can be as simple as filling up a form online, like the website says. There must surely be more. I don't know how to go about it. I message Puja and ask her if I can call.

She replies in a few minutes and I ask her if she knows anything about obtaining food licences. She says she will speak to her father and get back to me. Puja calls me after two hours, just as our evening rush is starting. She says it can be done easily through an agent. We will have to pay the agent his fees, which is almost as much as the licence fee. She tells me that an official from the food authority will come to inspect the place. The agent will handle all of it, including the bribes.

'Ha! I knew it wouldn't be so easy,' I tell her.

'It is easy. Nowadays it's all online and it takes only two weeks, maybe even less,' Puja says.

I smile, recalling that was exactly what I had told Thresiamma Chechi. Puja passes me the contact number of an agent and tells me that her father's friend runs a restaurant, and if I want any tips, she will connect me to him.

'My father said that when you speak to the agent, you can mention Mr Padmanabhan's name. That's my dad's restaurateur friend.'

I thank her and tell her I'll keep her informed. It is only after the rush hour is over that I am able to call the agent, Mr Radhesh Kumar. After introducing myself I mention Mr Padmanabhan's name.

'Yes, I do a lot of work for him,' Radhesh says. 'How do you know him, sir?' he asks. I sense that his tone towards me has become a bit more respectful.

'His close friend's daughter is a good friend of mine,' I tell him.

'Oh Mr Krishnan's daughter?' he immediately says.

'Umm, yes,'

'Okay, it will be done.'

'Your charges?'

'Don't worry about it.'

Radhesh doesn't even tell me how much it will cost me. A trickle of perspiration begins to form on my forehead. 'We're just a small business running from home. I don't have big budgets like Mr Padmanabhan,' I tell him. I don't want him to charge me an exorbitant amount.

'Is the turnover more than twelve lakh?' he asks.

'What? No! It isn't that much. We've just started.'

'Then it won't be much. We can settle everything within twenty-five thousand,' he says.

'That is a lot for me. We're really small. I'm just a student, who started this after my father passed away and I owe money to the bank also. I am doing this to make ends meet.'

I use every negotiation skill that I have learnt on the streets while dealing. If you want the other person to give you what you want, you have to make them feel important. You have to let them believe they are powerful.

Finally, I am able to convince him to being down the figure he quoted by more than fifty percent.

'I don't generally do this for so little, but since you are Mr Krishnan's daughter's friend and since you said your father passed away and all that's why—'

'I am really grateful. Thank you. Thank you so much,' I tell him.

After that, things move smoothly. There are several documents to be submitted like proof of identity, papers showing the house belongs to us, passport size photos, an FSSAI declaration form and many more such things. Radhesh handles all of it. He asks us if the business should be in my name or Amma's name or whether it is a partnership.

'My son's name. He has singlehandedly done all of this. I am just the cook,' Amma says. When I hear the pride in her voice, a sea of indescribable emotions washes over me. She may not have given birth to me but the way she has embraced everything about me makes me feel blessed.

I am on tenterhooks when the food inspector comes to our place. But Radhesh is with him. He inspects the kitchen. He asks us to show where we store the fish curry.

'We make everything fresh, sir. I buy the fish from the market, and it finishes by the end of the day. In fact, we cook only if the meal is pre-booked,' I tell him.

He just nods but I detect a glint of approval in his eyes.

A week later, Radhesh tells us that we've got our licence. I simply can't believe it. He sends me the link and I look it up online. I call Amma and show her. Radhesh says a physical copy will arrive soon. It arrives the very next day.

I am so proud I want to frame this. So is Amma. She makes payasam that evening—and we all have a quiet celebration. Ravi, Amma, Sindu and I.

The next day I call Puja to tell her all about it.

'Thank you so much, Puja, I owe you. Truly.'

'No need to thank me. I really want your restaurant to take off. You deserve it, Sujit, you really do.'

I feel weirdly emotional after hearing that. Perhaps it is because not a single person has said that to me before.

'Meet me for coffee?' I ask before I can stop myself.

She hesitates for a few seconds. I hold my breath; I don't even know why I asked her out.

Then she says, 'Sure, when?'

Now I feel a bit embarrassed. 'The only free time I have is between 2 and 4.30 p.m. I need to be back home to help Amma before the evening rush starts,' I tell her.

'Then you won't have enough time to come this side of town. You know what? I'll come over to your place. I do want to see your set-up,' she tells me.

Damn. What have I got myself into? My place is small, ordinary, plain compared to the grand palace she lives in.

'It's nothing to boast of,' I tell her quietly.

'So don't boast then.' She laughs, unaware of my predicament. She doesn't get it at all. Then I think she realises I am not laughing. She says, 'If you don't want me to come home then—'

'No, no, you can come over,' I tell her.

She is right. There really are no coffee shops in my part of town. At least not good enough to take Puja to.

'Alright. I'll come over in a few days. Send me your location,' she says.

'Sure, see you,' I tell her.

Inside I am dying. I don't want Puja to see my home, or worse, feel sorry for me. But I've put this in motion now, and I can't stop it.

16

Puja

Benny has made me a job offer and it takes me completely by surprise. He messaged me on Instagram and said that they are looking for a social media manager. He says the reel I made has helped them generate a ton of business, and Mr Nambiar and he both felt the need for a dedicated social media manager after they saw what it could do for the business. I told him that I'll think about it, as it will mean I will have to move to Varkala. While it's good for a holiday, compared to Kochi it is a small town. I am really not sure if I want it and so asked for some time. I want to talk to Divya about it too.

She makes a video call to us when we're having dinner. She has a bright red bowl in her hand.

'What are you eating?' I ask.

'Maggi,' she says as she forks the noodles into her mouth and slurps. 'I have great news!' she says, waving the fork.

'Eat first and then talk,' Amma says.

'Amma, this can't wait! I cleared the final interview! They want me to join next week.' She says she is over the moon and can't wait to start working once again.

'Wonderful news indeed, Molle, just wonderful!' my mother says. Achcha is proud as well.

'Congratulations, Divya. I knew you would get it,' I tell her.

'Thanks, Puja,' Divya beams. 'Come and visit me here.'

'I will.'

'What are you all eating?' she asks.

'Fish fry. Shanti Chechi made it so well,' I tell her as I flip the camera around to show her the food.

'Yum! I miss home food. And that reminds me—what happened to Sujit's restaurant? How is it going?' She asks as she spoons in another mouthful of Maggi.

'It's going really well. Amma's colleagues have also started ordering from him,' I say.

'That's nice then!' she says.

She doesn't ask about Arush, because that comes under the category of 'love-life', which is something we speak about only to each other. It's an unspoken agreement between us that we don't share such things with our parents. I am dying to know what is happening between her and Vihan, but that will have to wait as well.

Amma asks her how Vihan is and Divya plays it cool.

'Right now, we're very good friends. I'm taking it slow Amma,' she says and Amma understands.

Once Divya hangs up my father says, 'Your friend who started the restaurant—the agent told Padmanabhan that he is a shrewd businessman and drives a hard bargain.'

Amma frowns when she hears that. 'Did I hear Divya say the name Sujit? Is it that same Sujit?'

I wince. I think I know what is coming. 'Yes, Amma,' I say.

'Which Sujit? Who is this boy?' my father asks.

'That same drug addict because of whom your daughter went to jail.' Amma's voice is icy now.

'What? Is it the same boy, Puja?' my father asks, shock and disbelief at what he is hearing becoming slowly evident on his face.

'Yes, Achcha.'

'What is this, Puja? I thought you had cut off all ties with him.'

'I had, but he got in touch recently. He wrote me an email explaining everything.'

'And you believed him?' Amma asks. 'And on top of that you decided to use Achcha's contacts to help him? How dare you, Puja. Are you making a fool of us again?'

When my mother is angry she turns into a very different person. She has no control over what she says or does. Right now, she is furious. The best way to diffuse her anger is to not say anything. So, I keep quiet.

'When you mentioned a friend needs help with food licence I never in a million years thought it would be this boy.'

'Achcha, it's not what you think. He has turned his life around.'

Amma scoffs. 'How naive you are, Puja. A leopard never changes it spots.'

'How can you say that?' I ask.

I am angry too now, with both my father and mother, for judging Sujit without knowing what he is going through.

'I know so many such cases. They give up for a year at the most and then they all slip back into old habits. You have no business at all even talking to him.' Amma's eyes flash as she speaks.

'I think I know who to be friends with and who not to be,' I tell her coolly.

I know a response like this will only trigger her more, but I feel like I *have* to defend Sujit. 'And your opinions aren't always right, you know.'

'As long as you're in my house, Puja, you obey my rules,' Amma says.

My father gives her a look and I catch it. He wants her to keep quiet. He knows the situation has gone out of hand.

'Look, Molle, ultimately it is your life and your call. But think about it calmly. Why would you want to be friends with him of all people and then help him too? Have you forgotten how I had to get you out of jail? That night, he ran away and was not to be seen. What kind of a person does that? Only a coward, if you ask me,' my father says in a pained tone.

'We've all changed, Achcha. That was two years back when we were stupid teenagers. I have changed so much since then. So has he. I'd even run away from home to a foreign country. But you all forgave me. I think everyone deserves a second chance to make things right.'

'You don't have to be that person providing that second chance. He has his parents for that,' my mother's voice is sharp. 'Don't you get it?'

I want to tell them that it is *they* who don't get it. Sujit lost his mother when he was a child and recently lost his father too. He really is working hard, and has apologised to me. I don't know how to make them understand that this is not that same Sujit they are presuming him to be. Even if I try, I know they won't even believe me. So, I say nothing and continue eating my meal.

My father takes a deep breath. Then he says, 'Let's not discuss this anymore.'

'Suits me.' I shrug, acting nonchalant.

No one speaks for the rest of the meal. I am burning inside. I know my parents think they are protecting me from all the bad decisions I've made. But I want them to understand that I am perfectly capable of making my own judgements about people. I want them to see that Sujit has changed.

I call up Divya from my room once we are through with dinner.

'What happened?' she asks as soon as she sees my face.

'Fight with both Amma and Achcha,' I tell her and narrate everything that happened.

'See, Puja, as long as you continue staying with them, you're going to keep having these clashes,' she says.

I catch a glimpse of movement behind her.

'You sly fox! Vihan is there, isn't he?' I ask.

'Yeah,' she admits sheepishly. 'We've been kind of together ever since I arrived here. But I am not sharing this with either of them. They will immediately want me to get married to him and stuff.'

'I know. Best not to tell them for now.'

Then I tell her about the job offer that Benny has made.

'What are you even thinking about? Accept it! Get out of home. Trust me, living on your own is a different feeling.'

'Yes, but it's not like Mumbai, which is a metropolis. This is almost a coastal touristy village I'll be moving to.'

'It doesn't matter, Puja. It feels terrific to live life on your own terms, under no one's shadow.'

We chat some more about how much she likes Mumbai and how happy she is. After we hang up, I sit in bed and think about what she has said. Yet, Varkala is not a place I want to move to. I decide that I'll talk to Arush about it. I look at the world clock on my phone. It is 4.15 p.m. for Arush.

'Hey, have time for a call?' I message him.

I get his reply only after forty minutes.

'Sorry, am at work. Anything urgent?'

'Nah, nothing urgent at all. Just need to talk,'

'Sure. Calling you soon.'

When he calls, I see that he is next to the coffee machine in his office.

'What's up?' he smiles.

My heart melts when I see him. He looks adorable with his shy smile as our eyes meet on the phone screen.

'Oh my god, you look so cute!' I am smiling widely now.

'Why don't you take a flight and come like last time?' he asks cheekily.

'Your turn, mister. I visited you. Now you need to visit me.'

'Let me save up some money. I am a working man and I need to get my leave sanctioned and all that,' he says as he runs his hand through his hair and glances at himself in the camera phone.

Just then someone walks up to him.

'Is this Puja?' she asks and a girl comes into the frame. She looks stunning as she smiles into the camera and says, 'Hiya! I am Naomi, Arush's colleague, and a friend, if I may say so.' She speaks with a British accent, exactly like Arush. I can't tell her ethnicity but she's probably Black.

'Naomi! We're having a private conversation,' Arush says. But the way he looks at her and smiles shows a level of comfort reserved for a close friend. It makes my heart sink.

'Puja, meet Naomi. Naomi, this is Puja,' he says.

'Hi, Naomi,' I say with fake cheer. I have no idea who she is. Why has Arush not mentioned her in any of the conversations we've had? Clearly, he has told her about me. I guess I should take that as a good sign, but I hate that she has interrupted our call. And annoyed about how friendly she is being.

'Sorry to interrupt, but we need to leave now. The tour starts in thirty minutes,' Naomi says.

'What tour?' I ask.

'This is a ghost walking tour. I am assisting Naomi for this one. There's so much that has happened in the past few days that we haven't caught up on. I've moved to the travel division. Can you believe it?'

'That's nice. What is a ghost walking tour?' I ask him.

'Look it up, okay? We take people to graveyards and a haunted hotel where seances were held and all that. I'll call you when I get home. Is that fine?'

'Sure, Arush, have a good time,' I tell him.

After I hang up, I feel stupid for having called him in the first place. I feel stupid for not knowing what a ghost walking tour is. And this new girl Naomi! First Jenna, now Naomi.

It occurs to me that it is after he moved to the travel division, he has suddenly become reticent. Is it because of Naomi, I wonder.

I watch a K-drama while waiting for him to call. It is past 1 a.m. when he finally does.

'Hey, what's up?' he asks.

'How was the ghost tour? Met any ghosts?'

He laughs when he hears it even though I was trying to be sarcastic.

'No ghosts, only humans,' he says. 'Listen, I've been meaning to tell you about Naomi.' Then he goes on to tell me how they have become very good friends, and how she lives on the floor below him. He tells me how good she is at the walking tours and how she encouraged him to speak to Olivia, who moved him to the travel division. He says he is really happy with the work now.

'But, Arush, this is not even what you trained for. I mean, your art? You're so good at it. You're leaving all that and doing this tour guide business?'

'Come on, Puja. You sound like you're derisive of it. That's such an Indian attitude. Just like my parents.'

'Ha! So your parents agree with me? And what do you mean Indian attitude Arush? If I have an Indian attitude, it is because I am Indian. I'm proud of it. Unlike you.'

'Puja, that last bit was unnecessary. We're discussing an issue here. There's no need to get personal.'

'You're the one who brought it up, saying it's an Indian attitude and all that,' I huff.

'Yes, I just wonder why there's so much emphasis placed on doing something related to what you studied. Does it really matter if you choose a profession completely different from what you did at college?' Arush asks. I detect exasperation in his voice.

'No, it doesn't matter really. All I was trying to point out is that you're so talented. I have seen your work. The mural you did at Ashwathy Bhawan was mind-blowing. Wouldn't you rather do work like that?'

'Of course, but that doesn't pay the bills, Puja. Jenna is lucky enough to get a job doing what she loves. While you are—'

He stops mid-sentence. I think I know what he was going to say, that I was rich. I decide to let it slide.

'That is because she pushed herself out of her comfort zone. But you've been pushed by your parents and you accepted whatever job you got.'

'That is so not true, Puja, you're just talking without knowing the situation. Yes, my parents set me up to take this job. But I wasn't at all happy sitting at the desk. Most days we didn't even have work. But the travel division is short-staffed and tourism is booming. They need me and I feel valued here. I am sorry if what I am doing isn't up to your exacting standards or my parents.' Right now, it is making me happy,' Arush says. There's an edge in his voice now.

I am taken aback by the anger in his voice. He has never lashed out like this. 'Yes, I am happy for you, Arush. That's not what I meant at all.'

'I guess I am also a little touchy about this as my parents have been giving me hell. They don't like what I am doing and they think its demeaning to accept tips,' Arush replies. His tone is slightly gentler now.

'I guess it is a cultural thing. Leave it,' I tell him. I don't want another fight.

'Yes, best to leave it. I think my parents will come around. You tell me, what's been happening at your end?' he asks.

I tell him about the fight with my parents, and that I am planning to visit Sujit. I am taken aback when Arush says he agrees with my parents.

'I think you're making a big mistake going to his house. Stay away from him. I thought we'd both closed that chapter.'

'He is my friend, Arush. We've known him since we were in school. Do you not believe what he said in the mail?'

'Yes, I do believe him. But I don't trust him.'

'So essentially, you're saying you don't trust the decision I am making. You accused me of being like *your* parents. But now you're being like *my* parents.'

'Just expressing what I feel. It's up to you,' he says.

I tell him it is late and hang up. It is only after I hang up that I realise I haven't even told Arush about the job offer, which was why I'd called him. I am angry with him as well as my parents.

I think about what their fear is. Can't people change? Why are they being so close-minded? Arush and my parents can say whatever they want. Now I am even more determined to meet Sujit.

17

Arush

The bright sunlight streams in, falling directly on my face. I shield my eyes and turn over to bury my face in the pillow, wishing I'd remembered to draw the curtains last night. It's when I turn that my hand brushes against something that feels like hair. Confused, I slowly open my eyes. I gasp in shock at what I am looking at. For a few seconds I lie still wondering if I am dreaming. Then I hurriedly slip out of the duvet as the previous day's events slowly come into focus inside my groggy, befuddled brain.

Naomi is sleeping next to me, her shoulders bare, my duvet covering her, which a few seconds ago was covering me as well.

I jump up in a raging hurry to get out of bed, now fully alert, my heart beating at a million beats per minute; I'm in my boxers. I rush to the kitchen on tiptoes.

Shit shitshitshitshit.

This is so messed up. What have I done? How could I have done this? How did it happen? What was I thinking?

I am freaking out now. To calm myself down and to give myself something to do, I switch on the kettle to make coffee. I glance back at my bed through the gap in the open door from the living room to make sure my mind is not playing tricks. Nope, she is there. Sleeping soundly. She is clearly naked under the sheets. I try to recall if I actually slept with her as I stir in the coffee and pour the milk. Absentmindedly I pour too much milk, and it is all milky now. But I don't care. I try hard to remember at least *something* from last night. To my horror it is all a blank in my mind.

Fucking hell.

My milky coffee tastes awful, reflecting what I feel inside. I have no one to blame but myself. This is all my fault. Entirely. I should have put a stop to it the moment I had the slightest suspicion of where this could end up. Naomi is easy to talk to, fun to be around. She also loves to drink at pubs, and every day after work it had become kind of a routine to have a drink at the pub and then head home. We usually ended up cooking together too. She loves Indian food, and I love the Jamaican stuff she makes.

But the thing is, I'd never thought it would end up like this—with her naked in my bed, and me having no recollection at all of anything. Did she roofie me? Even the thought seems absurd. Can guys even get roofied? What the hell happened?

I think about how it all started. She and I have been working together on all the tours for the past few weeks, and we've been spending an inordinate amount of time together. After accompanying her on many tours as her assistant, one day she suddenly told me to take the lead. I was nervous but managed fine, as I'd heard her do it many times. To my surprise, I discovered that I loved it as much as her. The jokes I made were different from the ones she cracked, and they came easily. It felt wonderful to have the attention of an entire group. Naomi said I was a natural, and she told Olivia and all the others at work about it. They all congratulated me and Olivia said they were all happy that I moved to the travel division. It made me feel important. After two years of being cooped up indoors without human contact, it now felt exhilarating to be around people that were not your family. It was a different high to have the whole attention of the walking tour groups who held on to every word I said.

She told me one day about how her grandmother, a White, British lady, got thrown out of her house when she decided to marry her grandfather, Jake, a Black man originally from Jamaica.

'It was the forties and Britain was not what it is today. Blacks were seen as dirty criminals. People weren't used to them. My grandpa came to England as a part of the American forces, which were stationed at Burtonwood base,' Naomi had told me one evening while we were drinking.

'I get it completely. My parents too came over when they were very young. My father too speaks of how he was discriminated against,' I'd shared.

'Can you believe nobody would rent out a home to my grandparents in Birmingham because grandpa was Black? Also, he couldn't work in an office, because a Black man working with White girls in the office was considered unsafe,' Naomi said.

'How did they meet?' I had asked.

'They were a part of the same technical college where my grandpa was sent over by the Air Force for training. He asked her to marry him when she was only nineteen, and later he moved here for her. They spent a happy sixty-two years together. She died in her sleep, and two months later he did too. I always feel he died of a broken heart and couldn't bear to be without her,' Naomi had said.

'They have really faced a lot. Did you face anything at all growing up?' I'd asked.

Naomi said that probably her experience was different from most people's but she was only aware of her mixed race when they had to write personal essays about family and she always wondered what colour her skin was when they had to make self-portraits. She'd spent most of her life in Nottingham and she had never faced any discrimination.

She asked me if I had.

'I never thought much about it either. As a teenager, I think I underwent a minor identity crisis. I thought I had to choose where "I'm really from", India or Britain. I felt England was home, and I felt British. But wondered if that was tantamount to denying my roots and my heritage. But now I just feel fortunate to have two countries.'

We'd talked about how only immigrants to a certain place would understand what it felt like, even though both of us considered the UK our home as we were both born and raised here.

Now when I think about it, all of what we shared was bringing us closer. It had happened so slowly that neither of us had realised it. At least I had not. I felt what we were doing was harmless—spending time together as colleagues at first, and then as friends. But in retrospect it is all very clear that it was leading to this.

Now that I am dissecting this situation, I think deep down I knew she was into me; the way she laughed at all my jokes, even the silly ones. Once she had a few drinks and was buzzed, all her inhibitions would vanish. She would be all over me. Hug me a bit too tightly when we said bye. Telling me how cute I looked in this jacket or that shirt. I should have put an end to it right then. But I guess I was flattered. Still, I'd never expected this—whatever it is, I still don't know—to happen. I don't even know how I am going to explain this to Puja.

Last evening, she'd come over with a Jamaican cassava that she had made. She also brought over some whisky. It was celebration whisky, she said. I'd asked her what she was celebrating, and she said she was celebrating her divorce.

'What? You were married?' I'd asked. I couldn't believe it.

'I was twenty and stupid. It was a whirlwind courtship. But it turned out we were not compatible. There were so many issues. I'm just glad I realised it soon and walked out,' she'd said.

She had smiled then. 'Let's change the topic. You tell me, what is India really like?'

We'd ended up talking late into the night. And even after we finished the delicious cassava she had brought, we continued drinking. I'd told her about Puja, and everything that happened when I visited India last time.

'Is she your girlfriend?' Naomi asked.

'Hmm, yes. But we haven't met for two years now. We're doing long distance, which comes with its own challenges,' I'd admitted.

'So do you love her?' Naomi had asked, as she moved closer and looked straight into my eyes.

We were both heavily drunk at that point.

'Listen, I think we shouldn't be doing this,' I remember telling her. 'We're both drunk.'

I had got the words out with great difficulty and tried to move away. But Naomi continued looking into my eyes, challenging me to resist her.

I had looked away, and moved to the sofa. She had followed me.

She wasn't stumbling. I remember thinking about how it was that she wasn't even slurring while my tongue was heavy and the words weren't coming out so easily. But she seemed to know exactly what she was doing.

After that it is all blurry. My head hurts as I try hard to reconstruct the events. I have only vague recollections of frenzied sex. I can't even tell for sure if that's what happened between us or whether my mind is joining the dots to fill in the blank spaces.

'Hey, good morning.' Naomi walks into the kitchen, startling me, wearing my T shirt from last night.

I try to suppress a groan. It all feels very wrong.

'Morning,' I force the word out.

'Any coffee for me?' She looks at the kettle.

I want to tell her to get out. I want to tell her to give me my T-shirt back. I want to tell her this is all a mistake and that we should go back to being colleagues.

But I say nothing as I sit still, sipping the rest of my milky coffee, which is now lukewarm, while she brews herself a strong black coffee. She then joins me with her cup in her hand and sits across me at my two-seater table. She looks into my eyes and smiles.

'Naomi, about last night,' I begin to say as I fidget with my coffee cup, unable to meet her eyes.

She laughs. 'You don't remember a thing, do you?'

'No, I don't,' I admit. 'Can you … can you tell me what happened?' I feel like a worm as I force myself to ask her.

'You kept yelling about how it was your first time and you kept calling me Puja,' she says.

'Oh, hell,' I say as I cover my face and slump against the table.

Naomi laughs again. 'Arush! I am only kidding. Do you really not remember?'

I am so shaken I don't know what to say. I shake my head.

'If you don't remember, then it doesn't count, does it?' she says unfazed.

'I need to know,' I tell her.

'Why does it matter?'

'It matters, Naomi. I am in a committed relationship.'

'With someone you haven't met for two years? What matters is how you *feel*, not what you do. People place a lot of emphasis on the physical aspect of this whole cheating business. They think if you have sex with someone other than your partner you have cheated. I don't agree with this view and I don't get it at all. You know you can cheat on someone without having sex with another person, right? Whether you cheat on someone or not—it has nothing to do with whether you have sex physically. You do it inside your head. You can cheat by merely having an emotional connect with someone other than your partner. You know what I mean,' Naomi declares. Then she sips her coffee.

For someone who has just woken up, her thoughts are clear and strong. And forceful. No arguments come to my mind.

'I don't know. I would just like some time to think, please I am sorry, Naomi,' I manage to say

'Of course. I'll leave now. But look, this doesn't change anything between us, okay? It's no big deal. Let's not be awkward about it,' she says as she slides off the stool.

I want to tell her that it is a big deal for me. I want to know if we really did it. I want to tell her I feel like a complete shit. Instead, I say, 'Could you please leave my T-shirt on my bed?'

She laughs like it is a joke.

I hear her go into the bedroom. When she comes out, she is dressed in her own clothes. 'My sweet, sweet Arush,' she says as she kisses me on the forehead, and walks out, shutting the door behind her.

I want to dive under the duvet and never wake up again. But I can't do that. We have a walking tour in exactly an hour from now.

Soaring

You start with a bag full of luck and an empty bag of experience. The trick is to fill the bag of experience before you empty the bag of luck.

—*Rules of the Air*

18

Sujit

I punch in the numbers into the calculator and stare at the figures. I cannot believe it. Amma can't believe it either.

'Do it properly. Maybe you made a mistake,' she says, her voice reflecting her incredulity.

Ravi, Amma and I are seated around the dining table. Sindu has gone to sleep.

'Read out the figures again, and let me recalculate,' I tell her. Even I am finding it hard to believe.

Amma painfully goes over every single day's total orders from the time we started the business. We've written all of it in an old notebook. She reads out the total number of orders as well as the selling price, just to be sure.

I punch in the numbers again. 'See, I have not made any mistake! I am right,' I exclaim triumphantly.

'*Ende Eeshwara*,' Amma gasps. 'What we've earned in three weeks is more than four months of Achcha's salary' she says. Then she begins crying softly.

Ravi and I stare at her in dismay.

'Amma, what happened?' Ravi asks.

'Nothing, Mone. It's just that I wish your father was alive to see this. He would have been so proud,' she says.

'Amma, this is just our turnover. It is not our profit,' I tell her.

'I know, I know. Your mother is not that foolish. But in my whole life I haven't earned this much,' she says.

I do some more calculations. 'We've made a profit of forty-three per cent.'

'Truly fantastic returns!' Ravi says.

'At this rate we will soon be doing over twelve lakhs rupees a year,' I tell them.

'That will be the day! Yes!' Ravi says as he makes a fist and punches the air.

'I think we have to add kappa also to the menu,' Amma says. 'See, we're offering only rice and fish curry right now. If we add kappa, it would be very easy to make. We can price it at ten rupees lesser than the rice. But the margin will be huge for us, as kappa is not that expensive.'

'Amma! Look at you go. Our Shankaran sir will say you have "business acumen" and he would be absolutely correct,' Ravi says.

'Ah-gyumen, eh? What is that?' Amma asks.

Ravi and I both laugh and Amma joins in.

'I think we should hire a helper. With this kind of profit margin, we can afford to hire one,' I tell them.

'I think you're right. We can easily expand and do double the capacity of what we're currently doing. Then the cost of hiring the helper will just get taken care of by the volume we can sell,' Ravi says quietly.

'Expand? How? It's just me and Amma doing everything. The only reason I thought of hiring a helper is because Amma can get some rest.'

'That's what, Chetta,' Ravi says like I am slow to understand. 'Amma can oversee the helper. But if we put tables and chairs outside the kitchen area, inside our compound. We have enough space there. We put up a tarpaulin roof. Then instead of having just six people at a time, maybe we can serve twenty? And in two batches we will be doing forty. Right now, space is our main constraint.'

'Don't forget we need vessels too if we are to do such large numbers,' Amma says.

'Getting vessels, that we can easily do. So, are you all up for it?' I ask.

'Let's just say my ah-gyumen is telling me it's a good idea.'

That night I am so happy I can't contain the happiness rising inside me anymore. I message Puja. She would certainly understand. I tell her about Amma crying with joy, and that we're thinking of expanding the business and how much it all means to our whole family.

Puja replies with about twenty emojis that show applause and twenty more that show joy. Then she messages: 'Talk?'

'Yes,' I tell her.

I look at Ravi. He is fast asleep. I can tell by the way he is breathing. So, I step out into the kitchen area and take her call. A million stars in the sky glitter down at me. Soon there's going to be a fully functional restaurant here.

Puja says, 'Congratulations to the big restaurateur! Well done.'

'Hey, Puja, it's not what you imagine. This is not some grand restaurant. We'll be putting up a tarpaulin tent inside the compound itself.'

'How do you know what I am imagining?' she asks.

'No, I mean, I don't want you to be disappointed when you come here.'

'Don't worry about it, Sujit, I am just happy to be a small part of your journey,' she says.

We speak for a long time. I don't feel the time pass. She talks about badly wanting to do something, yet not being able to gather the momentum or decide upon the direction. She says while she seems to be finding it hard to shake off the fog she is trapped in after the pandemic, she is also happy I figured out what I want to do. She admires what I have set up entirely on my own. I tell her not to worry and that she will figure it out too. She tells me that she will wait till the expansion at my place is done, and will come over to visit me after that.

'I look forward to it, Puja,' I tell her and I really mean it. Earlier I was worried about my home being tiny, my business not being good enough, and generally feeling somewhat inadequate. But now Puja feels like someone I can trust. A friend who will not judge me. I've never had a person on my side like her till now. I've only had people distrust me and judge me so far. While talking to Puja, I like myself a little bit more.

Perhaps it is the euphoria of making money. It is funny how a bit of money in the bank gives one confidence.

Every evening, after the day's work is done I either end up texting her or she messages me to ask how the day went. The messages lead to calls where we end up talking late into the night. It has become a kind of routine now. A part of me wonders if Arush will mind this. I know that if *my* girlfriend were talking to some guy every single day for a long time I'd sure as hell get mad. I want to ask Puja but I don't. It feels like if I talk about it to her, it will break this spell. That's what this is to me—a magic spell. And I don't want it broken.

I bring it up at my next session with Dr Harsh. Our sessions have now reduced in frequency; it is only once in twenty days now. Dr Harsh is happy with what he calls the 'tremendous positive changes' I've made in my life.

'Is it foolish of me to be in this Puja bubble, knowing fully well she is someone else's girlfriend? Do you think I should stop talking to her?' I ask him.

'Have you spoken to her about it?' he asks.

'No way! That's why I am raising it with you.'

'What do you think will happen if you tell her?' He looks thoughtful as he speaks.

'Tell her what?'

'That you think this is magical.'

'She might think I have a thing for her,' I say.

'Do you?' he asks.

'Come on, Dr Harsh, I can't answer that!'

'Why not?'

'I ... I don't know.'

'See, Sujit, it is only us humans who make all these distinctions in our heads about what other people might or might not do, think or feel. We decide this based on our past experiences. But the experiences other people have might be completely different from ours and they may not see a situation the same way that we do. So, as long as Puja hasn't said that she is uncomfortable talking to you every day, I don't think the onus is on you to steer this thing. If you feel like telling her what you have is special, then take that step and see where it leads you,' he says.

Long after the session I think about what Dr Harsh said. He is infuriatingly right. This is Puja's call. If she is okay talking to me, then what Arush thinks is not my business. I decide that I am not going to bring this up. But the decision is now coming from a place of contemplation and awareness, unlike before where it was coming from a place of confusion. Sometimes the best thing to do about something is simply nothing.

After a few days, we get a flat roof canopy tent put up outside our kitchen. Ravi had managed to get the contact details of a person in this business from his friend.

'Let's see. If it takes off, we can think of a more permanent structure. If it fails, we can go back to what it was before,' I tell Amma and Ravi, as the men put up the canopy and leave. Amma and Ravi both agree with me that it is a great option.

We also rent large vessels, stoves, chairs and tables for a month. Again, I've negotiated and got us good rates. The person renting it had said that they generally rent only for two or three days. But I had explained my situation and told him how we badly want to do something for my mother. I'd offered him one per cent of the day's earnings, and he was more than happy with that.

Amma, meanwhile, had applied for a commercial gas connection in her name, and the cylinders got delivered a couple of days back. When the vessels, stove, tables and chairs arrive, Ravi and I set up the whole thing. Amma wants to help but we tell her to relax.

'All of this makes it look like there's a wedding taking place in our home,' Sindu says when she comes back from school.

'Do you not like it?' Amma asks.

'I love it!' she says, clapping her hands, even though all we have are cheap plastic chairs and the cheapest metal tables that we could manage to rent.

'With all this set up, it's time we hire a help. Jayashri Chechi said they know someone really good who is looking for a job. She is sending him over today,' Amma says.

'I've also told the security people in the building down the road. They are also sending some people,' I tell Amma.

In between catering to our daily orders, Amma and I interview the candidates one of whom will potentially be employed as our helper. We ask them basic questions like whether they have had experience in an eatery or a restaurant, what their salary expectations are, and why they are looking for a job. I take down their contact details, and tell them I will let them know soon. By the end of the day, we have interviewed eleven people.

That night Amma and I discuss who to hire. Amma straight away dismisses most of them as she says they looked like they had never bathed in their entire lives. We both agree that the most promising of the lot was a young man his twenties—Chandran. Chandran has worked in a hotel in Malappuram district. When we asked him why he moved to Ernakulam, he had scratched behind his ear, blushed and said, 'Girlfriend.'

'No girlfriend visits or phone calls when on duty, okay?' Amma tells him when he reports for work the next day.

'No, no, Chechi, I will work properly. No calls on duty.' Then in the same breath he asks, 'During lunch break okay no?'

Amma looks at me and raises her eyebrows. I think about all the phone calls I have been having with Puja, and how important they have become to me. 'Yes, okay. But don't let the calls spill over to working hours,' I tell him.

'No, Sir, I won't,' he assures me.

It feels so odd when he addresses me as 'sir'. It's the first time in my life I am someone's boss. I can get used to this, I think as I sit at the dining table while Chandran makes tea for me and Amma.

Chandran proves to be an excellent worker. He does things fast and efficiently. His previous work experience proves to be invaluable. He is already adept at chopping everything, and he does it much better than me. He is also well-versed in cooking large quantities. The smell of the fish curry and rice permeates across the canopy, and spreads all over the street too. We've added kappa to the menu now, and kappa-fish curry soon becomes a popular item. I buy a standing blackboard, write the day's special on it and tie it to the gate of our home so that anyone entering the home can see what the day's special is. We've maintained the same pre-booking system, but now we have two batches—lunch as well as dinner. We are doing four times the quantity we were doing earlier.

We've told Chandran that he can eat whatever he likes from the restaurant. But he always eats the same thing: a small piece of kappa, a piece of fish and an ulli chutney, which he makes just for himself and us.

Chandran has taken it upon himself to accompany me when I go to the market in the morning. We chat on the way to the market and I learn that he has a family back in Malappuram. His father left his mother for another woman, and he can't stand his father because he took all of his mother's jewellery and cleaned out the bank accounts when he left. His mother worked as a house-help for many years to raise him and his two younger siblings who are still in school.

Chandran narrates all of this without any trace of emotions, like he is talking about the weather. He is also a huge movie buff, his favourite actor being Kunchacko Boban. He names many Malayalam movies and asks me if I have seen any. He is surprised when I tell him I haven't. 'You must watch them!' he tells me.

During lunch break, he quickly finishes his meal and then calls his girlfriend, Malini. His whole face lights up as he laughs and smiles. He stands taller, his shoulders pushed back as he speaks in a low voice. His whole personality is transformed. He later tells me that when he speaks to Malini, he feels more confident, like he can do anything in the world.

That night when I speak to Puja, it dawns on me that this is exactly how I feel when I speak to her. I don't know if this is love but whatever it is, it makes me feel invincible and on top of the world. It's been such a long time since I felt any of those emotions. It's a new high.

19

Puja

There's something off with Arush. I don't know exactly what it is, but I can tell from the way he is messaging me these days. They are all brief messages with a lot of heart emojis thrown in—something he's never done before. I ask him if there's something wrong and he says it's nothing, just that he is busy with work.

Usually, I stay awake waiting for him to get back from work, so we have a chance to talk. But these days he doesn't want to talk. He mostly messages saying he is exhausted, apologises and goes to bed.

He hasn't posted a single thing on his Instagram account either, but that's nothing new. I check out Jenna's profile. She has posted a few stories about a cat that she has adopted. She has also posted many illustrations she is working on. Other than that, there's nothing. I was hoping to find a clue to Arush's odd behaviour but I've hit a dead-end here as well.

Sujit, on the other hand, is texting me every single day. He is excited about his business and has daily updates for me—whether it is the new dish they added to the menu (kappa) or the new person they hired (Chandran), I know it all. It is almost as if I have a ringside view to Sujit's life while Arush has drawn the curtains over his.

Meanwhile, the days are just going past with nothing to do. I've looked at jobs for graduates on LinkedIn and none of them interest me. I feel lost, confused, useless. I talk to Divya about it.

'It is only because you are sitting at home and doing nothing, Puja. Take up that job at Varkala,' she says.

'I'm not sure about that either,' I moan.

She is back from work, and is curled up on the sofa. Vihan hands her a steaming mug.

'What's that? Coffee?' I ask.

'Hi! It is Belgian hot chocolate,' Vihan says as he appears in the frame and waves at me. 'Come visit us,' he says.

'Let me figure out my life first,' I tell him. I notice that he said 'us'. Then he walks to the bedroom and shuts the door.

'You idiot, I have been going on about how my life sucks and he must have heard everything. Why didn't you tell me he was around?' I ask Divya.

'It's okay. He is a sweet guy. I don't think he was even listening,' Divya says.

'He said to visit "us". So, what is it? You guys are together now? It's official?' I ask her.

'He asked me to move in, and I moved in here yesterday,' Divya beams.

'Ah! No wonder. I was thinking the house looks different!' I exclaim.

'Achcha and Amma will definitely not be okay with this. But half the time we were staying over at each other's place. Then why should we both pay rent?'

'True that ... but are you very sure of him?' I feel protective towards Divya.

'Yes, Puja. Much more certain than I felt about Kar-dick. I'm happy after a long time,' she says as she takes a sip of the hot chocolate.

'I just wish my life would work itself out too, Divya,' I sigh. Then I tell her about how Arush seems evasive these days and how I've been talking to Sujit almost daily.

'Is there something between you and Sujit then?' Divya asks.

'I've been asking myself that. I do feel a connection. But I think it is only because we're talking daily. With Arush too when we speak I feel a deep connection. But these days we aren't speaking. So that's that.' I shrug.

When I speak to Sujit that night he asks me when I'm coming over. He says things are running smoothly now.

'Any day between two and four-thirty in the afternoon is good,' he says. 'That's only time I can actually get some time off, even though we have Chandran now.'

The next morning, after lunch, I tell Shanti Chechi that I am going to Sujit's house. 'If Achcha asks where I am, tell him I've going to the beauty salon, okay?' I tell her.

'Yes, let me ask Antony to bring the car to the porch,' she says as she heads over to the intercom connected to the drivers' room in the basement.

Shanti Chechi is someone I can completely trust to be on my side. After Sujit's visit here, I'd told her in detail about how he set up the whole thing on his own, and she was as impressed as me.

Antony is waiting for me with the car door open when I emerge from the elevator. As I get into the car, I tell him where to take me. I've already planned out my excuses. I've looked up Sujit's house on Google Maps, and managed to locate a ladies' salon at the end of the street. I tell Antony to drop me off there. It is a busy junction and there's no place for Antony to park anywhere. As I get off from the car, I tell him that I'll call him when I am done and he can pick me up from the same spot.

It is only when I see the car disappear round the bend that I look around. This part of town is not one I've been to before. It seems like an unremarkable, ordinary lower middle-class neighbourhood. I look at the map on my phone and begin to walk towards Sujit's home.

The road is dusty, and the blazing sun beats directly down on me. I put on my sunglasses. At least I'm not squinting now. As I walk down the narrow untarred street I realise that the heels I am wearing aren't exactly appropriate for walking and neither is my flowing spaghetti dress. I had forgotten this little detail when I had planned the trip—that I would have to walk.

The small houses that line the street are very close to each other. Exposed cable wires crisscross from telephone to electric poles. Posters of all kinds are on the wall—ripped off movie posters, political posters and communist slogans in Malayalam that compete with paan stains. Though Sujit had warned me that it is not as grand as I might expect, I am still a little taken aback. I don't know what I had expected it to be like, but it is *very* different from the picture in my head.

It's easy to find his house—the aroma of fish curry leads me there. By the time I arrive, I am sweating. A blackboard announces the day's special: Ayala Fry.

Sujit bounds out of the house even before I enter the compound. 'Puja! Welcome, welcome,' he says with a million-watt smile as he rushes to greet me.

'Hi Sujit.' I remove my sunglasses.

'You look—'

'Overdressed?' I laugh.

'I was going to say amazing,' he says as he looks away. Was that a blush I detected on his face? I'm not sure.

When we enter, I see a large group of people having their meals in the tarpaulin tent.

'This is the last batch. They are just leaving,' Sujit says.

'Chetta, the Ayala fry was super,' one of the customers tells Sujit.

'Thank you, will let Amma know,' he says.

'Come on inside,' he says as he leads me into the house.

I look around for something to sit on to remove my shoes.

'Don't have to,' he tells me.

'Not a bother,' I say as I hold on to the grill door, unbuckle my heels one after the other and kick them aside. Then I follow him inside.

His house is tiny. There isn't any proper living room as such. By the side of the main entrance, a wooden bench with a backrest, serves as a sofa. A television is by one side of the wall. Then it opens out straight into the dining room, which leads to the kitchen. On either side of the dining room are two tiny bedrooms, both of which have their doors open. While it is not squalid, it is minimal, sparse and entirely functional. There's not an iota of luxury or comfort. I am properly shocked but I hope it doesn't show on my face.

Sujit leads me straight to the kitchen.

'Amma, this is Puja,' he says as he introduces me to his mother.

'Puja, Molle! I've heard so much about you,' his mother says as she hands me a glass of buttermilk. Her voice is gentle and her smile genuine. She is the kind of person who can hug you with their eyes. I feel her love for me, even though we've just met.

'Thank you, Aunty,' I tell her as I take the buttermilk. I don't want to drink it. I am not particularly fond of it, but I don't want her to feel offended either. Sujit leads me out of the kitchen to the tarpaulin tent, and I see Chandran cleaning up the tables. When Sujit introduces me, he gives me a big smile and a wave, and continues cleaning.

'Listen, you don't have to drink that if you don't want to, okay?' Sujit says as he notices the glass of buttermilk still in my hand.

'Thanks, I didn't want to seem rude. I don't want it.'

'No problem,' he says as he takes it from my hand and drains it in one gulp. I stare at him in surprise. He laughs.

'Working in the kitchen in this scorching heat—we need it to cool down,' he says.

He asks me if I will have lunch, but I've already eaten.

'Orange juice then? he asks and I nod.

He fetches a glass of orange juice from the fridge and leads me to his room.

'I share this with Ravi,' he says. I notice the beds perpendicular to each other, a single desk, and wardrobes on one side. There's hardly any space in the room.

'Sit!' Sujit says as he points to the bed and hands me the juice. He pulls up a folding chair and opens it, placing it opposite the bed.

I sit down, feeling strange to be seated on his bed. Sujit seems to sense it and he asks, 'Do you want the chair?'

'No, no, it's fine,' I tell him as I take a sip of the juice.

'You are probably wondering how tiny it is compared to your house,' Sujit says.

I almost choke on the juice when I hear that. God, is this guy a mind-reader?

'No, Sujit, I wasn't comparing it at all,' I tell him. He just smiles.

'Now you know why I was astonished when I came to your home. Anyway, it is what it is.' He shrugs.

'Yeah, it hardly matters,' I lie.

'Remember this? I dug it out when I knew you'd be coming,' Sujit says as he hands me a class photo. I laugh when I see it.

'Hahaha. Look at me—two plaits and all that. And attempting to look stylish in them. What class was this? Seventh?' I ask him.

'Eighth. Do you remember Mr Roy, our class teacher?'

'How can I forget? The first thing he said when he walked into the class was "I am Sushobhan Roy and I am a bachelor". All the girls thought he was a creep.'

'All the boys too.' Sujit chuckles.

I wonder how Sujit could afford to go to the same school I went to. It is one of the most expensive schools in the city. I don't bring it up as I don't want to hurt his feelings.

'Do you remember how I used to always act up in school?' he asks.

'Of course! Who can forget you riding into the school on your dad's bike, and your father chasing you while you climbed up a tree?' I laugh.

'Yeah, I was such an idiot. We used to live right next to the school then. My father hadn't yet bought this house. I think I did it mainly because I felt inferior to everyone else who was mostly wealthy. I felt the more outrageous I was, the more "respect" I'd earn.'

'Why did your father choose this school?' I ask.

'He wanted us to have the best education possible. I guess you don't know then how I got into this posh, prestigious school ...'

I think Sujit somehow knows what I really wanted to ask—how his parents could afford the school.

'No, I don't. How?' I ask.

'My mother took up the job of cleaning toilets at the school because my father came to know there's a staff quota. The children of the staff of the school could study there without paying any fees. A relative of mine knew the vice principal who recommended my mother's name and she got the job. Soon afterwards, she died. But yeah, she ensured school admission for my brother and me.'

I can't even imagine how it must have felt like for Sujit. My eyes involuntarily fill with tears that I blink back. I want to hug Sujit and tell him I am so, so sorry. I think about how fucking privileged I am in comparison to him. It is only by a chance of fate that I was born to my parents, and he was born to his.

'That must have been so hard for you,' I say. My voice is a bit unsteady and I clear my throat.

'Shit, I didn't mean to narrate all these emotional stories. Puja, all this is just past stuff. I don't even know why I brought it up,' Sujit says.

'You mentioned it only because I asked,' I tell him softly. I don't want him to see how moved I am by what he has said. But I think he knows.

'Hey, don't feel sorry for me, Puja. That was definitely not why I shared this. I don't feel sorry for myself. I was an idiot back then. But all of what I did—it's made me stronger, smarter and a better version of myself. My sessions with Dr Harsh have helped me accept myself for who I am.' Sujit is looking at the floor as he speaks.

How much this boy has been through. And how he has clawed and fought to get here.

'You're right, Sujit. You're absolutely right. But I want you to know this, I am I proud of you,' I tell him. I am so overwhelmed with emotions that I don't know what to say or do.

'Thanks. You're the first person I have shared all this with. It means so much to me' he says as he sits up straight and looks at me.

Looking at him, sitting in that chair, I feel all the pain he has been through, the unfairness of life he has faced and how much hardship he has suffered. The pain feels visceral, raw, unbearable.

Then he looks at me and smiles. What breaks my heart is the bravery in that smile.

20

Arush

A long time back, at art school—it feels like eons ago—Jenna had told me, 'You know that Billy Ocean song, *When the going gets tough, the tough get going*? What makes more sense is when things get tough, the tough hide.' She'd said it when she was going through a bad patch in her relationship with Josh. She'd kept putting off talking about the issues she had with him, because she wanted to be sure of what to say. Eventually she forgot about it and discovered it didn't matter anymore. I had laughed about it then and teased her, but it makes sense now. That's what I have been doing. Hiding. Simply because I don't know how to face Puja. Or even Naomi for that matter.

After the last walking tour, which was awkward for me to say the least, I knew I couldn't work with Naomi anymore. At least, not till I sorted whatever this was between us. I also knew there were escorted tours coming up to Scotland. I spoke to Olivia and told her I wanted to be shifted to the outstation tours. I said I was ready for the next challenge. Since I'd been getting great reviews for all the walking tours that I'd done in Birmingham, it helped my case tremendously. Olivia had said she would discuss it with Nik and get back to me. A day later Olivia asked if I could speak Hindi.

'Of course! I can speak it well and I can speak Punjabi too,' I'd said.

As it so happened, the group that had booked the Scotland tour was from India. Olivia knew if I was the tour guide, we would get excellent reviews especially, as I could speak two Indian languages. This was an important group, because the revenues from international tours were much higher than the ones from local walking tours. Olivia said I could assist Harry Shaw who normally did these escorted tours with Sakshi Govind. But Sakshi had quit a few months before I'd joined and Brian Coley, her replacement, couldn't speak any Indian language.

Olivia asked Brian if she could shift him to the Egypt tour. Brian jumped at the chance to go to Egypt, as he had never been there before. That was how I'd bagged this outstation tour.

The first leg of the tour is in London, from where the group will proceed to Scotland. For the past few days, I've been travelling with Harry Shaw, accompanying them all over London. The group consists of mostly middle-aged and elderly folks from India, including a few from Kerala as well. The elderly couple I am speaking to, Mrs and Mr Balachandran, are from Kochi. I chat with them about various places in India and what I loved about them. They are delighted to discover that not only have I visited Kerala but also know a lot about the state.

'So, when are you visiting Kerala next?' Mrs Balachandran asks.

'Oh, I want to. I've got a five-year visa because I'd applied through my college, for educational and cultural purposes. I did a course in Kerala mural painting. My visa is valid for another two years.'

They are very impressed when they hear that. 'Then you must make full use of that and come before it expires!' Mrs Balachandran tells me.

Chatting with them about Kochi takes me back to a different point in my life. It makes me long for Puja. I miss talking to her. I know I should call her soon. But not just yet. I am too ashamed right now and I want to sort out my tangled feelings of confusion, anger and guilt.

Fortunately, this group tour helps take my mind off it. There's always so much to do. Harry is good to work with, and he has a good rapport with me. 'Boy, am I glad you can speak the language. It helps a lot,' he says as he watches me chatting up many of the folks in the group.

We travel all over London and take them to all the usual touristy places beginning with the Tower of London. They are impressed by one of Britain's most iconic landmarks, which has been home to kings, traitors, bureaucrats and knights. It has witnessed many deaths and instances of treachery and cruelty, and yet been a constant part of London's skyline. Harry explains all of this well. I've been here a couple of times before, so it is nothing new to me. Still, it is fun to hear Harry speak. We've been given detailed information booklets about all the attractions we will be taking the group to.

An open bus awaits us after the Tower of London to take us to Piccadilly from where we walk to the National Museum, Trafalgar Square and the London Eye, which are all included as a part of the package. I am happy to take over when Harry is tired of talking. Because of the scripted notes I have and the history I've studied in school, I find that I can easily explain the history to the group; I'm enjoying it.

'You are good at this. Plus, this is a well-behaved group. It's a great combination to have,' Harry tells me.

'Do you have badly behaved groups?' I ask him

'Oh, some travellers can be nightmares. You know once, in an open-topped tour bus in London, an Indian woman tried to dangle her toddler over the railing. She was holding the kid around the waist and making the toddler sit on the railings. When I told her to stop, she said Indians are better at looking after their kids than White people. She ignored me and continued doing it. I had to stop the bus and get the driver to march her off before resuming the tour. Her husband got off too, and they were yelling, saying they did nothing wrong! Can you imagine?'

'Good lord, just one small slip and the kid would have died!'

'Exactly. Compared to some groups this one is very sweet,' Harry says.

At the end of the tour days, I am too tired to think about anything as I am exhausted after walking such a lot and taking care of the group. I send short messages to Puja and go off to sleep. Naomi has messaged me as well. She asks if I am angry with her, reiterates that it was no big deal. I don't know how to tell her that I am mostly angry with myself—for not remembering a thing. I don't reply to her. I am not ready yet.

After three hectic days in London, we take the group to King's Cross and then we're on a train to Edinburgh. I'd been to Edinburgh a few years back, in my first year of college. The group is fascinated by the English countryside whizzing by and I feel happy to see how even elderly people become like kids when they see new things. When we arrive at Edinburgh Waverly, I discover that all the memories I have of this place come flooding back.

The whole group is quite bowled over by the beauty of Scotland, just as I had been when I first arrived here. I remember how Jenna and I had sketched Edinburgh Castle, sitting side by side when we'd got here, as a part of our college outbound trip. I remember all the sites: the statue of Robert Burns whose toe people rubbed for luck, the irony being that he was a staunch opposer of such superstitions, the grave of the dog Bobby who was known as Greyfriars Bobby and many more. Jenna and I had sketched with carefree abandon.

Suddenly, I am filled with an urge to capture all of it once again in my sketchbook. I am taken aback by the urgency of the desire to make art, which has crept up on me out of nowhere. I hadn't felt this way in two whole years, ever since the pandemic started, but now I feel a pressing need. It is like I have to paint it all.

Since our train journey was four-and-a-half-hours long, the tour itinerary has the rest of the day free for the group to wander around. The guided tours begin only the next day. This gives Harry and me a break too. After we check into the hotel and after we've ensured that our whole group has checked in and are comfortable, I head over to the Edinburgh art store in old town. I smile as I remember how I, along with Jenna and some of the other students, had spent ample time here going over the art materials, talking about how expensive it was. The store owner overheard us and offered us student discounts.

I reach the art store and look around. Nothing has changed! It's exactly as I remember it. The owner is the same too and she is right there at the counter. But I am sure she doesn't remember me, so I don't introduce myself. I buy a sketchbook, some micron pens, travel watercolours and a large and small water brush and some tissues. I place them in my backpack and I head over to a spot by the side of the road, opposite the castle. This was where Jenna and I had sat last time, on the steps of a building that housed some shops and offices. I look up at the castle, and hold up my pencil to take some quick measurements. I sketch the outline fairly quickly, and then begin to paint. It feels exhilarating to be holding a brush again. I'd forgotten how much joy this brings me. It is as though something lying dormant in me has awakened. I feel the gaze of passers-by as they walk along, peeping into my sketchbook. But I am so focused, so much in the flow, that their voices seem distant.

At last, I am finished, and when I glance at the time on my phone, I realise I have been painting over one and a half hours. My legs are stiff as I stand up, and my nose is ice-cold and even my butt is freezing now. But this felt so satisfying. I am pleased with the painting I've made. Considering that it's been a very long time since I painted, I feel I haven't lost my touch at all, even if I say so myself. I click a picture and send it to Jenna.

'Remember this? Not dry yet!' I message her.

She calls within a few minutes when I am buying a hot chocolate at a café.

'You finally got your mojo back! And don't tell me you're in Edinburgh!' She is practically screaming in excitement so that I have to turn the volume of my phone down.

'Yes!' I smile as I walk out of the cafe, hot chocolate in hand, with the art supplies and sketchbook in my backpack.

She asks me how is it that I am in Edinburgh and I narrate the whole story to her, starting with the whole Naomi fiasco and then how I haven't even spoken to Puja yet.

'Oh,' she says when I finish. She doesn't say anything else.

'Please tell me I am not a horrible person, Jenna,' I say.

'You can never be a horrible person, Arush,' she says.

Something in her voice makes me pause. The Jenna I know would be telling me I was an idiot for even letting Naomi get close to me, and it was my fault for being in this situation. I am expecting her to tell me that. Instead, she sounds sad.

'What do you think I should do?' I ask.

'Whatever you think is right, Arush. Whatever makes you happy,' she says. Then she says she has to go and hangs up. On the way back to the hotel I keep thinking about why Jenna's mood suddenly changed. It was almost as if someone suddenly dropped her into a bucket of ice.

My phone buzzes just as I am entering the hotel elevator. I check it and see a message from Jenna. I read it as I open my room door and flop down on my pristine, freshly made hotel bed. Then I sit up and read it again. I can't believe what I am reading.

Hey, Arush! I'm sorry to send this longish message. But I think it's time I told you (in case you haven't guessed already). I have feelings for you. I presumed you felt the same way too, especially as you had been growing distant from Puja, and sharing all of it with me. I felt I had to do the right thing—by you and by her, and I kept advising you to make it up with her. But you never really made a big effort, so I thought that whatever you had with her was probably going to end soon. Silly on my part, I know. But what is sillier is that I thought we both had a chance. Now I know where I truly stand, and I feel so awful I want to crawl into a hole and die.

This is not on you, Arush—this is on me. I've been feeling this way for over two years now, and I didn't speak up. I felt over time the feelings would go away if I did nothing about it. But today, I realised I can't do this anymore.

It is hard to be just a friend to you, listening to everything you're doing with other girls and dying a little inside each time.

I'm sorry, Arush, I can't be your friend anymore. I truly hope you work things out with Puja—or Naomi, whoever you choose. You do deserve all the happiness in the world. Take care.

'Aaaaaah ...' I groan as I throw my phone on the bed and hold my head in my hands. How could I have been so blindsided? How could I have not seen this coming?

I think back to every interaction we've had. Jenna coming over often to my home, Jenna interacting with my parents, Jenna wearing Indian clothes and now Jenna sounding sad when I told her I might have slept with Naomi. Heartbroken, that's what she was. I feel horrible to have hurt her this way. Had I the slightest inkling of what she felt towards me I would have never in a million years told her about Naomi. But it's too late for that now.

I must be the world's greatest idiot. I've alienated three people who care for me—Puja, Jenna, Naomi. I have only myself to blame for all of it. I lie in bed for a long time and think about what I can do. Whichever way I look at it, there's only one way to fix it. It is not by running away. It is by talking.

I *have* to fix this.

I glance at the time. It's just past 11.00 p.m. in India. I have to do it no matter how hard it is. I can't run away anymore. I simply have to speak to Puja. With my heart pounding in my ears, I force myself to pick up the phone and call her.

21

Puja

The visit to Sujit's house has shaken me. Firstly, I had romanticised the idea of Sujit's restaurant in my head. I had imagined a large carnivalesque canopy under which would be colour coordinated, painted pretty wooden chairs amidst a lot of greenery. Why I'd presumed that I don't know. Perhaps it is all the Instagram reels I've been watching that show off such places. But Sujit's restaurant is functional and cheap. Secondly, I hadn't expected his house itself to be located in such a neighbourhood. I cannot imagine what it must have been like for him in school, where we all were from similar well-off backgrounds while he and his brother would have been the odd ones out.

The room he shares with his brother is smaller and less luxurious than Shanti Chechi's room in our home. He doesn't have an attached bathroom or even air-conditioning. Then again, we've always seen Shanti Chechi as family and provided her with every comfort that all of us have. The material comforts we're accustomed to, and take for granted, now rankle me.

I feel like a brat revelling in this luxury. My money had never bothered me before, but now, when I see how much Sujit is hustling to provide for his family, it does.

I can't imagine the pain he must have gone through when his mother died. His brave, sad, smile after he spoke about it—I can't stop thinking about it. The reality of his situation and what he has been through, the restaurant he has set up, his visit to my home when he was delivering the food, the enormity of it all is slowly sinking in. After the visit to his house, I get this feeling that my problems in comparison to his are not even real.

I feel useless sitting at my parents' home and doing absolutely nothing but enjoying my days, scrolling through Instagram, reading, messaging Arush and peacefully existing from one day to another. While Divya was here it was different. She had been 'my project' after she lost her job and after she broke up. But now even she has moved on while I am still here. It is time to change that.

I pick up my phone and message Benny. 'Hey, that position of social media manager still open?' I text.

That's when my phone rings. My heart leaps up when I see Arush's photo (with me) flash on the screen. It's my favourite picture of us, clicked when we were at the camp in Wayanad. We both look so much younger than we do now, and his arm is around me. It always brings a smile to my face.

'Hey, hey, busy man! Finally, you make time to call,' I greet him.

'Hey, Puja,' he says. His voice sounds heavy, sad. Like he is struggling to speak.

'What happened? Is everything okay?' I ask.

'Yes … Actually, no … Oh, Puja, I don't even know where to begin,' he says. He then goes quiet. I am beginning to worry now. He has never been this way.

'Hello? Are you there?'

'I'm still here, Puja.'

It sounds like he is in a lot of pain. Each word he utters seems to be with great effort.

'You're scaring me, Arush. Are you okay? Is everyone at your home okay? What's happening?' The questions just tumble out because I am properly scared now.

He sighs. 'Yes, everyone in my home is okay. I am okay too.'

'Thank god! You had me worried. Then why are you so quiet?'

A big pause again. Then he says, 'Puja, I messed up … I've messed up big time and I am sorry.'

My heartbeats increase a hundred-fold. I knew it. I knew there was something off. My mind races and makes connections. If his family is okay and everything else is okay, and he is saying he messed up, then it can mean only one thing. He slept with Jenna. How in the world could he do that to me?

My throat goes dry. I grit my teeth. 'Jenna?' I ask.

'How did you know?' The surprise is evident in his voice.

'I mean, it's obvious, isn't it? The girl is in love with you. And I have been really jealous that she gets to spend time with your family, and be with you … but … but you've always told me she is nothing more than a friend to you. So, I don't understand how you could sleep with her. I thought—'

I'm speaking very fast. It is as though if I keep talking I can make this thing go away. But he interrupts me before I can say anything more.

'Puja, I didn't. I haven't even *met* Jenna after I moved to Birmingham,' he says. 'I don't know how you think her feelings for me were obvious, but I swear I didn't know she was in love with me. She has just sent me a message saying she doesn't want to be my friend anymore.'

'Oh!' I say. 'Oh … I see.'

That has stopped my runaway train of thoughts. I wasn't expecting that at all. I heave a sigh of relief that I'd jumped to the wrong conclusion. Is he just upset about Jenna deciding that she doesn't want to be his friend anymore? If so, what I have presumed is so ridiculous that I might just end up laughing. That's how relieved I am.

'Then what it is that you messed up? Anything at work? Hope all is fine?' I ask.

'Puja, I am really sorry. It's not Jenna … it … it's Naomi,' he says.

'What? You slept with Naomi?' My mouth twists into a grimace and I inhale sharply. I wonder if I heard him right. 'Arush, you're making no sense at all. Are you drunk?' I am hoping he will say he is.

'No, Puja … I am completely sober, let me explain,' he says.

Then he begins to talk. His voice is full of remorse as he talks about how he and Naomi got close and how they started spending a lot of time together. I hear him taking a deep breath. He tells me how he blanked out completely and doesn't remember a thing. He says he is not working with Naomi anymore. He tells me about his whole move to the outbound travel division, explains why he is in Edinburgh right now and what led to Jenna's message.

Even though he is talking about how much it has been eating him from inside that he let things go too far with Naomi, each sentence he utters feels like a hard blow to my chest. One part of my head is processing everything that he is saying, the other part is reeling in shock at everything I am hearing. In a strange way I completely get why Jenna doesn't even want to be his friend anymore.

Arush has stopped talking now and is waiting for me to say something. But I have no words really. I am burning, drowning, dying, with the pain of betrayal. This is my worst nightmare coming true. I'd sensed there was something going on when I'd seen Naomi behave like that, but then I'd just attributed it to my jealousy.

'Puja, listen, I am sorry ... I'm not even speaking to Naomi.' His voice is almost a whimper now. But my heart has turned to stone.

'Why?" I ask, swallowing my pride and every single emotion that is rising to my throat.

'Why I let it happen?'

'No. Why aren't you speaking to her?'

'Because ... because she doesn't mean anything to me.'

'Why did you spend so much time with her if she didn't mean anything to you?'

'Puja, I fucked up. I didn't realise that it would lead to this.'

'You mean you fucked her.' I laugh bitterly. I don't even know why I said that. I want to hurt him the way he has hurt me.

'Puja, I don't know what happened. But please know I am sorry and I deeply regret it, okay? I truly am.'

'So, what am I supposed to do? Pretend everything is okay, and tell you that we can move on? Sorry, Arush, that's not how this works,' I say and hang up

I am not able to speak at all.

Arush calls me back immediately but I cut his call. When I see notifications popping up, I switch off my phone. I don't want to listen to anything he has to say. All I can think of is how he could do this to me. This negates everything we've had, everything we shared, everything that existed between us.

We'd both accepted that long-distance was hard and decided that if we ever got close to other people or if we ever got the feeling that this wasn't working out, we'd be honest and discuss it with each other first. But he hasn't done that. He's got so close to someone else, behind my back.

I think that's what hurts so much, that I have been cheated on. How can it be a mistake? If you have allowed yourself to be in that position then it certainly means at least some part of you wanted it too.

I sit in bed and stare at the sea through my window. The moonlight shimmers on the waves and a few passenger ships with cheerful lights sail in the distance. I stare at them for long and think about who might be aboard those ships. I wish I was with them ... far, far away from all of this. I wish it didn't matter to me what Arush did or didn't do. I wish I didn't care.

I think about these last two years. We've been so close ... chatting, video-calling and even emailing, sending each other cards, links and funny memes throughout the pandemic. Things only changed when he started working.

What does that mean? Was the relationship we had one of convenience? I was available when he needed me, and now that he has others around him, he doesn't need me anymore?

I think about the amount of time he and Naomi must have spent together, and it makes me sick to the pit of my stomach. He'd mentioned she lives in the same building. Which means he is bound to see her again. What is the guarantee that it won't happen again?

I was an idiot to wait around so eagerly for his messages. What a fool I have been!

I am unable to sleep at all. I toss and turn in my bed as I keep thinking about Naomi and Arush, and torturing myself with images of them together. I've switched off my phone but I am unable to switch off my thoughts.

It is only around 7.00 a.m. that I switch my phone back on. There are four missed calls from Arush. And a few messages saying he is terribly sorry. He wants to know what he can do to win my forgiveness.

(As though my forgiveness is a prize to be won.) He has pretty much repeated what he said on the phone—that he wasn't even sure what exactly happened and he wants to set things right between us.

I don't reply. I want to shut him out till I decide whether or not I want to continue in this relationship.

There are messages from Sujit as well. He wants to know if I want to talk. Then he has messaged asking if I dropped my phone in the loo. Then after a while there's another message: 'Tell me everything is okay? Please? I am worried now.'

I reply to Sujit immediately. 'Sorry, battery had drained out,' I type and hit 'Send'.

There's a message from Benny as well. I had almost forgotten the message I'd sent him amidst all of this.

> 'We haven't hired anyone yet. But we have been interviewing people for it since we didn't hear from you.'
>
> 'Sorry about not getting back sooner. I am interested and would like to take up the offer.'
>
> 'Sure. Let me inform Nambiar and I'll be in touch soon. Welcome aboard! :)'

That morning, I bring up the job with my parents. Achcha is reading the newspaper, and Amma is already dressed to leave for the hospital.

'What a pleasant surprise to see you waking up this early,' Amma says.

I don't tell her that I'm up early only because I've barely slept. 'I've decided to take up that social media manager job if they will have me,' I announce.

Achcha mutes the television. 'Eh? What job is this? What did you apply for?'

'Achcha, remember Benny? He offered me a social media job. I was thinking about it for long, and I think I should take it up. I just messaged him saying I will.'

'Doesn't it mean you have to move to Varkala?' my mother asks.

'Yes, Amma.'

'Is it really what you want to do, Molle? Varkala is okay for holidays and all, but to live there—it's not going to be easy.' My father looks alarmed.

I don't know how to tell him that was precisely the reason why I had been putting off taking up this job. I knew that it would be hard to live there. So, I couldn't make up my mind about it. But now after seeing Sujit's situation, and after Arush's confession, I feel like I have to get away from all this. I want to prove to myself that I am not a pampered, spoilt, rich girl.

I want to live on my own.

But there's no way I am telling my parents about Sujit. Or Arush. So, I tell them something which I know will strike a chord, at least with my mother.

'Everyone is doing something at my age. I am just sitting at home and wasting my time.'

'But that doesn't mean you have to take up any opportunity that comes. Do it only if you are passionate about it. All this social media manager and all that, what is the growth in it? Working for one tiny company too,' Amma remarks.

'It's not like Google or Amazon are waiting to hire me, Amma,' I say.

'Molle, you must seriously think about getting an MA degree. Now everything is opening up and colleges abroad are having in-person classes. Think about what you want to study. We can easily send you to any college you choose,' Amma says.

'At some point in the future, when I am sure of what I want to do, I'll pursue it. But right now I want to prove to myself that I can manage on my own,' I say.

'Where will you stay, Molle?' Achcha asks.

'I can speak to Nandakumar and get you suitable accommodation,' Amma says.

'I just want to do all of it on my own. It will just make me feel self-sufficient. Please give me that chance?' I ask them.

They reluctantly agree.

After Amma leaves for the hospital, I call up Benny.

'Hello, Puja! I am so glad you decided to join us,' he says. 'I discussed it with Mr Nambiar. We will be happy if you can start as soon as possible, but before that if you can give me a rough estimate of your expectations, we can probably work around it,' he says.

Expectations? It takes me a few seconds to understand what he is talking about. He means the salary. I'm so keen on just getting a job that I haven't even thought about a pay! The fact that I'll be earning real money hasn't occurred to me. I've never had to think of money. I've always had plenty of money in my name in the bank ever since I turned eighteen.

'Err ... whatever the market rate is?'

He names a figure that I know is lesser than what our electricity bill comes to each month. I know this only because I had glanced at the bill this morning when the security guard had rung our doorbell to hand it to us.

'Oh, that's a bit low,' I say. To be honest, I don't care. I am not taking up this job for the money. But I say it because I don't want to sound like a pushover.

'Puja, Varkala is a small place. It's not like Kochi. And you won't have to spend on accommodation at all. The building I live in belongs to Nambiar. It is by the backwaters, and he rents out rooms to tourists. It's a decent place. It's got built-in beds, seating, etc. It's also got Wi-Fi. He said you could take one of the rooms on the first floor if you wanted. I live on the ground floor there.'

'That suits me. I look forward to it,' I say.

'Does Friday suit you? We usually have a weekend influx for kayaking, and Friday will be good,' he says.

'Sure, I'll be there on Friday,' I tell him before I have a chance to change my mind.

When Divya calls, I tell her I am shifting to Varkala.

'Good! What made you finally decide to go for it?' she asks.

'Nothing in particular. I just got tired of sitting at home and thought I'd try it out.' I've decided not to tell Divya about what Arush has done. I know what she will tell me ... to break up with him immediately. I want to think things over, and when I make up my mind, it has to be my decision alone. I don't want Divya influencing me in any way.

Divya has a whole lot of tips for me on what to take to Varkala. She wants to know where I will be living, and whether I have seen it. I tell her what Benny mentioned.

'Oooh, so he will be close by. Are you sure he isn't the reason you're moving?' she asks.

'I am not you. I don't move to another place for some guy,' I tell her. It comes out much sharper than I intended and I watch her expression change. But she doesn't say anything. She just laughs it off and I feel even more miserable.

When I tell Sujit I am moving, he says while he is happy for me, he is going to miss me.

'What? Why will you miss me? It's not like we see each other every day,' I say.

'No, but the thought that I can see you anytime I want is comforting,'

'You can still see me anytime you want. Varkala is not that far away,' I tell him.

'Yeah, its 160 kilometres. Maybe I can rent a car and drive down. I'd done that once.'

'Really? Have you gone kayaking?'

'No, Puja,' he says. Then there's a few seconds of silence before he speaks again. 'Couldn't really afford a vacation back then. It was during my old days. Varkala gets a lot of foreigners who are willing to pay for good quality stuff. But those days are done. I would never bring that stuff anywhere near you.'

The steely determination in his voice and the openness with which he shares takes me by surprise.

'Come over once I am settled there and we will have some good fun,' I tell him.

'I hope it doesn't mean that you won't have time to talk to me every day. I've kind of got used to this now.'

He sounds so eager, like a child. 'Me too, Sujit,' I smile.

When I arrive in Varkala on Thursday afternoon I double check the address Benny has texted as the car pulls up. It looks so awful that I can't believe I'll be living here. It is a three-storied narrow building, which seems to have been constructed in the most economical manner. A long line of doors on the front façade lined up next to each other makes it look like a military barrack. Clothes hang outside these doors on the cement parapet. Though the building is freshly painted and the surroundings are clean, I don't know how it still manages to exude shabbiness.

Benny comes out of one of the doors and greets me with a big smile. 'Welcome! This is no Taj Mahal, I know, but you will see it is comfortable,' he says. He asks if he should help with my luggage but Antony has already taken out my suitcases.

Benny leads us to the staircase by the side of the building. It is so narrow that we have to walk in a single file. Benny then holds out the key to Room number 16 and Antony takes it from him.

'All yours,' he beams like he has checked me into a luxury resort.

Antony opens it, enters the room and looks around bewildered. Every single thing in the room is painted a dirty pink. It is as though the owner purchased pink paint at a bulk discount and decided to cover every surface with it. A pink cement seat which serves as a 'sofa', pink cabinets, pink counter and even a narrow pink built-in cement bed with an ugly deep pink mattress.

I manage to keep a straight face and say, 'Thanks, Benny, I'll see you around.' I then shut the door.

I look at Antony, he looks back at me and raises his eyebrows and makes a face. That's when I explode with laughter. He joins in too. We both continue laughing for a full three minutes. Ah! It feels so good to be able to laugh.

'*Yenta ithu?*' Antony asks. 'You want to live here? Shall I find a good hotel?'

'It's okay, I'll manage,' I tell him.

Antony helps me to unpack even though I tell him I'll do it on my own. Achcha and Amma have insisted that not only should Antony drop me but that he should help me set up the place. Shanti Chechi has made a list of all the things I will need and packed my bags for me. She has handed the list to Antony. He checks the list and unpacks everything meticulously. He goes to the car and fetches the bed linen and another large carton, which has the induction stove, a few pans and essentials like rice, dal and masalas that Shanti Chechi insisted I should take.

In less than two hours the whole thing is set up, and Antony has left. I check out the bathroom, and though it is clean, I hate the tiny mirror, the gaudy brown tiles the colour of poop, the bare washbasin and even the toilet with its black toilet seat.

I begin to miss my room back home like crazy.

That's when it hits me. This is my home now.

And I fucking detest every inch of it.

22

Sujit

'Are you sure we can afford to hire two additional people?' Amma frowns.

'Amma, you expressed disbelief last time when I told you the sales figures. Business has increased five times since then. It is no longer a question of *if* we can afford to hire. It is whether we can afford to *not* hire. It will be impossible for you, me and Chandran to manage this crowd,' I tell her.

We're having our routine family business meeting around the dining table after we've wound up for the day.

'It was your idea, Amma, to start the kappa and fish. And now that's the top selling item for us. You know someone from Coimbatore wanted to know if we can parcel it to them! Can you imagine that? That's how popular it is,' Ravi says.

'I did not even think in my wildest dreams that it would explode like an atom bomb,' Amma says. She looks so pleased that I take out my phone and click a photo.

'Eda! What is with the photo? I am not even dressed well,' she says, tucking a stray strand of hair behind her ear.

'Amma, you look beautiful even when you don't dress up!'

'Don't post it anywhere, okay?'

'Yes, yes, I won't post. In any case it is Ravi who controls the Instagram account.'

Amma turns to Ravi. 'Can you send me the YouTube link to that TV interview on WhatsApp? I want to forward it to the Kerala Samajam group.'

Ravi and I look at each other and smile about how tech-savvy Amma has become.

'You were hesitant to even do the interview. See how well it came out! It was a good idea, wasn't it?' Ravi says as he opens his phone to send her the link she has asked for.

The older brother of one of Ravi's classmates happened to be a reporter at Manorama channel, one of the biggest and most popular ones in Kerala. He was curious about the restaurant where people paid to get the food delivered. He'd checked out our Instagram, where we had just crossed 53 k followers, thanks to Ravi's carefully edited reels. He'd come over for a meal as he wanted to see what everyone was raving about. When he finished the meal, he had approached Amma saying he wanted to interview her and feature us in a food programme on television. It was with a bit of persuasion from Ravi and me that Amma had agreed to be interviewed.

'Shooting should not disrupt the daily meals. So many people now depend on us, you know? Especially students. We can't let them go hungry just because we are shooting something for TV,' Amma had said.

'Madam, we will be as unobtrusive as possible. You won't even know we're here. I will bring only one cameraman who will not disturb you in anyway. You can carry on with your usual routine,' he had assured her.

The next day they had a cameraman over who was wearing the gear on his body with some straps. The camera could shoot from many angles as it was attached to long flexible metal handles that he could adjust. I'd never seen anything like that. He followed Amma around as she chopped the fish, instructed Chandran and oversaw the daily processes. He took shots from the top as she prepared the masala, and he interrupted only once, to ask if we could wet the platform on which she was grinding the masalas, because it looked better in the shot. Other than that, as promised, he was almost like a shadow in the background and we didn't even notice he was there.

I said emphatically I didn't want to be interviewed or featured anywhere in any of the frames. But both Ravi and Chandran had no such qualms and gave interviews, which were recorded once the rush hour was over.

The film they made turned out to be extremely engaging and emotional. The reporter interviewing Amma was an experienced one. He was empathetic, easy to speak to and sensitive. He knew exactly what to ask and when to hold back. When Amma spoke about Achcha, she couldn't control her tears. We all felt moved watching it. Of course, it made for great television footage. Also, Amma's passion for cooking and feeding so many people, especially students, shone through. The short film made it seem like we were heroes, but all I was doing really was running a business like any other entrepreneur. After it was aired on TV, the influx of customers tripled almost overnight.

'Sujit, you are right. We can't hope to manage this crowd on our own. We do need to hire two extra hands,' Amma finally agrees. She takes out the list of names of the people we have interviewed that day and she chooses Chandran's friend's cousin, Reji, and a young bright-eyed boy named John. Reji, like Chandran, has worked in eateries ever since he ran away from his home in Morayur at sixteen to Ernakulam, where he had been working in a small hotel for a few years. He'd begun as a helper but soon graduated to being a cook. After it had recently shut down, he'd reached out to Chandran for a job recommendation. Chandran had promptly put him in touch with us.

John had been referred by Jayashri Chechi. His mother's sister has been working in Jayashri Chechi's house for many years now. John told us that he failed his tenth class exams thrice and had no wish to study anymore.

Both Reji and John begin work the very next day. It is a blessing that they already know what to do. Amma nevertheless gives them strict instructions. 'See that your hands are clean at all times. When you hold the glass of water, I don't want your fingers touching anywhere inside the glass. If you are taking more than two glasses of water, keep them on a plate. Wash your hands and wipe them well on clean towels. Clean the kitchen surfaces with disinfectant, boil the kitchen towels every day with a tablespoon of washing soda.'

Her instructions are precise and endless. She gets annoyed if these are not followed. Amma has turned into a little Hitler and all of us are her SS minions. But the boys don't mind at all. They take it in their stride and comply because while Amma is strict about all these processes she has a heart of gold. They know she genuinely cares for their well-being.

We see a massive difference in our workload the very first day. Amma and I don't have to do as much hard physical labour as we did before. I am ecstatic about it. The business runs like a well-oiled machine under Amma's watchful eyes. This leaves me with more free time than before. The change feels welcome.

That night I am more eager than usual to speak to Puja. In the morning I'd sent her a message wishing her luck for her first day at work and I want to know how it went.

When we get on our usual call, the moment I hear her voice I know she has had a terrible day and her mood is off.

'How was your first day at work?' I ask as I open up a folded easy chair and sink into it outside the house. The joy that fills my heart when I hear her voice at the end of the day is indescribable. I like sitting under the starry sky when we talk. I'd never in a million years pegged myself as a romantic but now I understand what the poets speak of when they talk about lovers being miles away from each other but gazing at the same moon. I know Puja probably sees me only as a friend. Yet my foolish heart hopes for something more. My feelings for her are probably one-sided, but a minuscule part of me hopes she feels the same way too. Not once has she talked about Arush, which makes me think that perhaps I stand a chance with her.

'I think coming here was a big mistake, Sujit,' Puja says.

'Oh no, what happened?' I ask as I stand up and start to walk around.

'I am exhausted and it's just too much work.'

'On the first day itself?'

'Yes, maybe it is just a matter of getting used to it. It's possible I am feeling this way as it's all new. But right now, I am not liking it at all.'

'What did you do? Did you not enjoy it even a little bit?'

'Well, maybe a little bit. Today, I had to kayak along with a group of awful people who signed up for the kayaking experience. When they saw me shooting videos, they kept giving me instructions. They didn't even bother to ask my name. They kept calling me photo girl.'

'Photo girl? That's hilarious!' I laugh as I sit down back.

'I thought it was funny too the first time, but after that it wasn't. Benny was annoyed with them but he didn't stop them either. Customer is king and all that. They were less interested in learning kayaking and more interested in photos. And on top of that I had to make a reel of those silly tourists and post it too.'

I think to myself that it doesn't sound as bad as she is making it out to be. All it seems like is she had to shoot photos of people she didn't particularly like. 'You know sometimes we just have to learn to get along with people we don't like. The good thing is you don't have to meet them again. In my restaurant here there are some obnoxious customers. They make a horrid mess after they eat. But we can't say anything as they are paying customers.'

'But for you it's your own business, here I am just working for someone.'

'Yeah, Puja, I know. Just leave it, maybe tomorrow you will get a fun group,' I console her.

'I hope so. This is just hard work. I'm burning a lot of calories for sure by kayaking so much. And I am using up tonnes of sunscreen because I don't want to get tanned in this heat.'

'Glad you're taking care of yourself. What do you do for food?'

'There's a local place nearby but it isn't all that great. I don't cook though Shanti Chechi has given me all the cooking equipment.' She laughs. 'I plan to get food from outside all the time.'

'What about the actual work? Has the reel you posted got good views?'

'Yes, it has. Benny is pleased with it and apparently so is Mr Nambiar. He asked Benny to tell me I'd done a great job.'

'That's good then, no?'

'I suppose so, Sujit, but I am so tired now, I am ready to drop dead. But enough of talking about me. What's up with you? How is it all going?'

I tell her about how pleased I am about hiring the two new people, and how well it is going.

'That's really nice, Sujit, I'm happy for you.'

I know she is but her voice sounds sad and tired.

'Puja, go to bed early today, okay? You have a long day tomorrow,' I tell her.

'Since when did you become my parent?' she asks, but I know she is pleased. I can tell. And that further fuels my foolish hope. *Maybe* this can be something more than just a friendship.

We talk for some more time, till she says she just can't keep her eyes open. After we hang up, I slowly tiptoe back to my room, but Ravi is not asleep.

'Why don't you go see her?' he asks.

'What?' I pretend to not understand.

'Chetta, you're so in love with her! Look at you glowing. I knew when she came home itself that you were crazy about her.'

'Is it that obvious?'

'Very much, to me at least. Didn't you mention she has moved to Varkala?'

'Yes, she has,'

'Take a weekend off, Chetta. Now we have additional help, I can manage along with Amma and Chandran. You deserve a break. What is the use of hiring all these people if you don't take time off for yourself?'

'Maybe I will,' I say.

I go to sleep that night with a song in my heart.

23
Arush

Not hearing from Puja is driving me crazy. I can't stop myself from obsessively checking for messages every fifteen minutes. It's almost unbearable, this waiting. I keep hoping to hear from her but there's nothing. Previously we used to quickly make up after any minor fights and disagreements. It was never a stonewall like this.

Every couple has a pattern to their fights and our is this. We go silent for a day or so and then the aggrieved party mails the other, telling them what made them upset. The other is quick to apologise. Then we talk. Every fight we've had during the time we've known each other has brought us closer, once we resolved it. But here, there seems to be no resolution in sight. She has shut me out completely and I am desperate to reach her.

I open my laptop and write.

My dearest, dearest Puja,

How are you? I know most people begin a mail this way asking 'how are you' but it doesn't mean anything beyond the cursory greeting. But for me, when it comes to you, it's not like that. I really, really want to know how you are.

I'm writing as you refuse to take my calls, refuse to reply to my messages and you aren't even checking my Instagram stories. I posted a few random stories (I know, pathetic!) just to see if you would check. But you haven't. You have posted nothing either—I am obsessively checking Instagram right now. Can you believe that?

Are you doing okay, my love? Are you eating well? Are you sleeping well? I am really worried. It feels horrid to not be in touch with you.

I know you're hurting. But please understand, I'm hurting too. So much. I'm hurting not because you aren't speaking to me anymore, but because I am the cause of your pain. I loathe myself for it. I've already told you multiple times how very much I regret it and how sorry I am, so I won't say that again. But if there's anything I can do to make this right, please tell me, Puja, and I will do it.

I'm at home right now. I've lately been having the luxury of time to think about things, because I've not been working the last five days. Apparently, we get four days of paid time-off when we complete an outstation tour. I combined that with the weekend, and got six days off, and came straight home. My family is overjoyed with this unexpected break. I leave back for Birmingham on Sunday evening.

I've been painting like a lunatic for the last few days. I am consumed by an urge to create. You were always telling me to take up the brush and paint. But I just couldn't. While I was at Edinburgh, the inspiration and the urge to paint just came back, and now it is overflowing as though making up for lost time. I have made two large oil paintings and four watercolours the last few days. I'm attaching the photos of the paintings with this mail. Perhaps you will see in them what I am going through because I have poured all my emotions (my pain, my regret, my love for you) into them. It's nothing like I've painted before.

In other news, my parents' shop has more customers than ever now and my aunt's restaurant is back on track. Business is back to how it was before the pandemic and I am delighted about that.

I've been going on long walks to the Derby Arboretum simply because I want to reflect upon what has happened between us.

Puja, I know you see this as cheating on you. But I want you to think about this (and please do give this some serious thought): what exactly constitutes 'cheating'? Western philosophy essentially tells us that if we have sex with someone other than our partner it is 'cheating'. But I think it is more than that. I think it is a violation of boundaries between a couple. What these boundaries exactly are depend on the couple.

What if you sleep in the same bed with someone and do not touch them at all? Is that cheating? What if you constantly think about someone while kissing your partner? Is that cheating? What if you spend a lot of time with someone other than your partner without having any romantic feelings for them, but they have feelings for you? Is that cheating? What if you spend a lot of time with someone and don't tell your partner about it? Is that cheating?

I hope you see the point I am making. Puja, I am not trying to justify what I did (or didn't do, because I really have no recollection of having sex with Naomi). But I am urging you to give it a thought.

Whatever has happened (or not happened)—it hasn't changed the way I feel towards you at all. I do agree that communication between us of late hasn't been too great. That is my fault. I promise to make amends for it. That shall not happen again. I will email daily if we are unable to speak. That I promise.

Puja, I do feel all of this has happened because we haven't seen each other for two whole years. That we could sustain it despite not meeting alone should tell us something, don't you think?

Have your feelings for me changed in anyway? If so, I need you to be honest with me and tell me. Please don't shut me out like this. Please talk to me.

I look forward to hearing your thoughts.

Take care, my darling Puja

All my love,
Arush

I read what I have written a few times. I don't want her to misinterpret what I am saying in any way. Her silence is worrying. I consider tracking down her sister on Instagram and messaging her, just to check if Puja is okay. But it seems too much of an encroachment to involve her family, and I decide I will wait for her reply. Maybe Puja just needs time, and I must give her that even though it's killing me.

I hit 'Send' on the mail, and I get back to the third painting that I am making. My parents are surprised by my frenzy to paint. But they haven't guessed why and I haven't told them it is to mitigate the pain I am drowning in.

They do ask about Jenna though. It is my aunt who brings her up when we are having a meal together. 'Why hasn't Jenna come over? Does she not know you're here?'

'I think she is busy with her work, Mami.' I evade the question.

'What work can keep her so busy that she can't come for a few hours? I'm going to call her up and ask,' Ma says.

'You can't call up people. It is rude. You have to text first.' Rhea gives Ma a disapproving glare. Though Dad, Mami and Ma laugh, what Rhea said is true. Phone calls are intrusive but Ma doesn't get that.

'All those rules are for you young people. Phone is for calling only. Not texting,' Ma says.

'Please don't pressurise her like that. If you call up, you won't be giving her the option to refuse. She will feel forced to drop her work and come over. She has an important deadline coming up. I'll speak to her and let you know.' I improvise on the spot quickly, before my mother dials her number. I don't want to tell my family what happened with Puja or Jenna. I want to sort this mess out myself. Fortunately for me, Ma buys it and doesn't pursue it further. I heave a sigh of relief.

There's no reply from Puja at all. Now in addition to checking Instagram I'm also obsessively checking mail. Later in the evening, Ma asks if I have spoken to Jenna. I lie and tell her that I have, and she is going to the Middle East for a book fair as her publishers are taking her there. I'd seen Jenna's story about how a book she is illustrating is travelling to the book fair, so it wasn't a complete lie.

'How lovely! Is she excited?' Ma asks.

'Very,' I reply and change the topic.

When I leave for Birmingham, I give strict instructions to my family that no one is to open the door to my room. The oil paintings haven't fully dried yet and I don't want them to be disturbed in any way.

When I get to my Birmingham flat, I run into Naomi on the stairs. It was to avoid her in the elevator that I'd decided to take the stairs, but clearly that plan hasn't worked. Naomi is in her sports bra and track pants.

'Oh, hi!' she says brightly upon spotting me, and removes her AirPods. 'I was on my way to the gym.'

I wave at her without meeting her eyes.

'Really, Arush, you are still mad? Come on! We can't skirt around each other like this you know. Let's talk about it and sort it out. Like adults.'

An adult is the last thing I feel like. I feel like a stupid teenager unable to cope with people not wanting to be my friends anymore. She is right though. I can't hide forever. I have to talk it out, as hard as that is.

'Yeah, Naomi, we will talk. But not right now, I presume.'

'No, not now. How about this evening?'

'We are not meeting in my house or your house anymore.'

She laughs. 'Are you that scared of me, Arush?'

I don't reply. I dislike how she seems to be teasing me, toying with me.

'Okay, sorry! I was joking. Guess it's too soon. Meet me at the coffee shop by the canal where we go during our walking tours in about an hour and fifteen minutes from now? I'll be done with my workout by then.'

'Sure,' I tell her as she waves cheerily and jogs off.

I don't know if she is putting on an act or whether it really doesn't affect her as much as it is affecting me. I'm not able to handle this at all.

The complete silence from Puja as well as from Jenna at the same time feels like a noose tightening around my neck. All because of Naomi, I think. One part of me knows it is incorrect on my part to blame her. After all, I did enjoy the time I spent with her. Only I was to blame. Yet I can't help feeling annoyed with her.

I have a leisurely shower and watch *Peaky Blinders*—it would be good to learn all the references from the iconic show which is set here, so I can use them in my guided tours—till it's time to meet Naomi.

When I arrive at the coffee shop by the canal, I find that Naomi is already seated on the wooden bench outside, waiting for me. 'Hi,' I say as I take the seat on the bench opposite her. We are separated by a long wooden table. The smell of coffee cuts through the cold air instantly, making me long for a cup.

'Hello!' she says as she smiles at me. I see fondness, affection in her eyes. Like she is greeting an old friend. She's already got her coffee.

'A minute please,' I tell her as I walk to the counter, get a black coffee and come back to the table.

'So?' she says as she swirls the stirrer in her coffee.

'You wanted to meet, Naomi. Why?'

'Because we can't run away from each other forever.'

'You pretend like nothing happened and that's not true. Something did happen that day,' I blurt out.

'We're both consenting adults and nothing happened that either of us didn't want, Arush. The thing I don't get is why it's such a big deal to you.'

'It kind of messed up my life, Naomi. Puja isn't talking to me, and my other good friend isn't either.'

'Wait, let me guess, your other good friend is also a girl?'

'Well, yes, how did you know what?'

'That's not hard to deduce. Many years in this travel business has made me good at reading people. See, Arush, the thing is whatever happened between us is something neither of us can do anything about. But what do we want to do going forward from here. That's what I want to talk about. Why are you avoiding me?'

It makes me stop and think. Why was I avoiding her? Because she wouldn't tell me what happened? Or because she was taking it all too casually? Then it occurs to me that probably the person I am angry with most is myself, not her.

'I guess I needed the time to process things, Naomi. You acted like it didn't matter at all. I felt you weren't respecting what I have, I mean had with Puja.'

'Wait, did she break up with you?'

'No. But she is on the verge of it, I think. I'm terrified she will soon. And I am freaking out. She isn't talking to me at all. Not picking up my calls, not replying. This has never happened before.'

'And what have you done about it apart from messaging her and calling her?'

'I have tried an email.'

'Ha, email! Arush, if you do love her as much as you claim, you need to do a lot more. You've got to fight for this thing you have. You *have* to make a big gesture. Not write a mail and sit back!' Naomi throws up her hands in the air and shakes her head.

'What do you mean by a big gesture?'

'Think about something she will never expect you to do. You need to show her what she means to you. A mail just won't cut it.'

'What? Like hiring a plane to write her name in the sky?'

'That's a grand gesture for sure.'

'But that might be impossible considering she is in India,' I say.

But Naomi isn't listening. She has a faraway look in her eyes. 'You know what I regret most about getting divorced?'

'What?'

'The fact that neither of us tried hard enough. I haven't told you about my ex-husband, Miguel. It hurts even to refer to him as my ex,' Naomi says. Without waiting for me to respond, she continues to talk. I feel like she wants to get this off her chest, so I listen. 'I expected Miguel to move to the UK. But he'd lived in Spain all his life. English is his second language. He presumed I would move to Spain. We were so young and crazily in love that we believed it would somehow work out. But things don't work out like that, Arush. You need to take actions to make them work. Neither of us took any steps and we both lost a great thing.'

We sit in silence for a few moments. What she has said is slowly sinking in. 'Yes, I guess you're right,' I tell her. 'Didn't you ever try to get back with Miguel? I mean, when you realised what you'd lost?' I ask her, curiosity getting the better of me.

'It was too late. He remarried and just became a father. The baby was born on the day I came to your place with the whiskey. Miguel now has a beautiful baby boy while I have regrets for company. You've no idea how it makes me feel. That's why I am telling you to pursue Puja if you really love her. Else, years from now you will be staring at her pictures with someone else like I am now.'

Naomi has spoken her heart. Even the thought of Puja with someone else is sheer agony for me. I can't imagine what Naomi must be going through, seeing pictures of Miguel's baby.

I do want to get back with Puja. I want her to start talking to me. I want things to go back to how they were.

Then I know what I have to do—the grand gesture that Naomi told me about. I will travel to India. I will surprise Puja, like she had surprised me all those years back.

If she turns me down, at least I'd have tried.

Touchdown

There are three simple rules for making a smooth landing. Unfortunately, no one knows what they are.

—*Rules of the Air*

24

Puja

Benny is a bore. There's no other word to describe him. I can't imagine how Divya and I thought he was cool when we first met him. Now that I am working with him, I've realised he is a one-trick pony. The same carefully rehearsed speech, the same instructions, the same jokes that he cracks, and the same way that he falls into the water to demonstrate how not to get into a kayak that I can almost hear in my sleep. Granted the instructions cannot differ; after all, he is teaching people to kayak. But can't he at least change the jokes? The tourist groups he is performing for are impressed, just as we were when we first came across him.

The job sucks. I have to begin shooting footage right from the time Benny is instructing to the time we finish the trip and pose for photos. In short, I have to be there throughout. The cabin where we have to wait when we have no bookings is like an oven. It's that hot. A tiny window with a dull green pane, an old pedestal fan, two metal chairs and a small desk take up almost all the space in here. The wall has a couple of old faded posters from Kerala tourism department which have visuals of Varkala. The cabin also has an attached toilet.

I also don't like the way Benny acts around me, a bit too familiar and over-friendly. He brings me stuff he cooks: omelettes, soups and fried rice. I thank him always, but I don't much like his cooking. It's too spicy. One time, he put his hand on my shoulder when we were getting back to the cabin and I made it clear I disliked it by removing it and moving away. If he didn't have a steady stream of girls who wait for him after our kayaking is done for the day, I might have thought that he was hitting on me. What these girls see in him, I do not know. I also wonder if he is two-timing—or maybe even three-timing—these girls, because the girls keep changing. But it's none of my business and so I don't comment.

One evening when we have a booking, I get to the cabin before Benny. The light streaming in is golden, and this is great natural light for photography. I put the self-timer on my camera and click a full-length picture. But when I look at it, I am shocked. I have lost *a lot* of weight. Ever since I moved here, I haven't seen myself in a full-length mirror. The image I have in my head of myself doesn't match what I am looking at on the phone. I also have a deep tan despite using sunscreen daily. My hair is so frizzy, I'm horrified.

Arush will be shocked if he sees me like this, I think. But I remember that we aren't talking anymore and a sharp pain shoots through me at this thought. It's so bad that I almost find it hard to breathe. My feelings drown me. Though he has written a mail to me, I have deleted it without reading. It's still in the trash. Icicles have formed around my heart and they stubbornly refuse to melt. I am still reeling with hurt.

One part of me wants to tell him it's over and move on. But the other part mocks me, asking me how will I break up when I long for his smile, his cute face, his voice, the way he kissed me, the way he said my hair smelled of vanilla and oranges and the way he gazed into my eyes.

Benny arrives then and announces that our clients are here. I am glad for the distraction.

I have become an expert at kayaking now and my arm muscles are stronger than they've ever been. Even Benny compliments me on that. But I do not care much for what he says at all. I wish the guy would just stop talking sometimes. He has nothing to say that I haven't heard before. I mechanically shoot the footage for that day's reel, as he instructs the group, which is like all the other groups we've got before.

We get all kinds of groups. A majority of the ones who come here aren't here for the sport but because someone in their group decided kayaking would be fun. There's always one person who is enthusiastic and others who are simply tagging along. Then we also get the Instagram influencer types. Most of them do their stuff, take pictures, shoot some videos and leave.

But today there is a girl who wants to a wear a Kerala saree and she wants to kayak in a saree! She has brought along an assistant, a young girl, who is helping her with the saree, touching up her makeup, holding her bag, fetching her drinks, etc. It annoys me to see the influencer acting like a spoilt movie star. She has another person along with her who is operating a drone, and she wants him to capture footage from above. She keeps yelling instructions at him at what angle to capture it from, till he tells her, 'Madam, please allow me to do my job. I will give you all the footage. Then you decide which ones to keep.'

Benny is relieved when she finally leaves and so am I.

'Want to come for dinner?' Benny asks.

Benny and I have eaten together a couple of times. We mostly have nothing to talk about. Benny doesn't have too many interests apart from kayaking and working out. The guy doesn't read at all nor does he watch TV shows. He tells me he doesn't have a Netflix or an Amazon Prime subscription. He hasn't heard of *Game of Thrones* or *Breaking Bad* or *Never Have I Ever*.

I'm in two minds whether to go with him for dinner or not. Accompanying him would mean enduring his insufferable company. But going home would mean I have to eat Maggi again and spend time in my stupid pink room. Sujit won't be free till nightfall, and I will end up constantly thinking about Arush, drowning in self-pity and anger, not knowing what to do.

I tell Benny I will come along. We walk to the only nearby place, a tiny joint with a tin sheet roof and faded grey walls that used to be white once upon a time. They blend well with the old worn-out wooden benches and tables. This place is so small that seating is along one side only.

I've tried almost everything on the menu here. The food is fresh but tasteless. It is as though the cook slapped some ingredients together in a tearing hurry. The puttu is hard, the kadala is watery, the dosas are drenched in oil and idlis are not spongy. I miss Shanti Chechi's delicious meals.

Before coming here I'd have never in a million years agreed to eat here. I'd have turned up my nose at such a place. But now I have no choice.

After we get back, Benny asks me if I'd like to smoke up. 'I have some good stuff, it's really good.' He grins.

'No, thanks, I don't touch that stuff,' I say.

'Never tried it? Not even in college?'

'No. There were others who did, but I find the smell itself disgusting.'

'Miss prim and proper.' Benny laughs.

I just roll my eyes and head to my room. Later that evening I speak to Divya.

'OMG, Puja, you look like a scarecrow. And you seem so sad,' she says as soon as she sees me. She is speaking from the terrace of her office building.

The real reason for my sadness is I am dying without Arush. But I don't tell her that. Behind her the Mumbai skyline looks magnificent with the setting sun.

'Are you okay, Puja-doll?' Divya asks, worry lines forming on her forehead.

'How can I not be in this gorgeous place?' I show her my pink room.

She laughs.

'I'd laughed too when I first saw it and so had Antony,' I tell her.

'Why don't you shift to someplace else?'

'No good rentals available in this area. There's only one lousy hotel nearby.'

'Do you want to go back home, Puja? And look for another job?'

'I've really begun enjoying kayaking. I don't much enjoy shooting these tourists, but to be able to kayak in these waters, it's something else.'

I don't tell Divya that I want to prove to myself that I can live and work on my own, and that I am not a spoilt, rich girl. Giving up on this job and rushing back home would mean that I have failed, and I am not ready to fail. Also, the job gives me something to do with my time other than be miserable about Arush.

Divya tells me she has big news. Vihan and she have decided to get married. She wants to come down to Kochi when she gets a long weekend, and then tell our parents in person. She asks me not to say anything to them. Before hanging up, she asks me to take care of myself.

That night when Sujit calls, he broaches almost shyly the possibility of him coming over for a visit. He says now that he has additional helpers he can get away.

'Come over! I will have to work but that's just for a couple of hours. We have only one booking I think, which is the next evening,' I tell him.

'Okay, then I will see you in the morning around 11 a.m. I will leave home early,' he says.

'See you!' I tell him.

I decide that I'll ask Benny if he can spare an extra mattress from one of the rooms not in use. While Sujit has not said that he will be staying over, I have presumed he will. It would be such a welcome change from the daily, boring monotonous life that I lead. Thinking about his visit uplifts my mood a great deal, and I eagerly look forward to Sujit's arrival.

25

Sujit

Puja greets me on the main road itself. She is standing by the side of the road and waving her arms over her head frantically like an aircraft marshaller. I grin widely when I spot her from a distance. I'd texted her the car registration and the make—it's a maroon Hyundai i20—as she had asked me to, but I had not expected her to meet me right on the highway. I pull up the car to a side. Even though I am driving a rented car, I feel like a king.

When I get a closer look at her, I am shocked at how much weight she has lost and how hollow her eyes look. She has a deep tan now and she looks a bit like a hippie in her sleeveless loose top and shorts. Her arms are super-toned though. If I hadn't known I was meeting her I might not even have recognised her. I don't comment on her appearance though I'm worried seeing her like this.

'Hey! Good to see you. Nice car,' she says as she hops in.

'Good to see you too, Puja.' I smile at her. My heart beats fast as I catch a whiff of the perfume she is wearing. It's a light floral, lemony fragrance. I can't believe I am next to her, and am going to be spending so much time with her.

She looks troubled. Whatever it is that is bothering her, I want to get to the bottom of it. I'll get it out of her slowly, tactfully, I decide. She chatters away, asking me about whether it was hard to drive, at what time I left and what my family thought about the whole visit. Amma and Ravi had mercilessly teased me and made fun of me when I blushed. Ravi had told me outright to tell Puja that I am in love with her. Of course, I don't tell her any of that!

I tell her what fun the drive was, and how good it feels to be finally making money, and being able to afford things like renting a car. She goes so quiet that I have to turn towards her and look to see if she is okay.

'Hey! Don't look at me. Eyes on the road please and slow down here, switch on your indicator,' she says.

'Yes, Ma'am!' I grin at her. Despite all the weight loss, she still looks stunning.

She instructs me to take the right turn, and then a turn to the left, after which she tells me to park.

'You have arrived at your destination,' she says, imitating the Google voice assistant.

'This building?' I ask, as we get out of the car. I take my bag and lock the car. The building looks drab to my eyes. I can't imagine Puja living here.

'Yes. Don't judge a book by its cover. You will see it's different inside,' she says solemnly, leading me up a narrow staircase.

I notice how some of the steps are chipped and cracked in a few places, but Puja just bounces up, deftly avoiding stepping on the cracked edges. I follow suit. She stops outside a door, fishes out a key from the pocket of her shorts and throws it open.

'Welcome to my humble abode. We believe in a monochromatic colour scheme, in case you didn't notice,' she says.

I enter and look around in disbelief. Puja collapses on the sofa laughing at my expression.

'Oh, Sujit, believe me, this is what I felt when I first saw it. Antony, my driver, asked if he should take me to a hotel,' she says.

'It, ahem, isn't ideal,' I admit and sit next to her, placing my bag on the side.

'No need to be polite. It's awful and it sucks,' she says.

'Guessing you chose this because it's close to the kayaking place?'

'Bingo. Let's click pictures in the pink room!' She pulls out her phone. I smile and pose as she makes a V with her hands. We make some more silly faces and click more pictures. She asks me if I'll have tea.

'That would be great. Let me help you,' I tell her.

'Why? Don't you trust me enough to make tea? I am not that spoilt,' she says as she walks up to the kitchen.

'No, I didn't think you were.'

'But tea is the only thing I can make!' She measures out two cups of water, fills up the vessel and keeps it on the induction stove. I hoist myself up on the kitchen platform and sit with my feet dangling. She looks so pretty tying her hair into a pony tail.

'God, even the platform is pink,' I remark, looking away, trying not to stare at her.

She shrugs.

'For lunch, we could go to the north cliff. Ever been there?' I ask.

'No.' She makes an exaggerated disappointed face. 'I've only been working and eating at the local eatery here.'

She looks so cute, it takes all my self-control to not comment on it.

'The north cliff is where all the restaurants are, and all the tourists as well. The view is beautiful, Puja. I'm surprised you haven't been there. Let's go.'

'Sure, give me five minutes to get ready.' She strains the tea and hands it over.

I take a sip.

'Good?' she asks.

'Perfect,' I tell her. I am not able to take my eyes off her.

She goes into the bedroom and shuts the door. When she emerges, she has changed into a light yellow halter-neck dress and is wearing lipstick.

'Too much?' she asks, smiling

'Oh, Puja, you look stunning!' It slips out before I can stop myself.

'I know I've lost a lot of weight and I look a bit crazy,' she says doubtfully.

'No, you look fine!'

'Don't lie, Sujit. I can see it myself. It's not that I am not aware. Do you not see any change in me? And be honest!' she says.

'Umm, well, I did feel you look a bit sad,' I admit.

'I am. I'll tell you all about it. Let's go,' she says as she steps out of the house. I follow her. She locks the door and asks me to keep the key in my bag, as she is carrying just a small purse.

'Sure,' I say as I slip the key into my pocket. This small little gesture of her trusting me with the key makes me feel so good that I have to remind myself to stop reading meaning into this tiny thing.

Just as we go towards the stairs, I see a well-built guy walking up and I wait by the side for him to pass as the staircase is too narrow.

Puja is right behind me. 'Oh Benny, meet my friend—'

'Sujit!' Benny says before she can complete it and I look at him again, in surprise.

'You two know each other? Puja asks

Benny gives me a knowing look. 'Let's just say we are old acquaintances,' he chuckles.

I shudder involuntarily. Fucking hell. This guy is the last person I expected to meet here. I wish the earth would swallow me up. And *this* is the guy Puja is working with? I am so disgusted I have no words.

'See you,' I manage to mutter. 'Let's go, Puja,' I tell her as I take her elbow and rush her to the car.

Puja is surprised by how I have taken charge and am steering her away. Actually, I am surprised too at how protective I feel towards Puja. I want to get her away from here as fast as possible. I feel Benny's eyes boring into us as we walk towards the car.

'What is it, Sujit? How do you know Benny?' Puja asks.

'Give me some time, Puja. I am in a bit of a shock. I'll tell you the whole story,' I say as I drive us towards north cliff. My mood is completely spoilt now and Puja senses it.

'Let's put on some music,' she says. She makes me pull over while she connects her blue tooth to the car stereo.

Soon Rihanna's voice singing *Shine bright like a diamond* fills the car. Puja starts swaying to the music and humming along with her arms in the air and that relaxes me instantly, and I smile at her carefree abandon, even if it's deliberate.

We park the car at the assigned space and walk down the narrow path on the cliff. On one side are all the restaurants lined up next to each other and on the other side is a sharp drop with gorgeous sea views.

'This is really lovely, Sujit!' Puja says as she half skips and half walks ahead while I hurry trying to keep up.

'It is, isn't it? Choose which restaurant you want to eat in,' I tell her hurrying after her. I feel so proud as though I have created all these cliffs myself just for her.

She makes me pose for a few pictures. Then she chooses a restaurant serving north-eastern food.

'I eat Kerala food all the time, let's try this one,' she says as she enters. The place is done up with a lot of Buddhist scrolls, tapestries and bamboo plants in long white planters. Bright cushions are scattered on colourful mats. The low open-air seating under a canopy made from long natural grass looks inviting. The place exudes serenity. Puja and I sit facing each other as we order iced tea, momos, jadoh and kelli chana.

Our tea arrives first and as we sip it, I think that I could sit like this and look at Puja forever. Her presence is intoxicating.

'So should I tell you first or will you tell me? she asks.

'What? I ask her, puzzled.

'What we discussed! You have to tell me how you know Benny and I will tell you the real reason I am sad. Fair trade.'

'Ah, that ...' I had almost forgotten about it. I'm mesmerised by Puja. She, of course, has no idea of the effect she is having on me.

'Ladies first. You tell me why you're sad.'

'Alright then. Listen,' she begins. 'This thing has been bothering me so much. The only person I can open up to is Divya, and I'm not ready to listen to what she has to say. I want you to tell me your honest opinion, okay?'

'Okay.'

She goes on to tell me how close she and Arush had become during the pandemic and how things changed after he started his new job; she tells me what happened between him and some girl at his workplace. She narrates it in great detail. She explains how much she misses him, and how she longs for things to go back to how they were. She tells me he has apologised a million times. Then she asks me if I think she should forgive him.

I am so shocked for a few seconds that I can't speak. It feels like someone is strangling me. I can see how deeply she is in love with him. Everything she has just said are bullets to my brain. I'd never thought her connection with Arush would be this deep, this intense. When she speaks of him her eyes light up and she is transformed into a different person. Till now I'd refused to think of him, and a part of me was content pretending that it was just me and Puja all alone in this thing we have going on. I was in my own Puja bubble. But now the bubble has burst. It is very clear to me she sees me only as a friend and nothing more. The small tender wisp of hope is crushed. A dull pain creeps up inside me and spreads all over my body. I never knew my heart was capable of such ache.

I take a sip of water to cover my shock, my pain and I pretend to think hard. My head is reeling. But I have to do right by Puja. I've brought enough pain to her in the past. She deserves all the love in the world.

I muster all my strength and I tell her, 'It seems to me that you are very much in love with him.' But I am unable to meet her eyes because it hurts so much.

'Yes, Sujit. Very much. I do love him deeply. But I feel like if I forgive him I might be losing my self-respect. I don't want to be weak-minded.'

'Puja,' I say, and this time I look her straight in the eye. 'Trust me, in love there's no place for ego. If ego wins, love loses. If you love him, just get back with him. Nothing else matters.'

For two seconds she says nothing. I hold my breath. Then she says, 'Oh, thanks, Sujit! I knew I did the right thing by asking you. Can't tell you how much this means.'

She sounds relieved and her eyes look brighter, as though a big burden that she was grappling with has been lifted off her. I feel like my heart has just been wrung out and thrown away. But I don't want Puja to know what I am going through. So, I pretend everything is great, and I pretend to enjoy the food when it arrives. Even though I am having a tough time swallowing it, I force it down my throat, smiling, watching the spark returning to her eyes.

26

Sujit

Puja and I have finished our meal. The food is gone. The empty plates lie on the table. When the waiter comes to clear the plates, she asks him to take a photo of us.

'Why so many pictures?' I ask. Earlier I was enthusiastic but now I don't want any more pictures of us.

'What can I say, I just love taking photos, and it is also my job now.' She smiles as she strikes a pose.

After he clicks the photo and hands back the phone to Puja, I ask him if he can call the cook as I want to thank him. He instantly breaks into a big grin, and the cook comes out. I tell him I really enjoyed the meal and I express appreciation. He gives me a big smile, bows and then goes back into the kitchen.

'That was so sweet of you!' Puja says.

'The cook would have toiled for so many hours to make this meal, and in a few minutes it is gone. It matters when people express their appreciation.'

When the waiter brings the bill, Puja says that she will pay. But I don't let her. I insist that it is my treat because my restaurant is doing so well. When she tries to grab the bill out of my hand, I hold it high above my head and she lunges towards me. She is so close to me that for a few seconds I am flustered. Then I remind myself that her heart belongs to someone else. I tell her I will be really mad if she doesn't allow me to pay for this meal. Finally, she agrees.

Just as I'm paying, her phone rings.

'It's my parents. They don't know we're friends. Excuse me,' she says as she hurries away to the other side of the restaurant and takes the call.

When she comes back, she says 'My mother has been invited for a medical conference in Jordan! She is presenting a paper and my father is going with her. They are so excited about it. They will take a vacation in Egypt after that. They're going on a cruise. They asked if I wanted to go along!'

'Oh, that's wonderful, why don't you go?' I ask her.

'Because of my job, Sujit!'

'But this is such a good opportunity to travel to all these places. Do you even know how lucky you are?'

'I guess. But they will be gone for over two weeks. I can't possibly take leave for that long. Also, I can travel to these places anytime I want. It's not like an opportunity of a lifetime,' she says as we talk towards the car.

I think about how fortunate she is to have that kind of money where she can just decide to take off any time to any country she wants to. I want to make enough money to be able to do that.

'Tell me about Benny. How do you know him?' Puja asks.

I think about how I should phrase it. How do I tell her that Benny is a worm? That I don't feel comfortable about Puja working for that scum.

'He is ... someone from my past life. He is not an okay guy, Puja. He is really not okay,' I say. I am struggling for words.

'What do you mean by "not okay"?'

'He is ... I don't even know how to say this to you, Puja. He is a pimp. Please forgive my language.'

'What?!' She has stopped walking and is looking at me to see if I am joking.

'He supplies girls, er ... sex workers ... to these politicians and foreigners,' I say and look away.

'Sujit, how do you know?'

That was the question I was dreading. This is so hard for me to talk about as that is the life I've buried and am done with. But I have to be honest with her. 'I was there at one of their parties at a hotel here in town. The guy I was working for, one of the suppliers, is good friends with this Benny. I was the one delivering the weed to these guys. High quality stuff they'd ordered. It was not only weed, there were other drugs as well. And our direct contact was Benny.'

I feel horrible to say all of this to Puja. It feels like she is 'pure' and I have to shield her from all this filth and muck, which had been my life.

'Shit. I can't believe it. He told my father that he had a corporate job and that he learnt kayaking in Italy.'

'Ha! Benny is a college drop-out, Puja. He has never even been outside India. He was trying desperately to get a job in the Middle East. I know this through common contacts. For a while I also thought I'd go to the Middle East and try to make a living there. This was just after that fiasco when you got arrested. I got a proper scare then. I was in touch with an immigration agent, and so was Benny. That's how I know.'

'He sure is a smooth liar then. He is very convincing,' she says.

'In this line of work you have to be. You have to know how to say the right things,' I tell her.

'How is he so good at kayaking then?'

'I think he did a course in Rishikesh or somewhere. The Middle East thing didn't work out. I heard that Benny beat up the agent and got his money back. I was fortunate I hadn't paid the agent, so I didn't lose any money there.'

Puja is thoughtful as we drive back to her place. She doesn't speak much. She plays some more songs from her playlist but she isn't dancing anymore.

'Hey, Puja, I didn't mean to upset you at all,' I tell her.

'No, I am not upset. I'm glad you told me, Sujit,' she says as we pull up in front of her building.

I am dreading running into Benny but he doesn't seem to be around. Once we're inside Puja's home, she says, 'See, Sujit, you have changed a lot, right? You are no longer the person you were back then.'

'Yes, I have.'

'Isn't it possible that Benny has changed too? That he has turned over a new leaf?'

I don't know how to explain that I find it hard to believe that someone like him can change. But then people would have presumed the same thing about me two years back. That I was a 'gone-case'. They would have written me off. Yet I managed to turn my life around. I know the effort I have put in, and the remorse I am feeling. A person like Benny simply doesn't strike me as the type of guy capable of self-reflection.

'Yes, of course it is possible,' I shrug.

Puja asks me if I will go with her to get the extra mattress for me. She says she had told Benny that a friend is coming over, and he'd said she could borrow one from the next room, and had given her the key.

I had originally intended to stay over, and had even brought a change of clothes. But after I heard Puja speaking about Arush, I've changed my plan. My heart feels like it's been ripped apart, and I feel a need to get away from her now. It will be difficult for me being around her knowing her heart is elsewhere.

'Actually, I have to get back home. I am so sorry I can't stay,' I tell her.

'Oh, I just presumed you'd be staying over.' Puja looks disappointed.

'Maybe another time. This was nice, Puja.'

'Alright then. I'll see you off,' she says, following me as I take my backpack and walk towards the door.

We reach the car and Puja hugs me tightly and I hug her back. Her arms around me feel so good, so comforting. I love how her hair smells. I want to hold her and never let her go. 'She sees you only as a friend, remember that,' the voice in my head tells me and I reluctantly pull apart.

'Thank you for coming, Sujit, and thanks for being so honest,' she tells me.

'Take care, Puja,' I tell her as I drive away with a heavy heart. I watch Puja getting smaller and smaller in my side-view mirror.

The sun is setting now, and the skies are a mix of blazing orange and crimson. I am on the coastal road, heading back towards Ernakulam. With the beach on one side, the scene before my eyes is picturesque. This would make a great backdrop in a movie, where the guy and the girl drive off into their happily-ever-after. I chide that little hope in my heart that had goaded me to think there ever was a tiny possibility of Puja being more than a friend. It was too good to be true.

As I drive on, all the feelings of inadequacy that I had faced in school come back to me. No matter how successful you become, you can never be 'one of them', the voice in my head taunts me. I try to think of what Dr Harsh would tell me. But no comforting words come to my mind. My mind is a complete blank. I feel broken as I drive mechanically, the kilometres flying by. After driving for over an hour and a half, I stop to take a tea break. I check my messages and Puja has sent me a little video with a whole lot of photos she has clicked of us together. She has edited it extremely well. The music is set to Rihanna's *Diamonds*.

'You're a diamond on earth,' Puja has written.

It hurts even to read it. I type a hug emoji, and get back to the car.

It is when I am crossing Purakkad, that I see an incoming call from Ravi. I wonder why he is calling. When I was leaving, he'd chuckled and told me he wouldn't 'disturb us' and had told me to have fun. I answer immediately, and the call gets transferred to the car's stereo.

'Chetta?' Ravi's voice booms through the speakers. It sounds like he is calling from a very noisy place. Either that or there's some kind of disturbance on the phone line or the Bluetooth connection.

'Yeah, Ravi, what is it?'

'Are you with Puja?'

'No, I'm actually heading back home. I'm driving.'

'Chetta, please pull over then.'

'Pull over? Why?'

'Please, Chetta,' Ravi says. Something in his tone makes me pull over to the side immediately. I switch on the distress lights and they flash in the darkness of the highway.

'Yeah, I've pulled over. What is it?' I ask

'There's ... there's been a fire at home, Chetta. Everything is up in flames. It's ... it's all gone,' Ravi breaks down.

'Oh my god!' I can't believe what I am hearing. For a second I wonder if it's a prank. But Ravi would never joke about something like this.

'Amma and Sindu? Are they okay.'

I wait with bated breath to hear his answer. I fear the worst.

'They are okay, Chetta. They will be fine.'

'They will be fine means what? Are they hurt? How bad is it?'

'It's pretty bad, but they are not hurt.'

I breathe then. If they are okay, then I can handle it, whatever it is, I tell myself.

'Drive carefully, Chetta. I don't want anything to happen to you,' Ravi says.

'Yes, I will,' I tell him. 'Is anyone else hurt?'

'No, Chetta, minor burns only. Very minor. Everyone is safe,' Ravi says.

'I think it will take me another two and a half hours at least to get there.'

'Just be safe, okay? Promise me,' Ravi says. I can feel the fear in his voice.

'Yes, I will be. I'm coming soon and safely.'

After that it seems like everything else has faded out. I can see only the road ahead of me. As the car moves forward the glare of the headlights light up just the part in front of me, the rest of it is dark.

'I have to get home. I have to drive carefully. They only have me. Drive carefully.' The thoughts go on inside my heads like chants. I drive with laser-like focus, more carefully than I've ever driven in my life. I curse the trucks passing me on the opposite side of the road for driving on high beam that almost blind me. I curse the traffic, inching slowly when I enter the city limits. I heave a sigh of relief as I finally take the turn that goes to my street. I smell the smoke right from the start of the street.

When I get closer, I spot a few scattered curious onlookers. As soon as I park the car, Ravi rushes out from the neighbouring house. I stare in disbelief at the sight before me. Inside our compound where our house once stood there is nothing. *Nothing*.

I can't believe what I am looking at—just ruins, a skeletal structure with half-burnt exposed beams, bricks black with soot and a pile of rubbish, dust and charcoal. It is still smouldering, angry black smoke rising up slowly, making its way upwards, merging with the dark night sky. There is no roof at all. It's all gone. It feels like a scene of bombing from a war movie I have seen.

'Fuck,' I say as I stand and stare.

'The fire engine could reach here only after an hour. By then it was all blazing. They took a long time to extinguish it,' Ravi says quietly.

'Where are Amma and Sindu?'

'Amma wanted to stay here till you came but Jayashri Chechi insisted that she should go there with Sindu. Amma stayed here till they put out the fire. After that I put them in an auto. It was difficult to convince her to leave,' Ravi says.

'You did the right thing.'

'Jayashri Chechi also told me to bring you and come over. She says we can stay as long as we want.'

'Get into the car, let's go,' I tell Ravi.

As we drive towards Jayashri Chechi's house, Ravi says in a strangled voice, 'What are we going to do? Apparently Achcha never took any insurance for the house.'

'I don't know, Ravi. I guess we will figure something out.'

When we get to Jayashri Chechi's house, Amma comes rushing out. It seems as though she was waiting for us.

'Mone, everything is gone,' she says as she breaks down, hugging me. It reminds me of the time when Achcha died. I've seen her distraught before, but never like this.

'Don't worry, Amma, I'll sort out everything,' I promise her with a bravado I am not feeling at all. 'Where's Sindu?' I ask as we enter the house.

'Asleep. She was worried about what she will wear to school tomorrow,' Amma says with a wry smile.

Jayashri Chechi is extremely sweet. She shows me and Ravi to our room. 'Don't worry. You can stay here as long as you like. The one good thing this old house has is enough spare rooms,' she says.

She insists that I eat even though I say I don't want anything. She says she has made idlis and I *have* to eat. Refusing is not an option. Amma too agrees with her. I am too tired to argue, so I eat. Strangely I feel better after eating.

'Thank you, Jayashri Chechi,' I tell her emotionally.

'What thanks and all? What is family for?' she asks.

Later, Amma comes into the room and tells Ravi and me to get a good night's sleep. 'There's nothing we can do today. Tomorrow, we will see how to start over,' she says.

I am barely able to sleep though. I lie in an unfamiliar bed thinking about the day's events. This is possibly the worst day of my life. In some ways it is even worse than when Achcha passed away. That was a finality I had to accept. But here we don't even have a home.

'I feel I shouldn't have gone to visit Puja,' I tell Ravi.

'Don't be silly. It's not that you could have prevented it.'

'What was the possible cause of the fire? How did it start?'

'That's what no one knows, Chetta. One moment everyone was eating. It was the evening peak hour rush. And suddenly the tarpaulin caught fire, from where it spread. Everyone ran out. I managed to take the important documents file, Amma's gold jewellery and I also managed to take out all the cash we collected for the day.'

'Oh, that was some smart thinking! How much was it?'

'About 28,000 rupees. I wanted to take some clothes too but Amma was screaming hysterically. By the way, we were all over television.'

'Oh, no!' I don't like the idea of the whole world knowing about our misfortunes, but it's not something I can control.

'Chetta, it is sensational news. Almost every TV channel was there to cover it. They even tried to speak to Amma but I chased them away.'

'Good, good. I wish I was there, Ravi. I feel so bad you had to handle it alone.'

'No, Chetta, my friend came over. He was there till I put Amma in the auto. Also, the neighbours were very helpful. They took good care of Amma and Sindu.'

'I guess we should be thankful we at least have a place to stay.'

'Yeah, Chetta, we're lucky we have kind people around us.'

The next morning, I am woken up by the noise of vessels. I look at the time and it's past 8.45 a.m. I sit up with a start and for a few seconds I am confused. Then I remember where I am. For many months now, my days began with a trip to the fish market after waking up at 5.00 a.m. Now I don't have anywhere to go, and it feels strange.

As I brush my teeth, a feeling of emptiness engulfs me. It's a feeling hard to describe—like the ground beneath my feet has given way and I am suspended in some kind of vacuum.

Yesterday morning, when I left for Varkala, I was feeling on top of the world. Everything was going well. I had hope in my heart. But now there's only emptiness, frustration and a sense of hopelessness. Just when things had begun going well too.

I've grandly promised Amma that we will sort it out. But the truth is I don't even know where to begin.

27

Arush

I've looked at the fares to travel to India. The cheapest one is an Air India one via Delhi. The total flight time is about 17 hours and 10 minutes, but I don't care about that if it means I get cheaper tickets. It lands at Kochi at 8.10 p.m. The thought of travelling to India fills me with indescribable joy, and it's not only because of Puja. I remember my time in Jew Town, the synagogue, the menorahs, the cobbled streets, the cafés and the little museum where I bought handmade soaps for Puja. I remember my lovely room in Mukundan's school, and how sweet and kind Shashi was. I feel like booking that flight straightaway and jumping into the plane to India.

But now that I am working there's the little problem of applying for leave. That too just after I've come back from a break. Before I set out for my walking tours for the day, I ask Olivia if she is free to speak.

'Yes, of course, Arush. What is it?' she asks.

I ask her what the company policy is regarding taking time off for personal reasons.

'Do you want to take a leave? How long?'

'About two weeks. I want to travel to India.'

'India? That's lovely. It's always been on my bucket list. When do you want to go?'

'As soon as possible.'

'Then you'll have to speak to Nik. Usually we have a lead time of two or three months as these things are planned when we do the quarterly meetings. Nik will be visiting us tomorrow as you know.'

I remember Olivia telling me that for Nik it was very important that he met all his employees one on one to understand their problems. He takes great pride in prioritising employee well-being. Since these meetings are of great importance to Nik the whole office had begun preparing for this before I'd left for Edinburgh.

'Oh, yes, I'd forgotten. I'll speak to him, thank you,' I say.

The thought of speaking to him fills me with trepidation. I do badly want to see Puja. If I don't ask him, the answer is anyway a no. I barely sleep that night as I worry about what I am going to tell him. I don't know what I will do if he refuses. I am a bundle of nerves as I reach office well in advance the next day even though my meeting with him is much later. Nik is meeting with the design team in the first half of the day after which he will meet with the travel division.

'What do people usually talk to him about at these meetings?' I ask my colleague Ruby.

'Career development, growth prospects, performance reviews, etcetera. If you have any problem with your boss, who is Olivia for you, you can speak to him about that as well.' Ruby winks.

But Olivia is the sweetest boss anyone could ask for. I've had no problems with her and I am happy to have moved to the travel division, which means that the only thing I really wanted to talk to Nik about is my leave. I've told Daljit to message me as soon as he finishes his meeting. And he does. He is pumped about it, as it went well. He tells me that Nik discussed his career plan in detail and he was most impressed about how Nik knew everything. In comparison to all the career stuff other people are discussing with him, here I am about to ask for two weeks' leave. It increases my nervousness so much that I feel like I might throw up.

When Nik comes to the travel division there's a flurry of activity as Olivia welcomes him and walks him to the conference room. The very air is charged with his presence.

'Hello, everyone! I look forward to speaking with each one of you,' he says before disappearing into the conference room.

My turn to speak to Nik comes almost at the end of the day, long after Naomi has finished. She comes over to my desk and says, 'Just be honest with him. He appreciates that.'

I enter the conference room to find Nik at the head of the table. He greets me warmly. 'Hello, Arush! I've been hearing such good things about you. How is the move to the travel division?' he asks as he indicates a chair for me to sit.

'It's great!' I also tell him about how much I've enjoyed Scotland and Edinburgh.

'I've been getting really good reports. I've read all the reviews and it seems like you're a huge hit, especially with our guests from India. Olivia told me that business improved a lot after you started doing the walking tours. Well done!'

'Thank you so much.' I beam.

'Going ahead would you like to undertake tours to other countries?'

'I'd very much like that!'

'That's good. Now the career path we foresee for you—in about two years from now, or perhaps even one and a half years, you can take over as Manager of Tours. By then you will have sufficient experience, and you can also train new recruits. Of course, that will be a promotion and the pay will be significantly higher than what you are at right now. How does that sound?'

'That really sounds great, and I am excited at the opportunity,' I tell him. Though I'm excited I still haven't asked him about the leave.

'Anything else?' Nik asks.

I take a deep breath. Then I say, 'I know this is an unusual request, but please could I take about two weeks off? I have to travel to India on some personal business.'

'What personal business? A girl?' Nik asks directly.

'Er ... yes,' I say.

Nik laughs. 'Oh, to be twenty-something and in love!' He looks amused. 'Why can't this travel to India wait? What's the urgency?'

'She might dump me and I can't afford to lose her,' I say.

I feel like the world's biggest idiot talking about my love life to a tycoon like Nik.

'Ah, we can't afford to have that now, can we? If you go through a breakup it means your productivity at work will suffer. And we want only happy employees here. So alright, go to India. Leave granted.'

'Thank you, thank you so much,' I gush.

'Good luck, Arush, with your job and with retaining your girlfriend.' Nik smiles and waves me out of the room.

I heave a massive sigh of relief. That wasn't as hard as I thought it would be. I've spoken to Nik and I've been granted leave. Hooray! I walk casually to my desk but inside I'm dancing. Naomi looks at me from her desk and raises her eyebrows. I nod and smile.

Then I go ahead and book my tickets, feeling elated.

Convincing my parents isn't so smooth though.

'Really, Arush? India? All of a sudden?' my father asks on the phone.

'When you have a job, you can't just drop things like that and go,' my mother says before I can even tell her that I've been granted leave.

'Also, you remember what happened last time, no?' my father says.

Both are on a video call taking turns to convince me that it is a bad idea.

'Dad, I remember. I promise you nothing like that will happen. I was a teen back then.'

'As though you're all grown up now,' Ma says.

'Ma! I am working, earning my own money, and I've got cheap tickets too.'

'You aren't telling us the real reason you're going. What is it? I know it has something to do with Puja. But why the urgency?' Ma asks.

'Ma, it's nothing. There's an art exhibition I want to attend, and I will meet Puja too. That's all.'

My parents are not convinced, but this is the best I can do. I don't want to share anything more with them. I check my mail to see if I've heard from Sashi, who I had met at the art course in Kochi when I'd visited last time. I don't even know if he is in Kochi anymore. I've mailed him and told him that I am visiting, and that we should catch up if he is around. I am delighted to see a reply from him. He's also given me his phone number and told me to call him.

I check the time in India. It's not late at all. So, I call him.

'Arush man! How are you? It's so good to hear from you!' his voice booms over the phone. He is still the same warm friendly guy I remember.

'Hey, Sashi, yes, it's been a while. What have you been up to?' I ask.

We end up chatting for over forty-five minutes. Sashi tells me that he is now an art dealer and trades in authentic and original art from Kerala and Tamil Nadu. He sources it and sells to select galleries in the Netherlands. He has his own apartment now. He tells me that I am most welcome to stay with him.

I'm happy to hear he has done well for himself. I ask him how Mukundan is doing. He says that Mukundan lost the elections but still runs his art school in Jew Town.

He asks me if there's any special reason I'm visiting Kerala, and I tell him the whole thing that has happened with Puja.

'Man, I'm sad that it's happened, but I'm also happy I'll get to see you. I'll pick you up from the airport, my man!' he says.

I smile when I hear that. I tell him I'll get a cab but he insists.

Before I leave for Heathrow, I knock on Naomi's door.

'Hey, thanks. But for you I wouldn't be doing this,' I tell her.

'You can thank me when you've got back together with her. Bring me spices from Kerala,' she says. She reaches over and hugs me and wishes me a safe journey.

As I board the plane, I can't believe this is happening. I am going to be in India in about seventeen hours from now.

I wonder what Puja is going to say when she sees me. Will she hug me? Will her jaw drop? Will she still be upset? Whatever her reaction is going to be, this journey is totally worth it.

India has a strange hypnotic charm, and I am overjoyed to be going back.

28

Puja

'Puja!' I hear a voice and for a few seconds I wonder if I imagined it. But there it is again.

'Helloooo ... Pujaaaaa.'

I go to the balcony and look down. Benny is standing next to the coconut tree in front of the building and looking up at me.

'What?' I ask, amused.

'We have two new additional back-to-back bookings in the evening. This is apart from the morning one. Are you okay with it?'

'Yeah of course. Why do you even ask?'

'I thought because your friend was there you might not want to.'

'He left last night.'

'I thought so, as I didn't see his car. But I wasn't sure.'

'Why didn't you text me? Why are you shouting from here?'

'I messaged. I called. No reply,' Benny says.

'Sorry. I think I put it on silent.'

'No problem. Be ready by nine for our first booking.'

'Yeah, see you,' I tell him and come back inside.

Is Benny being friendlier than usual or am I imagining it? I make myself a cup of tea. It's 8.15 already. Hell, if I don't hurry, I will be late. I'm still a bit groggy with sleep.

As I get ready, I look for messages from Sujit. There are none. It's unusual to get no messages at all. Last night I'd messaged to ask if he reached and he hasn't replied. Even to the video I'd compiled and sent there's just a hug emoji in reply. Which I'd attributed to him being on the road. But after getting home last night I thought he would text.

My phone rings as I am brushing my hair. It's Amma on a video call. She tells me they will leave for the airport soon and shows me the packed suitcases. She looks happy and relaxed. Achcha is right behind her, wearing a brown cowboy hat, a white shirt with bright orange flowers and khaki shorts.

'Achcha, what are you wearing?' I ask, shocked. He's never dressed like this before.

'I told him to change. It looks ridiculous.' Amma makes a face but she is smiling.

'Why don't we shoot a video, then you can make a—what is that called—reel?' Achcha says as he removes his hat and bows.

All of us laugh at his antics. He is such a serious person most of the time that it is refreshing to see his playful side.

'Amma, how did you get the visa so fast?' I ask.

'It's visa on arrival. There's a whole team of doctors coming there from all over the world. I wasn't supposed to go, actually. A colleague of mine was to present it. But one of his patients had to suddenly undergo a major surgery. Since I could also take time off to go on the Egypt cruise, I agreed.'

'You should have come with us, Molle. We're staying at a wonderful place,' Achcha says.

The pandemic has changed my parents' outlook, especially Amma's. Witnessing so many deaths up close changed the way she views life. Earlier my mother would never take days off; a vacation was rare. But now it is as though she has an insatiable thirst for travel.

'Another time, Achcha. You both have fun, and safe travels. Send lot of pictures, okay?' I tell them.

'We will make reels and post on Insta. I have been watching YouTube tutorials,' my father says and that makes us all laugh again.

Last night, after Sujit left, I'd thought long and hard about what he said about ego and love. I haven't reached out to Arush yet. I want to be very sure of what I am going to say. I want to be sure that I am forgiving him not because I am desperate, but because I genuinely love him. We both have to be clear about what we want from this whole thing. We've played too many games of 'hide and seek' by not communicating and not expressing expectations clearly. I remember the mail he'd sent. I login to my email and look in the trash folder. But his mail is not there. I frown as I look in spam. But there's nothing there either. Then I remember—a few days back I had got the notification of my storage being full and I'd deleted a whole lot of stuff to free up storage. Damn, I might have permanently deleted his mail. How awful!

It's almost 9.00 now so I hurry out. Benny and the group of tourists are already by the kayaking practice pool when I reach. This group is a family from France; two twin boys in their twenties and two girls, one eighteen and the other fifteen. The parents, fit and toned, mostly chatter in French. When they speak to either me or Benny they speak in a heavily accented English that is hard to understand. Their English sounds like French.

Benny does the usual demonstration where he falls into the water, and I get a lot of good shots of the family's reaction—amusement and surprise. Since I know what is coming, I am ready to film it. Before filming we always ask permission. Most are happy to oblige.

It is unusually hot today, and by the time we finish it is past 1.30 p.m. 'The next booking is at three. Sorry, there's hardly any gaps between bookings,' Benny tells me when we finish.

'This isn't a daily occurrence, so it's fine,' I say.

'And you aren't that prim and proper as you pretend to be.' Benny winks.

'What do you mean?'

'Sujit is your friend. Ha!'

I have no idea what he means by that but I am too exhausted to argue and I don't care.

'See you at three,' I say as I walk back to my place.

I drink an entire bottle of water and lie on the sofa. When I next open my eyes, it's a quarter to three. I hadn't intended to sleep. 'Oh, hell,' I mutter as I quickly heat water in the kettle and make myself a cup of coffee. I gulp it down quickly.

The 3.00 p.m. booking is a fairly easy corporate group. They are all having fun, and there's so much banter back and forth that it makes me smile. It is always easier to get good shots when the group is genuinely having fun.

Even before we're done with this group, the next group is waiting. I am pleasantly surprised to see a group of senior citizens. We rarely get them. Usually, the senior citizens we get are the ones who come with their children. But this is such a cool, fit group. They tell us that they are members of a club called Sassy Seniors.

'People think to grow old means blood pressure and diabetes. Not a single member of our group has any age-related health conditions,' Wing Commander Bhalla tells us.

'That's wonderful to hear, Sir,' Benny replies.

'Don't call us sir or ma'am. That again is ageism. You know, age doesn't automatically bring respect.'

'How would you like us to address you?' Benny asks hesitantly. This is the first time I've seen him thrown off his game a bit.

'Just address us by our names, young man! I am Jeetu. Meet Bina, Amar, Vijaynath, Sheelu and Gayatri,' he says.

I find it strange to call them by their names. It is hard! Yet I can see why he said that. Addressing them by their names closes the gap in how we perceive them.

'When you call us by our names, it makes me feel young,' Gayatri tells me as we set out in kayaks after the instruction and demo is done.

I'm enjoying filming this group. We are going to have some great footage, I think, as I furiously kayak alongside them, trying to get as many shots as possible. I have a professional gimbal now and I can shoot from all angles. I'd debated whether to buy a professional camera but, in a kayak it is easier to shoot with a high quality iPhone.

The senior group thoroughly enjoys kayaking through the mangroves. They are happy to pose for videos. They are so enthusiastic, I am astonished. So is Benny.

'What a group! I think the best we've had,' Benny tells me at one point, when we row back.

'Yes, I'm getting some great footage,' I tell him.

'Be sure to interview a couple of them once we're done. It'll be good publicity,' he says.

'I won't miss it. It's great content,' I tell him.

As I row behind him, I suddenly feel my hands going numb. I panic as I am unable to move them. I feel light-headed and I see little red dots. Then darkness slowly closes in from the edges. It all happens in a span of a second and I know there's something seriously wrong.

'Benny ...' I manage to shout and then everything goes black.

When I open my eyes, I am lying on the shore on my back and many worried elderly faces are looking at me. I've just felt something cold splashing on my face and I blink as I try to focus.

'She's going to be fine. Move, please give her some space to breathe,' I hear someone say.

My life jacket is still on me.

'Are you okay, Puja?' I hear Benny's voice as I slowly sit up. I touch my forehead and it hurts. I feel a little bump. I nod.

'Here, have some water.' He hands me a bottle.

'What happened?' I ask.

'You blacked out completely. Luckily, I heard you and turned back. I towed your kayak. Has it ever happened before?'

'No. This is the first time.'

'Hmmm,' he says and gives me a strange look. Like he doesn't believe me. Then he says, 'I will see the group off and put away all the stuff. You go home and take rest.'

'I'm okay now,' I say though I am not sure. I stand up and I expect to feel wobbly but surprisingly I feel fine. Once home, I make myself some Maggi and I also fry two eggs. As I eat, I realise how ravenous I am. I haven't eaten a thing since morning. No wonder I'd blanked out like that. It was terrifying, but apart from the extreme tiredness, which I attribute to kayaking such a lot in a single day, I feel okay. I take a selfie and enlarge the photo to look at the bump on my forehead. It's beginning to fade now. I'm horrified at the dark circles under my eyes. I need to sleep early tonight. My body needs a lot of rest. I change into my night clothes, and get into bed. I look for messages from Sujit. There still aren't any. I once again look for the mail from Arush—but it's nowhere to be found. Since I am too exhausted to think clearly, I decide

I'll message him in the morning. The last thought that occurs to me before I fall sleep is that it is such bliss to tune out the world and escape.

I am woken up by a loud knock on the door. I sit up with a start.

'Hey Puja—I got something for you,' I hear Benny's voice.

Frowning, I get out of bed, annoyed at being woken up like this.

I open the door a tiny bit. 'What is it, Benny?'

'I made chicken soup. It'll help,' he says. He is holding a tray with a steel vessel on it covered with a plate. It seems rude to refuse, so I open the door fully and Benny comes in and places it on the table. I expect him to leave but he sits down without saying a word. His eyes are bloodshot and he seems slightly breathless. Something about this whole thing just doesn't feel right.

'Come, sit and have,' he says as he pats the place next to him.

There's only a single built-in sofa in the whole house, and if I have to sit it has to be next to him.I feel underdressed in my nightdress, a T shirt which I sleep in, even though it falls below my knee.

'Thanks, I'll have it later,' I tell him.

'No, have it now. You need the strength,' he says

'Benny, it is late. I've already had my dinner,' I say. I want him to leave.

'What late? Don't act so innocent Miss Prim and Proper.' Benny gives me a knowing smile.

It instantly puts me on high alert. He is behaving strangely and I don't like the way he is looking at me. Like he is stripping me naked with his eyes. Tiny beads of perspiration begin to form on my forehead.

'See you tomorrow,' I tell him. I continue standing, hoping he will leave.

'Drop the act. I know what kind of a girl you are. You acted all high class and everything,' Benny sneers.

'I don't know what you're talking about. This is not the time or the place to have this conversation,' I tell him.

'Here, take this. Very good quality,' he says. He holds out his hand and I see a triangular reddish pill and a square-shaped orange pill. 'Imported stuff from Germany. Hits hard. That's why I am telling you to have the soup first. It's better to roll with food in your stomach.' He looks like he expects me to applaud him.

I am terrified now.

'Look, Benny, you've made a mistake. I don't even know what this stuff is. Just go,' I tell him, pointing to the door, my heart pounding.

'Why? Is it that only he is good enough for you? I am telling you this is better than whatever shit he deals in.' Benny stands up and walks towards me.

'I want you to *leave*, do you understand? Don't take another step forward.' I am screaming now.

But Benny just laughs. 'Playing hard to get, eh? So classy you act. Trust me you will enjoy it.'

He suddenly reaches out and squeezes my breast. I freeze. I feel so violated.

'No bra even. I see you are ready. You playing innocent is such a turn-on. We can take it slow. Have the chicken soup,' he smiles.

The knot in my stomach tightens and fear rises up inside me. If I don't act now, I'm likely to be raped. I have to think on my feet.

My brain is working furiously. I remember everything I've read about rape victims. If I resist, it is only going to excite him more. I have to use my head here, I tell myself. My palms are icy with fear and my heart is in my mouth.

'Let me get a bowl for the soup,' I say. I turn and walk towards the kitchen.

Benny stands right behind me, watching me with a crazed expression. Like a cat toying with a mouse. My hands shake. My stomach churns and I feel every single muscle in my body tense. I shift my body weight on my heels. I can't let him see I am trembling. I am wearing only a long t-shirt and my panties. Never in my life have I felt so exposed. My back is turned towards him. I slowly unplug the induction stove.

'You know, I've been watching you for many days now,' he says. 'What do you think that wireless router is?' he asks. 'There's a spy-cam in here, Puja. And you're so sexy. I am sure you knew it too, didn't you? You were putting on a show for me, weren't you?' he says.

He has walked into the kitchen, and is standing right beside me now, smirking.

I can't believe what he has just said. Something inside my head explodes. The guy has been shamelessly spying on me. How fucking dare he do that? And he is standing here proudly proclaiming it too.

I clench my jaw. The fear that I felt earlier is replaced by a red-hot blinding rage. I slap him hard across his face with my right hand. It takes him completely by surprise and he staggers back. Before he can recover from his shock, I lift the induction stove and bring it down on his head. He ducks but he isn't fast enough. The stove makes a loud cracking noise as it makes contact with the side of his head.

'Aaaaaaah,' he screams as he sways, loses balance and tumbles backwards, his body landing on the floor. He is in a seated position, leaning against the kitchen wall in complete shock. I lose complete control after that and my hands bring down the induction stove once again on his head. I am clenching it tight as I smash it down. This time the stove shatters and he slumps sideways, falling fully to the floor.

I stop only then. I am breathing so hard and staring at him in anger. What a fucking pervert. What the fuck did he think?

I see blood flowing out slowly from above his left ear. His eyes are closed.

Benny's hand is open now and the two pills are still in it.

The magnitude of what I've done is slowly sinking in. It feels as though I am coming out of a trance. I begin shaking so violently I don't know what to do. My legs feel weak as I walk to the sofa and collapse. I force myself to take deep breaths. Slowly.

Oh, fucking hell. Have I killed him? What am I going to do?

29

Sujit

When I finish brushing my teeth and step outside I find Amma and Jayashri Chechi seated around the dining table shelling peas.

'Amma, why didn't you wake me up? It's so late,' I tell her.

'You were sleeping like a baby. Anyway, it's not like we have anything to do,' Amma replies.

'Let me get you coffee,' Jayashri Chechi says as she heads to the kitchen.

'Where are Ravi and Sindu?' I ask Amma.

'Sindu's friend came over this morning with a spare set of uniform. Sindu was delighted that she could go to school. Ravi's friends also came over with some clothes. Mone, there are spare clothes for you also.'

'Ravi could have waited for me to get new clothes. Why wear other peoples' hands-outs?' I ask. I feel miserable about taking those clothes. We do have enough money to afford clothes. Jayashri Chechi comes back just then and hands me the coffee.

'I know how it feels. I am wearing Jayashri's sarees. But tell me, if your friend's house burnt down, wouldn't you rush over and offer whatever help you can?' Amma asks.

'Yes, of course, I will.'

'That's exactly what their friends are doing. It's not about hand-outs. There's nothing wrong in accepting help when we need it. Ravi is wearing his friend's clothes. What's so bad in that? Let's graciously thank them,' Amma says.

'True. But I don't want to wear Ravi's friend's clothes. I'll go shopping and get new clothes for everyone.'

Amma nods. 'By the way, I spoke to my sister this morning. She is asking us to move to her place in Pune.'

Jayashri Chechi jumps in. 'You can stay here as long as you like. Please don't go to Pune.'

'Amma, what will we do in Pune? Our life is here,' I tell her.

'That's what I told my sister too. Also, one more thing—the phone has been ringing non-stop. All our customers saw the fire. Almost every single person has called. Do you know what they are doing?'

'What?' I ask.

'You are not going to like it, but they are raising a fund.'

'What? Amma, we can't accept it.'

'Mone, that's exactly what I said to them. But do you know what they said? They said they are not doing it for us but for themselves. They said they miss eating food at reasonable prices. You know Jacob and his friends? They have been coming almost every day since we started the restaurant. He is the one leading the online campaign.'

'What? Is it online?'

'Yes, wait, let me show you the link.' She hands me her phone.

Jacob has sent her the link on WhatsApp. I open it with mixed feelings. On the one hand, I am pleased that they care so much. But on the other hand, I hate to be at the receiving end. It makes me feel like a beggar.

But when I read what Jacob has written, I change my mind.

Dear friends,

All fish-lovers would be aware of the restaurant A Fishy Business. A family-run eatery started by Sujit Nair, his brother Ravi Nair and their mother Devika Nair, won our hearts (and stomachs!) in a short span of time.

Everyone who has had food here knows how much effort goes into each meal, which they make with so much love and care. For hundreds of hostel students, single people far away from their families, and people who have lost their loved ones during covid (like me) craving for a good home-cooked meal, this establishment was heaven. I've been a regular customer here ever since it opened and so have many of you.

Yesterday, most of it was burned down in a fire. It is not only the family that has lost their home but we too. A Fishy Business was home to many of us.

If you want to see this restaurant back on its feet as fast as possible, please contribute generously. Don't think you are helping just one family, you are helping hundreds of people like me.

Watch their story in the video below.

All contributions are tax-free. No amount is too little or too big.

If you believe in this restaurant and only if you think it is a worthy cause, open your hearts and your purses! Donate now.

Jacob has put up the video of the short film the Manorama channel had made.

His name also appears as the first contributor, and he has contributed Rs. 15,000. I can't believe how generous people are being. Someone has anonymously donated Rs. 50,000! One person who owns a well-known garment shop has donated Rs. 20,000. Some have given Rs. 2,000, and a lot have contributed Rs. 500 too.

So far, Jacob has already managed to raise over Rs. 3 lakh. The list of contributors is growing by the minute. I am so overwhelmed that tears fill my eyes. I blink them away quickly. Till now I'd felt that I couldn't even breathe but now a small sliver of hope is shining through.

'I don't know what to say, Amma. He just went ahead and did it? He didn't even ask you?'

'I guess he knew I wouldn't agree if he asked. Also, read what he is saying, that he is doing it for people like him.'

'I can't believe they like our food that much.'

'It's not just the food, Mone. It is the community you've built,' Jayashri Chechi says.

'I agree. That's what makes us different from other people in the business. It's not like they can't get fish curry and rice elsewhere. But it's the love and care that we put into it,' Amma says. 'I think we should shed our false pride and accept this help in the spirit it is being given.'

Despite my profound sense of loss, Amma's words and Jacob's fundraiser both inspire me. I'd always thought of the restaurant as a way to make money but I now see how it is so much bigger than just that. So many supporters! It's on me now to take it forward.

'The first step is to hire a bulldozer and clean up all the debris. Let's see how much money Jacob manages to raise. I will get an estimate from a building contractor, and after that maybe I can get a loan from the bank. We will build a new place, Amma,' I tell her.

'Yes, let's take one small step at a time.'

'And it begins with me shopping for clothes for all of us.'

I'm glad I have the car. I tell them I will be back soon and head to the nearest mall. I buy a couple of dresses, shorts and T-shirts for Sindu. For Ravi and me I buy trackpants, shorts, T-shirts, shirts and a pair of jeans for each of us. I pick four cotton sarees for Amma. And though I buy undergarments for Sindu, Ravi and me, I don't get any for Amma. Not because I am shy, but because I don't know how to. I will leave that to her. As an afterthought I get a saree for Jayashri Chechi as well. It's a different kind of high to be buying all this stuff, because we can easily afford all of it now. I feel like Santa Claus as I drive to Jayashri Chechi's house with all the shopping bags.

When I get there, Chandran, Reji and John are waiting under the tree opposite Jayashri Chechi's house. Their faces look grave and sombre.

'What happened? Why are you guys here?' I ask.

Reji speaks first. 'We heard that the fire was deliberate. They say the restaurant on the next street started the fire, as they were losing customers.'

'Who said this?'

'There are rumours. Word gets around,' John says.

'Look, it doesn't matter. We're going to start building everything from scratch. You know our regular customer Jacob? He is organising a fundraiser and we will rebuild everything. But I don't know how long it will take to set up the business. Meanwhile if you all want to find employment elsewhere you are free to.'

'No, no. We are not going anywhere. We're with you,' all three chorus.

'Devika Chechi said we needed to clear the debris first. That's the other reason we came here. Reji knows people who do it. They can be at the site in an hour,' Chandran says.

'Give me their number, I'll speak to them,' I say.

After that things move fast. I negotiate a good rate with them. It's much cheaper than we expected. The contractor says he will clear the whole thing with a 5-tonne 55-z mini excavator.

I tell Chandran, Reji and John to hop in the car. I decide to rent the car for at least the next fifteen days. It will be useful to go back and forth from Jayashri Chechi's house to our site. Earlier it was a home, but now it is just a site. But still, it is *our* site.

While we wait for the mini excavator, Reji and John walk into the debris and ask if they should pick up whatever they can salvage. John holds up a pressure cooker black with soot, and Reji is holds a blackened large cauldron. Then I spot my old cycle, which is now a melted mess. The tyres are gone, only a small bit of the frame remains. I feel sad to see all our belongings like this.

'No, let them take it all away. We will begin fresh,' I tell them.

The contractor comes an hour after the work starts.

'What will you be constructing here?' he asks.

'I want to build a home. Hopefully something good at minimum cost,' I say.

'I know of someone who has built a 800-square feet house in Thrissur. It's a two-bedroom built on four cents of land. The total cost is just seven lakhs,' he says.

'Only seven lakhs?' I am astonished.

'Yes, it's not the usual method of construction. They've eliminated a lot of costs they believe are unnecessary. It's a pioneer project that will revolutionise the industry. I had attended a conference and if I hadn't seen all the videos and photos, I myself wouldn't have believed it. You must check it out,' he says.

'Please pass me the name and details, okay?'

Most of the day goes in watching the mini excavator clear the debris. I tell Chandran, Reji and John to not hang around, but they won't hear of leaving.

The contractor has also brought a tipper truck. The neighbours and people living on the street come out to watch. Some make videos. I wonder what they are going to do with the videos.

One of them brings food packets for all of us. Another brings tea in a flask.

The machine clearing the debris also comes equipped with a dozer, and by the end of the day, we have a clean, level plot. I have no idea what the plot size is but it appears massive to me. And this piece of land is ours. A fresh canvas to begin our journey.

I take pictures and videos and send to Amma

She replies immediately with a thumbs-up emoji. Just then the message from the contractor arrives with links to the video of the low-cost house. It looks incredibly stylish. It is well-designed, and it's hard to believe that it is actually an economical project.

After the excavator leaves, I tell Chandran, John and Reji to come next only when the construction at our place starts. 'Till then, there's really no work for you all,' I say.

I tell them that out of the funds Jacob has raised, I'll continue to pay them their full salaries. But they tell me they aren't here for their salaries, but out of love and respect for my family.

'Still, you need money. You can't survive on love and respect,' I tell them.

'You will be so surprised how much it matters. A job we can get anywhere. But love and respect, that's something which can't be bought,' Reji says. Chandran and John nod, and it brings tears to my eyes for the second time that day. At this rate, I will appear on Oprah's shows.

When I get home, I gift all the clothes to my family members. They love what I have chosen. Jayashri Chechi is moved and says it is very kind of me. I tell her it is nothing compared to the kindness she is showing us.

After we have dinner and after Sindu has gone to bed, Amma comes to our room. We have a family business meeting like we used to, before the restaurant burnt down. I tell them about the low-cost house and when I show them the video, they're incredulous.

'It looks stylish and it's designed to withstand the warm humid climate. It will be very cool inside the house,' Amma says.

'Chetta, if we manage to get this done, there's enough space for a proper restaurant in our compound itself. We can incorporate open seating. And this time we're not using a tarpaulin. We'll get a proper roof,' Ravi says.

'I'm going to make this happen,' I tell them.

It is only after Amma leaves and Ravi turns off the lights that I remember I haven't messaged Puja at all! I've been so busy. Though it is just yesterday that I was with her, and it's just yesterday that our house burnt down, such a lot has happened that it feels like weeks have passed.

I wonder if I should message at all. Perhaps this is the way to gently ease out of her life. She can go back to Arush and be happy together.

Just as I think that, the phone rings.

And Puja's smiling face flashes on the screen.

30

Arush

Every minute that I am on the plane, I find myself replaying all the memories I've made with Puja. I remember our first kiss, how small her hands felt in mine, how my heart felt like it had burst in my chest. Each time a new memory emerges I grin. I am grinning a lot to myself. I hope the flight attendant doesn't think I am a nut job.

I tune into the inflight entertainment service and end up gravitating towards a Malayalam movie, *Kumbalangi Nights*. It makes me long for Kerala even more.

Once I land in Delhi, I change planes after a slightly longish layover. I remember how the last time I was here I was a student, and I had scuttled around the airport, getting an Indian SIM card. Now I'm here as a working professional, and I've taken an international roaming plan. It feels good to be earning enough money and spending on things I want to. I message my parents and Sashi that I've arrived at Delhi.

'Welcome to India, bro!' Sashi replies. I smile when I read this because Sashi is Indian only in origin. He is from the Netherlands, adopted as a baby from India. He'd come to India in search of his biological parents, who he discovered were dead. Yet, he felt a connection powerful enough to stay back, and he has made a success of his life here. I wonder if I will ever be able to leave Britain, the only country I've known all my life, and move to India. I feel at ease in India this time, and it doesn't feel like a foreign country anymore, like it had first felt when I arrived here last time.

I wander around Terminal 3, looking at various shops at the airport. I buy an overpriced sandwich and a chocolate shake, the earlier enthusiasm and euphoria now replaced by impatience and restlessness to get to Kochi. One part of me badly wants to call up Puja and let her know I'm coming. Another part of me tells me I'm being foolish to travel all the way to meet her when she hasn't even bothered to reply to my messages. What if she has decided not to forgive me? But it is a chance I simply must take so I don't end up regretting it in the future.

At last, I am on the plane to Kochi. I sleep for a while, exhausted by the long travel. When I wake up it's almost time to land in Kochi. I feel excited as I see the city lights from the sky. As soon as we land, I switch on my phone, and check for messages. There's one from Sashi saying he is waiting outside.

It takes less than an hour to clear immigration, and when I walk out of the airport I can't believe I am here. In Kerala! And soon I will be with Puja!

'Yo!' I hear a yell. Sashi's voice reaches me before I spot him.

I turn in the direction of his voice and see him holding up a sign that says 'ARUSH, welcome home, my BROTHER!' He also has a flower garland on his arm.

'Good lord!' I mutter as Sashi dances towards me to some catchy Malayalam song playing loudly on his phone. Then he garlands me. I am embarrassed by his over-the-top gesture. A lot of people turn to look at us but Sashi doesn't care. He has put on a tonne of weight since I last saw him. He also has a beard and a moustache now, and he looks every inch the successful businessman that he is. He does a little jig around me after he garlands me. I stand rooted to the spot, turning a beetroot red. Sashi hugs me tight and says, 'Never mind me. I'm just very happy to see you.'

'Same here,' I say as I remove the garland and we walk towards the car. Sashi tries to take my suitcase from me, just like he'd done when I'd first met him. But this time I flatly refuse. I ask him if he remembers how he had fooled me the first time we'd met when he said it was an insult if I didn't let him carry my luggage. He laughs when he hears that. 'Yeah, you were so gullible then. I hope you have wisened up now,' he says.

I see that his car is a red BMW M4. I've never been inside one before, and it feels luxurious.

'This car is brilliant,' I tell him.

'It is, isn't it? I just had to have this. It does zero to sixty in 3.5 seconds,' he says.

'Woah! Tried that out?'

'Of course. I drive to villages near Salem in Tamil Nadu all the time to acquire village art. This drives like a dream on the highway.'

As we drive from Cochin International Airport in Nedumbassery towards Ernakulam, Sashi tells me that he lost his mother to Covid-19. And three months later he lost his father too. 'I couldn't even go back to the Netherlands for the burial, bro. I was depressed for months. I would just say home and order pizza and watch TV shows.'

'Oh, Sashi, that's really hard. I am so sorry,' I say.

When my uncle died the grief was unbearable. I can't imagine how it must have been for Sashi to lose both his parents.

'I met a girl from Russia, Daria. Daria had moved to Kochi at the start of the pandemic to study Kerala art. She is the one who pulled me out of the slump. Helped me get back on my feet,' he says.

'I'm glad. Also, I'm happy to see how well you've done, Sashi,' I tell him.

'You should see my apartment. And please, I'm not boasting. It's just that I am proud of where I am now compared to the mess I was earlier. This car, my apartment—I bought all of it just after my folks died. It's as though I am trying to fill a void that can never be filled. I wish my parents could have seen how well I am doing,' he says with a sad smile.

'I think the one thing the pandemic taught us is to value the people we have in our lives.'

'Absolutely.'

Then he asks me what I want to do. Since it is already past 9.00 p.m., I ask him if it's too late to ring Puja's doorbell.

'I can see how eager you are to meet her. Let's do this. Let's pull up outside her apartment, and you call her, and tell her to come out. Sounds good?' he asks.

'Perfect!' I tell him.

'Okay, put the address in the GPS and we'll drive there,' he says.

I already know where Puja's home is from my visit last time. We also have sent each other gifts that we ordered online and so have each other's addresses. It takes us about fifty minutes to reach. Sashi pulls up on the side of the road opposite her building.

'Puja must be a billionaire, bro. This is where all the rich folks live,' he says.

'Yes, her father is a business tycoon. I've seen her home on our video calls. It is spectacular.'

'My next address will be this one. If things go well, maybe in a few years, I can move here.'

I think that he is joking but he is dead serious. That's the thing about Sashi. Once he decides he wants something, he does everything he can to get it.

'Are we allowed to park here?'

'Yes. Don't worry about it. Go on then, make that call,' he says.

'I am terrified, Sashi. This is the deciding moment. What if she says she doesn't want to meet me?'

'Either way you won't know unless you make that call, will you? If she breaks up with you, I'm here, bro. We'll hit all the pubs in town, and I'll introduce you to Daria's friends.' He laughs.

'Okay, here goes.'

'Wait, you need privacy,' he says and gets out of the car.

I pick up the phone and with my heart tripling in speed I dial Puja's number,

She picks up almost immediately.

'Arush?' her voice is a whisper.

'Hey!' I say.

'Thank god you've called. I'm ... I'm terrified ...' she whispers.

'Hey, hey, what happened?'

'Arush, I ... I might've killed Benny—'

'Benny? That guy Benny whom you met while you went kayaking?'

'Yes.'

'Haha! Come on, Puja! You've got to try a better prank!' I laugh.

'I'm not joking, Arush,' she whispers and then she starts crying.

That's when I know it is not a joke.

'Listen, calm down, okay? I'm here for you.'

'What can you do sitting 5,000 miles away?'

The sound of her sobbing is unbearable. I feel a tightness in my chest. 'Puja, I'm right here, outside your apartment, come outside. I'm here, baby.'

'What?'

'I wanted to surprise you. I flew into Kochi a little while ago. Sashi picked me up and we're both parked outside your apartment.'

She doesn't speak for a few seconds.

'Hello? I'm not kidding. Just come outside and you'll see me.'

'I'm not in Kochi, Arush, I'm in Varkala. And I've just spoken to Sujit and he is on his way here.'

Then she goes on to tell me what happened. She tells me how she moved to Varkala and took up the job, how she had been getting a bit of a creep vibe from Benny but how she wasn't sure till now. She tells me about Sujit's visit and what Sujit told her about Benny. Then she narrates what has just happened.

My blood boils when I hear what Benny has done. I want to beat up that worm and rip him to shreds.

'Puja, I'll be there. Send me your location,' I tell her.

She says she has left her apartment and is sitting by the backwaters because she is too frightened to go back to her place. Because she is crying, she is finding it hard to speak. 'It will take about four hours to get here from Kochi. How will you come? Maybe you can come with Sujit? But he left about an hour and a half ago ...'

'Puja, don't worry about it. I'll see you soon. Hang in there,' I tell her.

After I hang up I furiously gesture to Sashi and tell him I need a huge favour.

'You look ashen. What's it, bro?' he asks.

I tell him what has happened and that Sujit is on the way there.

'God! Say no more. I'll get us there super quick. Maybe we can catch up with this Sujit dude on the way,' he says.

Puja has sent me her location: a kayaking centre in Varkala. I send it to Sashi who puts it in the GPS. As we begin to speed away from Kochi, I can see that Sashi means business. He is an expert driver and he is clearly enjoying zig-zagging through Kochi's lanes. As we hit the highway, Sashi drives even faster.

'This car can handle the speed. But, please, just drive carefully,' I tell him. The last thing I want is an accident when Puja is waiting for me.

'Don't worry. I'm fast but not rash. Trust me,' he assures me. Then he says 'By the way, you did say Sujit, right? Isn't he that same druggie because of whom you landed up in the hospital?'

'Yeah, the very same,' I say. 'Puja says he has turned his life around. Apparently, he runs a successful restaurant now.'

'Really? What's the name of the place?'

'Not sure, let me google' I say. When I type in Sujit Nair Kochi restaurant, I find it immediately. I tell him it is called A Fishy Business.

'My, my! Yes, it is well-known indeed. Their story is quite inspiring. I've ordered tonnes of times from there. Their fish curry rice is outstanding, bro! And, you know, it burnt down and there's a fundraiser that someone has started. I just contributed fifty grand. And it didn't occur to me that it's owned by our pal Sujit. He never appears on any of their social media.'

'What? His restaurant burnt down?'

'Yes, it was tragic. And let me tell you this, bro, and I'm sorry I am being very honest. If he is rushing to Puja's aid as soon as she called despite his restaurant burning down, you can be sure he is in love with her.'

I don't say anything as I stare at the highway ahead. Sashi is focusing on the road and the car is zooming ahead so smoothly that I don't realise he is driving at a 120 kmph till I look at the speedometer.

As we zip ahead, it slowly sinks in that what he has said is absolutely right.

Fuck. Maybe Puja is in love with Sujit too.

31

Puja

God or whoever is up there has a cruel sense of humour. Of all the days that Arush decides to land up in India, it is this day. What a fucking mess. Or maybe it's all god's plan. To help me bury the body.

Who knows.

Either way, I am glad my friends are rushing to my aid. I look at my phone and Arush has texted that he is with Sashi, and they are headed my way.

I've had a lot of time to think while waiting for Sujit—and now Arush and Sashi as well—to get here. I've left my apartment because I can't bear to look at that asshole's body and I'm hiding here by the backwaters, behind a bush. I had to step over his body to enter my bedroom to wear a bra and change into pair of jeans and a T-shirt. I was shaking while getting dressed at the thought of that creep popping up and trying to molest me again. But, of course, nothing of that sort has happened. Now I don't want to think about him at all as I wait. I'm seated on a cement block and have made myself as comfortable as I possibly can. There's nothing I can do till they get here—Sujit, Arush and Sashi.

Sujit has been calling me nonstop while he is driving, making sure I am okay. He keeps updating me on his location. He has called me at least five times now while on his way here and he knows that Arush is heading here with Sashi as well. I told him as soon as I knew. It is only on the third call to me that he tells me about his restaurant burning down. I couldn't believe it when I heard it.

'Why didn't you tell me that as soon as I called?'

'And what? Leave you all alone to deal with this? No way, Puja. I'll be there soon. Don't worry.'

As I sit hidden behind the bush near the cabin, I think about what a solid, dependable guy Sujit is. He has told me about how he has the situation at his end under control, how the whole site has been cleared of debris and how he is hopeful about getting a low-cost house constructed. I'm crying softly now as I think of it.

I'd spent nearly five lakhs on my impulsive trip to the UK before the pandemic. I had felt so guilty about having that much money—I remember it was almost thirty-five lakhs that my grandmother had given me, shortly after which she passed away. Perhaps she knew the end was near. God bless her soul. A few weeks after I returned from the UK, I told Achcha I wanted to transfer it all back to his account. But Achcha insisted I keep at least ten lakh in my account. The rest, he said, he would invest in my name, in mutual funds. And that's how much liquid cash I have right now, in my account, fully at my disposal, to do whatever I please. I feel like telling Sujit that I can easily give him the money he requires, and that he can have his house. But I know he will never accept it.

I think about how Arush didn't even know what has been going on in my life. Granted, it was because I had cut him off. I'd told myself that I wanted time to think. But sitting here, I am questioning if that it is really true. I recall Sujit's expression that day, as he told me to go back to Arush. There was a strange kind of resignation in his eyes. That is when it slowly dawns on me—Sujit is in love with me. I was blind to have not noticed it earlier. Looking back, it all adds up. Suddenly it is clear to me why he didn't stay over when he'd visited. His mood had shifted after I told him I was in love with Arush. But am I really? Deep down I don't know anymore.

I think about all the conversations Sujit and I have had. I've actually been feeling happy talking to him. And I was disappointed that he didn't stay over. Have I been deluding myself that I am in love with Arush while actually having feelings for Sujit? Or am I just confused because I'm not in the right state of mind just now? I'm finding it hard to tell.

It's a warm night but there's cool breeze blowing from the backwaters. I am shivering despite wearing a full-sleeved T-shirt. The phone rings just then, and Sujit tells me he is taking the turn towards my building. I direct him to where I am.

He pulls up and parks. He gets out of the car, and I stand up from behind the bushes. He looks so worried. The moment he spots me immediate relief washes over his face. I run to him, and hug him tightly. He hugs me right back, his body pressing into mine. His hug is so strong, stronger than anything I've ever known, and it feels like he is my shield, my armour. I can feel his love for me. Pure, strong, warm. I don't want to let go. I want to hold on to him forever. We stand that way for a minute or maybe two, I don't know. It's as though time stands still.

We stop hugging only when the phone rings. I reach into my pocket and see it is Arush. He says he and Sashi have reached the kayaking centre. I direct them to where I am.

When a BMW pulls up Sujit and I are both surprised.

'Hey, Puja, you okay?' Arush says as he gets out of the car.

Seeing him brings back a thousand memories. I can't believe he is actually here. I walk up to him and he hugs me quietly. It is a familiar hug, a feeling of comfort. I feel cocooned, cherished, loved.

'Hey, Puja! So good to see you,' Sashi says and I break away from Arush and give him a quick hug too. I can't believe this is happening—Sujit, Arush and now even Sashi is here.

'Hey, Sujit,' Arush says.

'Hey, man,' Sujit replies.

The silence that follows is so awkward I want to disappear. I have to take charge. They are here because of me.

But before I can say anything, Sashi says to Sujit, 'Your restaurant is superb, bro, I've ordered from there many times.'

'Thanks,' Sujit says, his face lighting up. 'But it burnt down yesterday,' he says.

'Yes, I saw that, but I'm sure it will be up again.'

'Okay, guys, we can talk about that later. Let's decide what to do,' says Sujit.

'Is he dead?' Arush asks.

'There is only one way to find out. Let's go check. Puja, do you want to stay here?' Sashi asks.

'As much as I hate to see that fucker, I'm coming along,' I tell them.

'Let's go then,' Arush says.

'Wait, not like this,' Sujit says as he walks to his car. He opens the boot, and takes out a machete and a big iron rod flattened on one end.

'What the hell, bro?' Sashi looks shocked.

'You don't know what kind of a guy this is. I do,' Sujit says quietly. There's steel in his eyes now.

'We don't know if he is alive,' I remind them.

'I've also got two spades in here. I came prepared,' Sujit adds. It shocks me how practical he is. 'If he is alive then we have to be prepared. I could find only these at my aunt's house as they use these to dehusk and peel coconuts. Else, I'd have brought hockey sticks. Sashi, go open your car and take out the tool kit. You might have a lever rod in there.' Sujit has taken charge now.

Sashi does as he is told and comes back with a rod.

Sujit nods and hands over the large iron rod to Arush, holding the machete himself. He takes out a cloth bag from the boot and gives it to me.

'Hold on to this,' he says.

'What's this?' I ask.

'Ropes and a blindfold. Intimidation weapons,' he says.

Oh, bloody hell. This guy is a pro.

With Sashi, Arush and Sujit by my side, I am not scared anymore. We march in a single line to my apartment with Sujit leading us, Arush behind him and Sashi behind me.

The door to my apartment is open and Sujit enters first.

'There's no one here,' he says as he looks around. I see the shattered induction stove and I shudder.

Arush and Sashi look around. 'Why is everything pink here?' Sashi asks puzzled.

'Yeah, strange,' Arush says.

I cannot suppress a laugh and neither can Sujit. Perhaps it's the sheer relief of not finding Benny's body.

'I asked the same thing when I came here,' Sujit says.

'Can't imagine you living here, Puja.' Arush shakes his head.

'He isn't here, which means he might be at his house. If the bastard has been recording Puja secretly, we need to get it out of him. I'll do the talking. You guys just follow my lead,' Sujit says. 'Puja, you stay here. Please don't insist on coming.'

'I am coming. I got you guys into this. There's no way I am hiding here. Also, you don't know his apartment.'

'Okay, let's not lose time now,' Sujit says.

We march quietly down the stairs. When we're outside Benny's door Sujit puts a finger on his lips and looks at us. He gestures us to stand aside.

Then he knocks on the door.

'Police, open up!' he says authoritatively. I draw in a sharp breath. He sounds so different.

I hear a scuffle inside and then the door opens slightly. Sujit kicks it open and raises the machete, his eyes aflame. I hold my breath as I see Benny, fear writ on his face, putting his hands over his head.

Benny's voice is a whimper. 'Please ... please don't,' he says.

'Sashi, blindfold him. Arush, tie him up.' Sujit's tone is terse.

I give the blindfold to Sashi and the ropes to Arush.

Sujit pushes Benny down on a metal chair and I watch part in shock and part in horror as Sashi puts the blindfold over Benny's eyes and Arush deftly ties his hands together tightly, and his legs to the chair.

'Please ... please spare me,' Benny whimpers. I see the gash on his head where I struck him. One part of me feels sorry for this pathetic human being. But another part of me feels vindicated.

'Have you been recording Puja?' Sujit asks as he pokes Benny under the chin with the edge of the machete.

'Yes, I am sorry. I'll give you all the footage,' he bleats.

'Have you uploaded or streamed it anywhere?' Sujit asks.

'No ...' Benny says.

Sujit hits him hard on the head with the handle of the machete. Arush, Sashi and I gasp in shock. Benny's head bobs forward with the impact and he screams.

'Tell the truth, you fucking bastard, else I'll finish you off right now,' Sujit says, once more pressing the sharp edge of the machete to Benny's throat.

Benny is quivering in fright now. 'I am telling the truth ... I haven't. It was ... it was just for me,' he says.

Sujit hits him again with the handle of the machete when he hears that. 'Where the fuck have you been storing it?' he asks.

'Laptop,' Benny manages to say.

'Where is it?' Sujit asks as he looks around. Sashi points to it. It's on the table to our right.

Sujit walks up to the laptop. 'Password?' Sujit asks

Benny immediately tells him.

Sujit unlocks it and asks him which folder it is in. I am right behind Sujit as he opens the folder. Arush, Sashi and I stare at the crystal-clear footage of me in the living room. I feel sick to the pit of my stomach when I see it.

Sujit walks back to Benny. 'Is there a copy anywhere else, you scum?' he roars.

'No, no copy ... only here,' Benny says quickly this time, before Sujit can hit him. Sujit hits him anyway but this time he punches him with his fist. The impact throws Benny's neck sideways.

I am so scared I begin shaking.

Sujit walks to the laptop and smashes it on the ground. Then he hacks it again and again with the machete till it breaks. He looks around for Benny's phone and he does the same thing.

'Dare you fucking do something like this again ...' He leaves the threat hanging.

He gathers the broken pieces of the laptop and the phone, and puts it into the bag that held the blindfold and the rope.

Then he tells us, 'Let's go.'

'Do we leave him like this?' Arush asks.

'What do you want to do? Free him?' Sujit says.

'What if he goes to the police?' asks Sashi, who is sweating profusely.

We are all shocked at what we've just witnessed.

'Ha, trust me, a police station is the last place he will want to go to,' says Sujit.

We walk back up the stairs to my place.

'Puja take that wireless router with you. Hold on to the memory card inside it. If ever he goes to the police, we will have evidence against him,' Arush says.

'Good thinking,' Sujit says.

'I don't want to touch that horrid thing,' I shudder.

'I'll hold on to it, don't worry,' Sujit says as he unplugs the router and places it in the bag. I am shaking so much that I have to sit.

'Are you okay, Puja?' asks Arush.

I nod in a shaky way.

Sujit is silent. 'Look I am sorry you had to see all that,' Sujit says. 'But we can be sure now that no secret recording of you will ever emerge anywhere.'

'The good thing is I have never changed my clothes or anything over here. Still, it is beyond horrible.'

'You were incredible today. Respect, boss,' Sashi says to Sujit, saluting with two fingers.

'I agree with Sashi,' Arush says.

'I'm not proud of what I did today. But I had to. I simply couldn't bear the thought of that pervert having anything to do with Puja.' Sujit is staring at the floor as he speaks.

'Guys, I don't want to stay here another minute. Let me pack my stuff,' I tell them as I walk to the bedroom. I shove all my clothes into a suitcase. Arush and Sujit both offer to help me pack.

'No, guys, I got this,' I tell them.

'What about these vessels?' Sashi asks, inspecting the kitchen.

'I don't fucking want them. The next occupant of this room can keep them. I am never coming back here again.'

'So shall we leave then?' Sujit asks.

'Yes, let's leave,' I say.

Arush insists on carrying my suitcase down the stairs. Then he takes it to Sujit's car and places it in the boot.

'Puja, you travel back with Sujit, I'll follow in the car with Sashi,' Arush says.

'Puja, you can go back with Arush and Sashi if you want to. I'm sure you guys have a lot of catching up to do,' Sujit says.

'With Sashi in the car?' I ask.

'Ha, thanks, guys! You travel in my car and I am the third wheel now?' Sashi says and we all laugh.

'Go, Puja, I'll see you tomorrow. I'm staying at Sashi's place,' Arush tells me.

'Yes, see you,' I say as I get into the car with Sujit, and we drive off.

The dawn is just breaking and a gorgeous sunset spreads across the sky, a flaming bright orange-crimson as we make our way towards Ernakulam.

32

Arush

By the time Sashi pulls into his building's parking lot, I am ready to drop down dead. 'What a crazy welcome to India I've had!' I exclaim.

'An ordinary one just wouldn't have sufficed. We did it the *Fast & Furious* way. We were fast and Sujit was furious.' We both laugh.

'Oh, I was furious too. But his rage was on a different level altogether. God knows if someone found Benny and untied him.'

'Not my circus, not my monkeys.'

'Touché.'

The lobby of his building resembles that of a five-star hotel. Sashi wasn't boasting about his apartment.

Sashi and I had overtaken Sujit and Puja last night. Puja waved at us, Sujit saluted us. Sashi had driven extremely fast, and got us here in record time. While in the car with Sujit, Puja had created a group: Pirates of the Arabian C. So clever! With Johnny Depp from *Pirates of the Caribbean* as the group display picture.

'How are we pirates?' I had posted in the group.

'Should it be laptop and mobile *chors*?' she had replied.

'Stealing one laptop and mobile doesn't make us chors. Also, shh, don't leave evidence here,' I'd typed.

Since Sujit and Sashi were driving they'd missed out on this little banter. I am happy that Puja is already joking about it. I was worried she would be too traumatised. It had taken a lot of effort last night to ask her to go along with Sujit. The thing is I couldn't ditch Sashi after he drove all the way for me, and Sujit had driven all the way for Puja.

Sashi is now reading the messages on the group and he guffaws as we get into the lift, which has mirrors on all sides and smells nice like it's made of lemon peels.

Sashi opens his apartment door with a flourish. 'Tada! Welcome to my humble abode.'

'It is anything but,' I tell him as I walk in. His three-bedroom apartment is luxurious with spacious balconies overlooking either pristine greenery or a river. He lives on the highest floor and the views are magnificent. He shows me to my bedroom, a beautiful room done up in white and beige. The bathroom has all natural materials: skylight, plush linen and a standalone bathtub. Plants and scented candles complete the look.

'What a beautiful room!' I say.

'Daria did it up.' Sashi beams with pride.

'Do we get to meet her?'

'She is in Russia, visiting family. Else, I'd have loved for you to meet.'

By the time I've showered and changed into clean clothes, Sashi has whipped up omelettes and toast.

'Bless you, I was ravenous,' I say.

'Me too,' Sashi says.

After we eat, he says that he is going to sleep for a while.

Since we haven't slept the entire night, and since I've travelled as well, I too am ready to sleep. I get into bed and text Puja. 'What did you and Sujit talk about?'

But before I can read her replies, my eyelids are already closing as my head sinks into the pillow.

I wake up by noon, and head over to the kitchen. Sashi is still asleep. I open his kitchen cabinets and make myself a cup of tea. When I check my phone for Puja's messages, I find four.

'Why do you want to know? Are you jealous?' And she has put a wink emoji.

The next one says, 'Hello—no reply?'

The third says, 'Yooohooo, are we meeting? Do you want to come home? My parents aren't here. You can meet Shanti Chechi too.'

The fourth says, 'Call me when you see this, guessing you are asleep.'

I immediately call her. She asks me if I want to come over. I tell her that Sashi is still sleeping.

'So what? Leave a note for him. I'm sure he'll understand,' she says. She says she'll send her driver, Antony, to pick me up, and asks me to text her the location.

'Puja, I'll take a cab.'

'No, Arush, I'll send the car for you. Antony is free as my parents are out of town. Be ready! I'll send you his number and he will meet you outside your condominium,' she says.

I message Sashi saying that I am leaving for Puja's place. I shave, apply some cologne and change into a fitted smart casual grey shirt and black jeans. I spray a liberal dose of my favourite perfume—the one she likes. After about twenty minutes, I get a call from Antony saying he is waiting outside. When I go downstairs, I am shocked to see a black Rolls-Royce Phantom.

Good lord! I can't believe it. While I knew Puja is wealthy, I had no idea this wealthy. Antony, dressed in a white chauffeur's uniform, smartly salutes me, and then holds the rear door open.

I've never been inside a Rolls-Royce, and I know young royals ride in these cars. I am blown away by the interiors of the car and the way it almost seems to float over the roads.

'Do you like driving this?' I ask Antony.

'Dream car,' he says.

Antony's English is limited to mostly 'Yes, sir' and 'Of course, sir', and I know no Malayalam at all. So, we mostly drive in silence.

He parks in the porch leading to the lobby and rushes to open the door for me.

'Penthouse. Top floor. Puja mol is expecting you,' he says.

In the lobby, the security personnel welcome me, and apologise for the security checks I have to undergo before they wave me through. It is like entering a high-security mansion.

Puja is waiting outside the lift, and as soon as it opens, she darts forward and hugs me.

White spaghetti top, denim shorts, freshly washed hair, arms toned and tanned—she looks different from the last time I saw her. I hadn't had a chance to even properly look at her last night, and now I can't take my eyes off her as she leads me inside.

The interiors of her house, especially the sea view, look even more stunning than they did on video. She introduces me to Shanti Chechi, to whom I have spoken countless times on video.

'Arush, hello. Very tall.' She smiles approvingly.

I smile back. 'Nice to finally see you in person, Shanti Chechi,' I say, and turn to Puja. 'The feeling of seeing this in real is exhilarating.'

'The feeling of seeing *you* in real is exhilarating,' she imitates my accent and I laugh.

Puja takes me to her room. 'Sit!' she commands. I sit on the sofa facing the bed. She sits cross-legged on the bed and places a pillow on her lap.

All this while I was waiting to see her, but now that I am actually here I find that words have vanished. I sit in silence.

'What?' She laughs as she looks into my eyes.

'Oh, Puja. I need to calm down a bit. Seeing you in person, I have to get used to it.'

Shanti Chechi knocks on the door. 'Tea, coffee or orange juice?' I am glad for the interruption.

'Some orange juice would be great, Shanti Chechi,' I tell her.

When she leaves, Puja says, 'Arush, the last mail you sent, I never read it. I deleted it by mistake. Can you send it again, please?'

'Oh! Of course.' I open my phone and send it to her.

She reads it, takes a deep breath and says, 'My god, Arush, they are stunning! Easily your best work.'

For a few seconds I don't even know what she is talking about, then I remember I had sent her the paintings.

'Ah, yes, you weren't talking to me then. I was desperate. I had to know if there's still something we have left—you know, if we still have a chance. Is there someone else, Puja?'

She and I both know I'm referring to Sujit. Before Puja can answer Shanti Chechi appears with the juice and some snacks on a trolley.

'I'll take it, Shanti Chechi,' Puja jumps up. She shuts the door and wheels in the trolley. She hasn't answered my question, and it is making me nervous.

'Puja, you have to be honest with me. Is there something going on between you and Sujit?' I ask again. I simply *have* to know.

'Arush, I could have sworn there wasn't till two days back. But yesterday, I mean after yesterday's incident, I am questioning myself.'

I feel crushed to hear that. But at least she is being honest.

'So, you and I—are we over?'

If she is breaking up with me, I want her to say it. I want to be clear here.

'Arush, no. I am sorry, I am so confused right now.'

'How can there be confusion in what you feel, Puja? I know exactly what I feel for Naomi. She is nothing but a friend.'

'Yes, Sujit is a friend too. A very good friend. But I think he is in love with me.'

'Of course, he is. It is evident. The guy will give his life for you.'

'When I know that—how do you think I will feel?'

'That's on you, Puja. How you feel is on you. I can't control that. But what I want to know is how you feel towards me. Has that changed?'

'No, Arush, that hasn't changed in anyway. But like I told you, I need some more time. I don't want us to be the way we were, playing games and not talking, and then talking, and then not talking. I am done with that.'

'Me too, Puja, me too,' I say fervently.

'How do you think this long-distance thing will work? You will go back to the UK and get busy with your work.'

'Yes, and unless we make time for each other, and unless we are both very sure of what we want going forward, it won't work.'

'What do we do, Arush? I can't imagine breaking up with you, let alone go through with it.' There are tears in her eyes now.

'Neither can I, Puja, neither can I.'

I want to hold her and kiss her and show her how much she means to me. But I am unable to move. The fact that she had admitted that she does have some kind of feelings for Sujit has crushed me.

She walks towards me now and sits next to me. She takes my hand in hers and leans on my shoulder. She smells so sweet, the same familiar scent. Having her next to me feels so good, feels so *right*.

She holds my hand tightly and says in a small voice, 'What are we going to do, Arush?'

I can't stop myself anymore. I turn towards her and take her face in my hands. We kiss. I feel the tension leaving my body, and I feel her relaxing into me. The desire that lights up within me is instant—like a match to gasoline. I can sense that she is feeling it too. She is kissing me fiercely, like she can't have enough of me.

We kiss for a long time, and the whole world vanishes. It is as though the possibility of losing each other has intensified our desire.

She reaches under my shirt and places her hands on my bare chest. I groan. She smiles and looks at me again, and I disappear into her eyes. She lifts my hands and places it on her bare shoulders. And then her hands wander further down, towards my boxers.

'Puja, stop,' I tell her.

I am so scared I won't be able to resist if she starts this.

'Why?' she asks as she nibbles down my neck.

'Puja, we have to be sure. Let's not do this ... I want you to be very sure of where we stand. I am sorry. I am really sorry, but this thing between us, it means something to me. You mean something to me.'

She pulls away with great reluctance. So many feelings rise inside me—I fight them. I want to throw her on the bed, rip off her clothes and make love to her. But I don't ever want her to feel I've taken advantage of her when she is in this state of mind. I want her to be sure. I feel having sex will change things between us, and I don't want anything to change.

'You know what, Arush, you're right. We have to be sure,' she murmurs as she walks to the balcony. She is taking deep breaths now.

I follow her and stand beside her; we both look at the ships.

'I guess with time we will figure it out,' she says softly.

Both our phones buzz at the same time as we step back into her room. Sashi has messaged on the group. He wants the four of us to meet at 7.30 p.m. for dinner at his place.

'Don't say no. That's not an option for Pirates of the Arabian C,' he has texted.

I look at Puja and raise my eyebrows. She nods.

'I'll be there,' I type.

'Me too,' Puja types.

Sujit's reply comes in a few minutes: 'See you soon, my pirates. Don't be late.'

Puja and I spend the rest of the day just talking; there is so much to catch up on! Shanti Chechi lays out a sumptuous lunch for us, and makes me taste every single dish she has made. Puja laughs when she sees my eyes watering because I bite into a green chilli. Being in her home makes it so special, as she shows me everything that matters to her. She takes out her notebook, the one she wrote in when her parents had taken away her laptop and phone, and she gives it to me. We sit side by side and read it together.

'Oh Puja,' I say as I read some of her entries and kiss her on the forehead. She kisses me back on the cheek. Being together is heaven. At four, Shanti Chechi serves tea on the terrace.

'What does it feel like to be living here?' I ask Puja.

'It's just home for me, Arush,' she shrugs.

We talk about our future plans. Puja says she isn't sure yet but she will look at videography courses. 'I kind of enjoy making reels, but not of dumb tourists. Editing and filming was great.' She asks me, 'Will you ever get back to art?'

I tell her that at the moment, I am enjoying the tours. I tell her about what Nik has in mind for me.

'But I plan to paint on the weekends and on my off days,' I tell her.

'You must, Arush. Please don't give up on it,' she says passionately.

When it is time to go to Sashi's house, Puja asks me to wait in the hall as she gets dressed. She takes an unusually long time. I text Sashi and tell him we might be late. When she emerges, I can't stop staring at her. She is wearing a sleeveless navy-blue, V-neck dress that falls to her feet. It's got a bow on both shoulders and the top portion of the dress has pleats that wrap around her perfectly. Glittering hoops in her ears and a matching bracelet compliment the dress. She has put up her hair in a chignon, with long strands in the front, left loose to frame her face. Puja looks elegant, sophisticated, chic.

'Oh my god, Puja, you're killing me,' I tell her.

'Just felt like dressing up. It's been a long time,' she smiles impishly.

When we get to Sashi's house, Sujit is already there. He waves at us casually, but I can see that he is stunned by Puja's transformation too. The guy can't take his eyes off her, and I don't blame him. Jealousy rises inside me, but I remind myself of everything he has done for Puja.

'Welcome, Puja!' Sashi greets her.

'No welcome for me?' I ask.

'I already welcomed you at the airport, bro.'

'Well, you did and what a welcome it was.'

I narrate to the others what Sashi did at the airport as we both walk in and sit in his living room. I sit on one end of the sofa and Puja sits on the far end, next to Sujit who is on a single-seater.

Sashi asks us what we will have. 'Whiskey, vodka, the finest rum, I have it all,' he says. He has also laid out a lot of starters on the centre table which look tempting. The guy really knows how to entertain.

Sujit says he will have just a beer as he is driving back.

'Bro, stay here! You can leave tomorrow,' Sashi says immediately.

'No, I have an early start tomorrow. I am meeting with the house contractor. Looks like I might have a new home in a few months,' Sujit says.

'Amen to that,' Sashi replies.

I tell Sashi that I'll have a vodka, and Puja says she will have one too. Sashi pours a whiskey for himself. He gets the drinks for all of us, and then settles down next to Sujit.

Puja says, 'You know what, I am so fortunate to have all of you. I can't imagine what I'd have done if I didn't have you guys yesterday.'

'No thanks needed, Puja,' Sujit says. The way he looks at her with so much tenderness in his eyes makes me feel that even if Puja does break up with me and go to him, I can be sure this guy will look after her and be willing to give up his life for her. Strangely enough, that thought brings me comfort.

The conversation flows smoothly. Sashi is a great host, and he has many funny stories to narrate. He keeps refilling everyone's drinks. Time flies.

During dinner, Sashi says, 'You know what we should do? The four of us should start a company together.'

'A company? Doing what? Is that the whiskey talking?' Puja asks.

'No, Puja, it's not the whiskey talking. I can drink a whole bottle and it won't affect me. Think about it—Arush can set up a company in the UK, and bring people for art and culinary tours to India, Kerala in particular. Just think about all the places you've travelled to. Wouldn't you say that food is a big part of the experience?'

'Yes, of course. People travel as they like new experiences —whether it's food or culture, they want to have it all,' Puja says.

'Exactly! So we offer them a unique experience where we blend both. I take them to rural places where they see original art being made. Sujit offers curated dining experiences, maybe near a waterfall or something. Think candlelight dinners under the stars, hand-crafted menus and impeccable service in a tranquil atmosphere. Puja, you head marketing and publicise it and all of that. We really can make it work, guys!'

There's a stunned silence at the table after that, each of us thinking about what Sashi has just said.

Sujit is the first to speak. 'It's really a great idea. Of course, we'll need to work on it a lot more. But, yes, it is a possibility sometime in the future.'

'Yes, in the future for sure!' Puja agrees.

'Cheers to that!' I say.

'Cheers to Pirates of the Arabian C,' we all say at the same time, and the sound of our collective laughter reverberates through Sashi's apartment.

33

Puja

When Achcha and Amma get back, they are horrified by what happened in Varkala. I have waited for them to come back to India to tell them as I didn't want to spoil their vacation. We're all on the terrace having tea.

My father is both relieved and furious at the same time. Amma is just shocked.

'That bastard. I'm going to use my contacts with the police and get him arrested,' my father says.

'Achcha, he got what he deserved. Also, Sujit destroyed his laptop and phone. Let him be.'

'How could my judgement about the guy be so wrong? I thought he was an enterprising fellow. But he turned out to be a disgusting con artist, and he fooled me.' Achcha is pacing up and down the lawn, hands clenched behind his back. He does that when he is disturbed about something.

'Sometimes you can't tell at all. Humans are the most complicated animals,' Amma says. 'Anyway, thank god, Sujit came immediately. How we misjudged him too. Looks like he has really turned his life around.'

'He has! His restaurant and home had just burnt down. Yet he came. He said he can't leave me alone to deal with that. He drove all the way there as soon as I called,' I tell my parents.

'What? His house and restaurant burnt down?' Achcha asks.

I tell them about it and how he is raising money to build a home, and his restaurant. I tell them what it costs, and how I want to give him that money but that Sujit will never accept charity.

'Yes, no self-respecting person will ever accept charity. But what if he got in an investor? An angel investor?' Achcha looks at me.

'What do you mean?' I ask.

'You know what angel investing is?' Achcha asks. 'It's the opposite of a venture capitalist or a seed fund investor. An angel investor offers more favourable terms than the bank in exchange for equity in the company. They are interested in seeing the company succeed. You know what? You please invite Sujit over. I want to propose a business idea to him.'

'That's an excellent idea. Why don't you invite your other two friends also, Molle? We would really like to meet them and thank them,' Amma says.

'Arush left for the UK last week. He had come only for a week.'

'Oh, I see. Why had he come to India?' Amma asks.

'He had some work. His company sent him,' I lie. Though I am very close to my parents now, this is something I don't want to discuss with them.

'Oh-ho, I missed a chance to meet the hero for whom my daughter had run away from India,' Achcha teases me.

'But now she has a new hero, Sujit!' Amma puts in.

'Please, you guys, stop it!' I tell them. But they're both smiling at each other.

'Call Sujit, I want to speak to him,' Achcha says.

I call him immediately and tell him my father wants to see him. 'Oh, god, Puja, why did you tell your parents?' he asks.

'Then what reason can I give them about why I quit my job? Also, it's a huge thing what happened, Sujit. How can I hide it from them?'

'That's true. But why does your father want to meet me?'

'He wants to be an angel investor in your restaurant. He wants to discuss business plans.'

'What? Shit! I haven't prepared any business plan. I need to prepare if I have to meet your father. Also, I'm not sure I'm big enough for an angel investor.'

'Just come, Sujit, and speak to him. Achcha's business expertise is something that will really help.'

'Of course. No doubts about that. Your father is like a business guru, Puja. The fact that he is interested in my restaurant itself is such a big honour for me. May I speak to him, please?'

'Now?'

'Yes.'

I give the phone to my father and I hear him tell Sujit that he doesn't want to hear any business plan or pitch. Only what Sujit has in mind. He asks him to come over that evening and that they will discuss it.

'Now that you don't have a job, what are you going to do with your time, Molle?' Amma asks me.

Ever since I've been back, I've been thinking about what I want to do. There's this idea growing inside me. The more I think of it, the surer I am. So, I have my answer ready.

'I want to start my own social media agency for small entrepreneurs like Sujit. I can help them grow. Right now, Sujit's brother, Ravi, handles the social media. But his final exams are coming up, and he needs to focus on his college work. That's when the idea occurred to me. I've even drawn a list of potential clients and all that.'

'I think it's a fantastic idea, Molle. You should definitely do it,' Achcha says.

'If you have to travel to shoot videos, then you must ensure that you stay in a five-star hotel. No more staying in shady places,' Amma says.

I am not sure about five-star places, but I'm definitely not putting myself at risk again!

'Once it grows, you can think of scaling up, employing people and all that for editing videos. You can handle the client relations bit of it, and get people to do the shoots,' Achcha says.

'Yes, let me start off first. I wanted to discuss it with you all and hear what you think.'

'You know what they say—a journey of a thousand miles begins with a single step. I am glad you've taken this first step, Puja,' my father says tenderly.

Sujit comes over around 4.00 p.m. He is dressed smartly in a white shirt, dark brown trousers and shiny brown leather shoes; I also spy a belt. There's a folder in his hands.

'You've dressed up!' I tell him when I see him.

'This is a business meeting, Puja' he says, and he doesn't smile at me in the usual way that he does.

My father greets him and takes him to his office, where he meets all his business associates. I'm a little miffed when they don't invite me to the meeting! That's when I know that my father truly means business.

They talk for over an hour. I am dying to hear what they are talking about. I can see Sujit speaking animatedly through the glass panel of my father's business room. I notice that my father is stroking his chin and nodding in approval. I wait at the dining table, designing my business cards using Canva, a graphic design platform. I have decided to call my company 'By Your Side'. That has a nice ring to it.

Puja Krishnan
Social Media and Digital Marketing
By Your Side

It feels fantastic to make my own business card!

By the time Sujit and my father finish their discussion I have my own website set up. I've also opened accounts on social media. I am so pumped.

Sujit and my father both come out looking very pleased. 'We're going into business together!' Sujit announces.

'I now have equity in A Fishy Business. We have solid expansion plans over the next five years. I have to get my equity to grow,' Achcha says.

'By any chance if your business needs a social media consultant, I am available. Here's my card, and this is my website I say,' and turn my laptop around.

Sujit and my father both look at it.

'That's really cool, Puja! I'd love to work with you,' Sujit says.

'We need to discuss my terms and my charges,' I tell him tartly.

'Of course. I wouldn't dream of making you do free work,' Sujit says.

My father tells me that he is going to invest in a good property to house Sujit's restaurant. Sujit knows an empty plot on the same street that can be taken on lease. It's been lying vacant for many years, and he is sure the owners will lease it out. He and his mother can easily walk to the restaurant.

That night when I talk to Arush, I tell him the latest developments. He doesn't sound too happy about the fact that I will be working with Sujit once his restaurant comes up. He asks whether I will take on other clients.

'Of course. Sujit is not going to be my only client!' I tell him.

He tells me that he is going to be taking a three-week tour to Spain soon, and he is excited about it. He has been reading up on Spanish history and is looking forward to it. Almost as soon as he comes back, he is travelling to Italy for the next three weeks. On both tours he is assisting, and so the onus isn't on him. He is delighted about getting to see the world, and immersing himself in history and culture. He says he will make sketches at all these places.

Now that I have my business card and website—where I have showcased the best videos I have shot—I send out emails to almost every person on my contact list. My father too puts out the word, and I am immediately hired by his restaurateur friend.

'Is he hiring me because I am your daughter?' I ask Achcha.

'Perhaps. But he is a shrewd businessman. If they don't see value in what you deliver, you will be out on your ass,' my father tells me.

I enjoy setting up social media accounts and handling it for my father's friend. They have had no presence on social media at all, and soon there is an improvement in footfall. Then he refers me to his niece, an upcoming boutique owner who sells premium bed linen from Jaipur. I have a lot of creative ideas to showcase the bedsheets, and I enjoy the shoots that I do. All the courses that I did during the pandemic are helping me, and I invest in a high-quality camera, tripod, light kit, studio backdrop, box lights and a few more things.

His niece refers me to her friend who runs a home bakery, and I do the social media for her. I shoot at her home, with her two small kids. I love watching her bake, how she transforms every cake into a work of art. My reels about her business tell her story. She is delighted with how I have showcased her. She refers me to another friend of hers, a couple who are into real estate. And so my business grows. Never a dull moment.

When I speak to Sujit, he tells me that he had his concluding session with Dr Harsh a week back. The doctor felt he didn't need the sessions anymore. I tell Sujit about the different kinds of people I work with. And he says he can't wait to see what I do with his restaurant. He tells me that construction has begun for both, his home as well as his restaurant. I also tell Arush about all my clients. Sometimes I forget whether I've told Arush or whether I've told Sujit!

After Arush returns from Italy, he calls me during the middle of the day when I've just got back from a shoot. He can hardly contain his excitement.

'Did you see the link I sent you?'

'Not yet.'

'There's a new scheme that has just been announced. Beginning next year, there's a new India-Britain partnership under which 3,000 degree-holding Indians between the ages of eighteen and thirty can apply for British visas under the Young Professionals Scheme. Puja, I am going to speak to Nik about it!'

'About what, Arush?'

'You can shift here, Puja! You can do social media for us when we travel. We do need a social media presence if we are to attract the young crowd. Nik has come up with some unique travel opportunities for young people. And he is always looking to hire deserving Indians.'

'It is tempting for sure. But I have clients here, Arush.'

'But we get to travel the world together. What can be better than that?'

I tell him I will seriously consider it. The scheme has yet to come into effect, and we do have time until next year.

When I speak to Divya that night, I ask her whether it is possible to love two people. I really like Sujit, and I like Arush too. I tell her what Arush has said.

Divya says that if I am enjoying my work then I should focus on that. She says travelling to the UK and working in a foreign country is likely to be a terrific experience. 'But don't think too much about it for now. When the time is right, things have a way of working out.'

34

5 months later

Group chat: *Pirates of the Arabian C*

Puja: Hearty congrats, Sujit! The videos you posted of your new house as well as of your restaurant are fantastic. Can't wait to see it in person.

Sashi: I am coming along too! And I love your restaurant set-up!

Sujit: Yes, I love it too. The architects have done a stunning job, incorporating earthy elements, and choosing the right plants.

Sashi: It's heaven, bro!

Puja: The greenery and the ambience!

Sujit: Everything is even better than before. Also it's very close to home. I can't believe the numbers we're doing. We're running full and it's impossible to get a table unless you book at least a week in advance.

Sashi: Hope that doesn't apply to your friends.

Sujit: Of course not. Special table for you always reserved. And your table is not at the restaurant. It is in my home

Puja: We will come over for sure.

Arush: I wake up and I see all these. Unfair that we are five and a half hours behind India time. Sujit, it looks absolutely stunning. You deserve all the success and joy, dude. Well done!

Sujit: Thanks, man. It feels so satisfying. When are you coming to India next? Pirates of the Arabian C need some British flavour.

Arush: I am coming there in two months' time. I'm leading a tour group to India. Mostly rich White British folks have booked this tour.

Sashi: That's great! What all places are they visiting?

Arush: The usual touristy route—Delhi, Agra, Jaipur, Jodhpur. But the thing is I will be able to take time off after that.

Sashi: Great! Keep a close watch on what they like and what they dislike on the tour. These are all great learnings when we set up our own company.

Arush: Of course!

Puja: Sorry for the delay in replies. I am also chatting with Divya. She is getting married in 3 months so lots of stuff to plan.

Sashi: Congrats to Divya!

Puja: I want all three of you at my sister's wedding, okay? Arush, I'll send you the dates in advance. No excuses, book your tickets. It's likely to be a destination wedding, and they are looking at Havelock island in Andaman or perhaps Udaipur. It's not finalised yet.

Arush: I'll be there.

Sashi: Won't miss it.

Sujit: Will come.

Puja: Yay! A grand reunion of Pirates of the Arabian C

Sujit: As long as you promise not to kill anyone, we're good.

Puja: But you will bring the spades anyway, no?

Sujit: Always.

Acknowledgements

My heartfelt thanks to my father K.V. J. Kamath for instilling in me the deep love for books, and to my mother from whom I inherit my sense of humour and a pragmatic approach to life.

To Purvi for the countless phone calls where we spoke for hours about Arush, Puja and Sujit, for being in love with the book as much as me. She would eagerly await the chapters as I wrote them and urge me to send it to her fast, as she couldn't wait to read. Her inputs made all the difference as she gave me great insights into young people's minds. To Atul for the super sticker design.

To the fantastic team at Westland, Gautam Padmanabhan, Karthika V. K., Sanghamitra Biswas, Satish Sundaram, Usha Jha and Madhu B. I can't express how elated I am to work with the whole team once again! A special thanks to Amrita Talwar who believes in the book much more than I do. Your enthusiasm is so infectious and I am lucky to have you do the publicity and marketing.

To Shinie Antony for the precise edits.

To Saurabh Garge for a fabulous cover.

To Satish Shenoy for always being there for me. You're truly my rock!

To Rathipriya, my soul sister for the late night phone calls, laughter and the strength we give each other.

To Jayashree Chinne, my closest friend. Your presence in my life means the world to me.

To Pranav Shah and his super responsive team for the technical support.

To Hrithik Agarwal, Haritha V. Rhea Melwani, Mona Thammaiah, the young people in my life.

To Arup Bose and J. K. Bose, who were the first to believe in my work.

To my closest friends who I am in touch with on a regular basis–you know who you are!

To my sweetest readers who shower so much love on me that I am sometimes overwhelmed. Thank you for reading all that I write.